MY CRIMINAL WORLD

Henry Sutton is the author of six previous novels, including *Get Me Out of Here* and *Kids' Stuff*, which became a long-running stage play in Latvia. He is also the author of a collection of short stories, *Thong Nation*. He has worked as a journalist and critic, and is now Senior Lecturer in Creative Writing at the University of East Anglia. He lives in Norwich.

ALSO BY HENRY SUTTON

HENRY SUTTON

My Criminal World

VINTAGE BOOKS
London

Published by Vintage 2014

2 4 6 8 10 9 7 5 3 1

First published in Great Britain in 2013 by
Harvill Secker

Vintage
Random House, 20 Vauxhall Bridge Road,
London SW1V 2SA

www.vintage-books.co.uk

Addresses for companies within The Random House Group Limited
can be found at: www.randomhouse.co.uk/offices.htm

The Random House Group Limited Reg. No. 954009

A CIP catalogue record for this book
is available from the British Library

ISBN 9780099578567

The Random House Group Limited supports the Forest
Stewardship Council® (FSC®), the leading international forest-
certification organisation. Our books carrying the FSC label are
printed on FSC®-certified paper. FSC is the only forest-certification
scheme supported by the leading environmental organisations,
including Greenpeace. Our paper procurement policy can be found
at www.randomhouse.co.uk/environment

Typeset by Palimpsest Book Production Ltd, Falkirk, Stirlingshire
Printed and bound in Great Britain by Clays Ltd, St Ives plc

To Rachel

'I was supposed to, you know, really write nice, serious books. And . . . I don't know, got derailed, and here I am.'

James Patterson

Not Just the Facts

I know things I don't want to know, as someone once wrote.

And there are things I don't know and don't want to know, but often find out knowing anyway. Failing that, it's not hard to imagine them.

Who can resist?

When it comes to crime, to violent acts, the mind is more than capable of elaborating on the details: stretching the facts and adding some colour. In many ways I believe we have become overly conditioned to accepting all manner of horror, to expecting it and then adding that little bit extra too. Life would be so boring without it, wouldn't it? There's nothing like fear to make the heart beat faster.

And I'm very much involved in making hearts beat faster. I'm not the best at it or the most popular, but I've been doing OK. Have made a living, of sorts. Not bad for someone with rather sketchy qualifications. What's more, something like a team of aides and helpers has grown up around me; I'm almost a mini-industry, in this zippy, digital world. And then of course there's my family who have become used to, reliant really on, the way of life that my rather particular – nasty, some might say – but popular work provides.

For a number of years I believe I thought I was someone else, doing something else. I thought I was not just a craftsman (pretty skilled, it has to be said), but, and I'll say this quietly, an artist. All right, a writer with poetic, literary even, tendencies. A *writer* writer. Or is it a *writer's* writer? But lucky fool that I was, I didn't see how good things were. I didn't see what I really was.

Until one day – how resonant that phrase seems to have become – until one bright, shiny morning actually, when I was informed in no uncertain terms, by someone who has long been a key (the key actually) component of my team, that I was in great danger of letting slip all that was good, all that was working.

I needed to take a good look in the mirror and realise just who I was and what I was capable of. 'David,' this key person said, 'time to take stock. Time to believe in yourself, for what you really are. Not what you might want to be. Get real.'

I was, so I was told, not just a writer, but importantly, crucially, an entertainer. A writer who aims to lighten the burden of people's daily lives. A writer who provides distraction, escape.

There can be no higher aim, where I'm coming from. If only I had realised this a little sooner, I might have – what: gone further, climbed higher?

Be thankful for what you've done, for what you've got – this is what I need to keep telling myself. I haven't just been lucky, I've been blessed. Yes. What's more, being an entertainer, nowadays at least, can be particularly prophetic. We're at the leading edge of thought and taste. To a certain extent we're dictating. At the very least we're making narratives that count, that get noticed. Plus we're having fun while we're at it. It's been a blast.

Sure, the entertainment business is a wide and wonderful thing. Dynamic too. It's what makes the world, our world, tick – all this downtime we have, this leisure time, this redundancy and unemployment and endless retirement. And so mirroring this free world, this free market, the entertainment industry operates on a supply-and-demand basis.

What I supply is murder. And murder is very, very popular. The world over.

Murder comes in all shapes and sizes. Over the years I've incorporated many other areas of criminal behaviour too: racketeering, blackmail, extortion, fraud (which is of course so extraordinarily expansive), arson, theft (again another massive umbrella), kidnapping, rape, torture, and so on. But there always has to be a murder (in my mind), or a suspicious death (note the subtle difference).

And, as far as I'm concerned, it should always be as lifelike, as believable, as true as possible. Authenticity is more important than accuracy (another subtle difference). The thing has to feel, to smell right, almost regardless of the facts.

Though perhaps I should add, just before we begin, that I was once warned (by that most persistent, prescient – yes, she's that also – member of my team) of investing too much in this particular world, of taking it all too seriously.

'For fuck's sake, David, it's meant to be fun,' Julie said. 'It's not meant to actually kill you. Or anyone else.'

PART ONE

The Wrong Beginning

One

As ever, I'm probably staring out of the window, at flowers, at foliage anyway – a few straggly roses, clematis possibly, ferns perhaps, a vine maybe, and plenty of other stuff, weeds notably. Or I'm looking at the sky through the long, slim, slightly grimy panes above the French windows – watching clouds build and threaten, while urging my mind to race off elsewhere.

Or I'm just looking at my screen, my chapped, chubby hands hovering lamely over the keyboard. Perhaps I'm glancing at the books and paperwork stacked up on my desk, the mounds of receipts and bills, invoices and remittance slips, contracts and invitations, the odd bit of fan mail too, having arrived the old-fashioned way via my publishers and through the letter box. I like to hang on to these cards, these letters. Some, I guess, have been sitting there for a while.

So in many ways, while trying to avoid these things that'll never get properly dealt with or filed, and trying to concentrate, trying to think about what I do best, while panicking a little because a deadline is looming, more bills have to be paid and my brand enhanced, an image appears as if from nowhere. Thank God – not, of course, that I believe in one. In my game?

This, then, is how I'm going to begin it.

* * *

First light Christmas morning. A thin, freezing fog was drifting in from the sea, across the tideline, the frosted dunes, and curling around the decrepit hotels and guesthouses, the long-since-shut and boarded arcades and amusements. A funfair from another era lost further up the Golden Mile.

He crossed the road, his dog trotting obediently by his side. Out of habit he looked behind him, in front again, scanned every which way – not that he could see far. But far enough to tell he was the only fool about at this time and in this place. Why he liked it.

His grey Hugo Boss puffa was zipped tight, his orange beanie pulled low, yet still the air was getting straight to his bones.

Once on the sand, Baz, his black-and-tan Boxer, immediately bounded out of view.

Increasing his pace, not because he was worried about the dog, but to try to generate some warmth, he headed straight towards the sea on a faint path. They always went the same way, across this Area of Outstanding Natural Beauty. How it had been designated as such was a mystery.

'Baz,' he shouted at last. 'Where the hell are you?'

What is it with Christmas? Why did I have to say it's Christmas morning? The added pathos? No, that's not the real reason. Normally I'd run a mile from anything to do with Christmas. The expectation, never truly met. The expense – actually that more than anything nowadays, with Maggie and the children, and their increasing appetites for posh consumer goods. It was because Christmas was the deadline I'd set myself to begin this book. The very last deadline I'd set myself. Now we're well into February. I'm weeks behind already – I don't want to think about the other deadline, the one to finish it. Funny how deadlines, my deadlines, used to be all about finishing things. Now I can't even make deadlines to start things. But at least here it is. Something.

I'm on my feet, which are cold in their knackered slippers, and am now standing behind my desk, having pushed back my chair. With the excitement? The adrenalin rush? Relief more like. I stretch, doing a sort of doubled-armed Olympic salute, arch my back, pull my dressing gown tighter around me, then sit again. Shut my eyes for a moment. I could have done with more sleep. I could always do with more sleep. But it seldom comes, of course – not long, restorative bouts of undisturbed unconsciousness. Not for a while.

Perhaps I should start knocking myself out. Maggie would probably have it that I already do, courtesy of Majestic. Or more recently, because even Majestic's bulk-buying bargain prices seem to be less of a bargain, the Co-op. Specifically their house claret. It's OK, when you get used to it.

I stare at my beginning some more. It'll do. It'll have to do. But what next? All cannot be what it seems. This middle-aged man out walking his dog on Christmas morning: a man who's happy to be in such a deserted place, though he's not so happy about the cold, or the fact his dog's run off.

Middle age. Despite being warned, it still creeps up on you. And then it does your head in. Maggie might say that's also the claret – diminishing your powers, making you fat – but it's not. It's the simple, physical (and mental) lack of youth, of vigour, of being attractive and original, of being a new-ish thing. But this man out there in the freezing cold might be middle-aged, though he is not me.

While my feet are cold – bad circulation – the rest of me is pretty warm; there's quite a layer or two of fat nowadays. And I don't have a Hugo Boss puffa; it's not my style. Nor do we have a dog. Yes, the children have begged for one, keep begging for one. Though fortunately Maggie and I have remained resolute on the issue. We don't have the time. I certainly don't have the time – being the one who's at home, working from home, most days. It would have fallen to me to walk the thing. To keep it exercised and entertained.

Perhaps the company would be good. What I've needed.

Though I am not lonely, surely. And no more distractions, please.

* * *

He scanned the foggy distance. 'Baz,' he shouted again. 'Come here.'

He thought he could hear the dog, sniffing excitedly at something. The fog seemingly amplifying sound, though playing havoc with any sense of distance. 'Baz!'

Baz isn't short for anything. This man who's not me has only ever called Baz Baz. He's not a man of many words (unlike me – though Julie might disagree with that; my agent would probably say that actually I am a man of very few words right now, at least words that have been put down on the screen, one after the other, in some sort of order, which might constitute a book).

Relax, David, I tell myself. Stay calm. Or stay excited, if you want, which would perhaps be more appropriate. This man out on those desolate dunes, laughingly referred to as an Area of Outstanding Natural Beauty, is the start of things, finally, I can feel.

And yet in my ear I can already hear the noise, chatter, advice (if you want to call it that) coming from Julie Everett: oh yes, the awesome, legendary, award-winning literary agent, whom I was fortunate enough to secure at the very beginning of my career, with my very first novel. Things have shifted between us. She used to read and listen. Now I do the listening. She's particularly sharp (and has become particularly persistent) when it comes to telling me what my audience wants and has come to expect. But she would know. She's out there in the real world. I'm just in my bubble, as she likes to remind me. More recently it has become a 'little bubble'.

Conviction's one of her things at the moment. 'Ultimately we have to believe,' Julie will invariably say. 'But most importantly we have to have a vested interest in the main characters' plights from the word go. Keep surprising us, surprise us all you want with those fancy little plot twists and turns of yours, but always keep us hooked. And how do you do that, David? By keeping us emotionally involved, of course.

That's sympathetically involved, not just empathetically involved – of course.'

Julie's always saying 'of course'.

'We have to care, and not just for the victims,' she might then continue, before sighing contentedly, perhaps even sniggering gamely down the line, or over the lunch table – she should have been an actress, indeed she wanted to be an actress – before adding, 'I don't know why I'm telling you this, David. You're the one who's done it time and time again. And that's why I love you.' If we're together in person she'll lean over and peck me on the cheek, theatrically. But the truth is we haven't had lunch for a while. We mostly communicate via email. Unless she's especially cross. Then she rings me up. Threatens, too, to come all the way over to see me. She hasn't yet. Because, thankfully, I always seem to pull it out of the bag just in time. Like now – I'm hoping.

He felt Baz against his leg before he saw him. The dog was warm and excited, snuffling and quietly yelping, and taking the lead. He followed the dog, over the hard sand and through the frosted marram grass – Baz gathering pace and excitement.

Baz suddenly stopped, dropping his head.

'Shit!' the man said aloud, crouching by the body, but keeping his distance, and most definitely not touching.

While she was definitely dead, he didn't think she could have been dead for long. Her body, though unnaturally contorted, and noticeably emaciated, didn't appear to have started to decompose at all. The cold might have been a factor, but nevertheless there was a terrible reality to the corpse. That life wasn't far away.

Though, more disturbingly, what struck the man was not the fact that her limbs were twisted wrongly, or that she was so thin, but that she was naked. Her body had clearly been dumped here, perhaps she had been murdered here, and not very long ago.

Standing, studying the immediate area, seeing his footprints, and Baz's, he could feel his heartrate rise. Quickly he backed away, not wanting to look at the girl and just staring at the ground immediately in front of him, which is why he spotted something. It was almost glinting.

He didn't think twice before bending down to pick it up in his gloved hand. Carefully he put it into his pocket.

'Baz,' he said quietly now, very quietly, but forcefully, 'come here.'

Julie likes that mix of sympathy and shock, of emotion and violence; she says it's very feminine. And of course who are the majority of my readers? Women. Women, she'll smile knowingly (or used to, when we lunched), make up the vast majority of my audience, my readership.

'David?'

But it's another voice I hear now. A loud, determined female voice for sure, though not Julie's. Yet I ignore this voice because suddenly the vast majority of my audience is bothering me. Is the phrase *vast majority* even applicable any more? If the whole isn't very big (now), can a majority within that whole ever be, strictly speaking, vast?

Words, of sorts, might be my trade, but this sort of analytical stuff is more Maggie's game. She's the academic, whereas my education was pretty patchy at best. I know, or think I know, about suspense, about pace, about keeping your foot down and, to a lesser degree, about originality. Issues of originality are often being aired by Julie, and my publishers. And I remember doing a residential writing course many years ago, where we were all urged to forget writing about what we knew, or for that matter what we didn't know, and do some automatic writing; how automatic writing was the window into the subconscious, and where the real truths and preoccupations lay.

I never went back. That was the first and last course I ever undertook. Who knows why I go down a certain route. Why particular images and subsequent leads, pointers and storylines develop the way they do. Who

12

knows how much of myself, my life, I'm really exploring. Where indeed my literary voice comes from. Literary? Who cares anyway? Julie doesn't like me to think about such things. 'You're not fucking Dostoyevsky, thank God,' she once said.

Except sometimes, in fact quite often really, I have not been able to avoid thinking about such things. While Julie doesn't expect me to be another Dostoyevsky, thank God, she does expect a certain commitment, a certain panache, a certain success.

I look at my screen, reminding myself of exactly where I am: this man out walking his dog on the frozen dunes and coming across the naked body of a young woman. OK, Julie?

'David?'

But this is not Julie's voice, it's Maggie's. I look at the time on my laptop screen, flicking away in the right-hand corner of the bar, forgetting exactly how slow it is, how out of sync with the real world. All I know is that it is, by some margin (but don't ask me how or why); so I glance over at my watch, which as usual I've taken off and have placed amid all the detritus, near the desk phone. I can't work wearing a watch, even if, unlike the time on my screen, it's usually correct.

Shit, it's later than I thought. Much later.

'David?' Maggie shouts much louder this time. She's in a hurry. Of course she's in a hurry. She's overslept, and now it's already nearly eight and, suspiciously, there is no sound from the children, and I seem to remember that Maggie has a departmental meeting at nine, and because it takes her, well, a certain amount of time to dress for these meetings and then first drop into her office to gather her thoughts and papers and quickly attend to the endless stream of emails she receives, it looks like it'll be my turn to take the children to school. Again. And first dress them and feed them endless bowls of Cheerios – or is it Sugar Puffs this week? – and make their packed lunches, prepare their school bags, check they have their PE stuff, their hairbands, their water bottles, their homework.

But my God, my children, like their mother, can be particular dressers.

And that on top of their stylistic and comfort quirks, the battlefield that is their bedroom floor, the carnage that lies within their cupboards and chest-of-drawers. It's impossible to find anything.

A nanny would be good, I used to think. Or, more realistically, an au pair. Though whenever I raised the idea, Maggie as quickly dismissed it. She felt guilty enough as a full-time working mother. Always said that while I worked from home – one of the perks of my job – I could at least make myself useful (as if, frankly, my work wasn't useful). They were my children too – oh yes. Didn't I want to spend time with them? Wouldn't I miss them growing up?

Maggie and I have always been somewhat competitive when it comes to work time. And I'm not sure she's ever understood the nature of me being effectively freelance, shifting from one contract to another. Why should she? Plus she has the salary, the security, now earns more than me.

And we do now have someone, Emily, who picks the kids up from school a couple of days a week, and helps out on the odd other occasion too.

I push back my chair and stand, trying to smile, trying to banish any negative domestic thoughts. Because, just as I love my audience (first thing Julie insisted: 'Make time for your readers, love them madly, because if you don't love them they're not going to love you back'), and just as, in a way I suppose, I love Julie and the rest of her colleagues at the agency, and my editor and publisher Peter too for that matter, and his vast team (because, so I learned and have never forgotten, it pays to love everyone in this business – not that it's always that reciprocal), so I love my children, naturally, even if their love doesn't always feel that reciprocal, either. Still, I firmly believe that I do my best for my kids, that I do all I can, when I can.

And Maggie as well, of course, I love Maggie very much; despite – perhaps even because of – her desire to be so stylishly groomed and attired, regardless of whatever else is going on, of what other demands people, young people mostly (in one form or another), are making on her.

I'm out of my study, finally, pleased at the distraction, the need to engage with my kids, with daily life. It's always good to abandon my desk, abandon work, on a sort of high, at last. Pace, pace, pace, I'm thinking, indeed I'm reiterating to myself cheerily, as I pause for breath in the hall.

So what if it takes Maggie a certain amount of time to get ready, to throw together a look. Maggie is miles better-looking, and miles more stylish, than any other woman in her department, in her faculty, and that's including most of the students I've seen when I've occasionally ventured onto her campus.

'David, where the hell are you?' Her voice zooms downstairs.

'Coming,' I say, heading up, nearly as fast as I can go. Pace on the page is one thing, but on the stairs? Forget it. With one foot on the landing I pause, yet again, wondering whether somehow my lack of fitness, the fact I'm physically slower than I used to be, is rubbing off on my work. Maybe, as Julie has been implying, I'm spending too much time on the description, on the small, inconsequential detail. 'David, you write beautifully,' she said, when we were going over my last book, 'but I don't want to be reminded of it on every page. Get to the fucking point.'

I once had a chat with a crime writer, one of the best-selling crime writers on the planet – having cornered him at Bouchercon – and he said, 'The thing is, David' – he must have been reading my name badge – 'my books took off when I stopped putting in so much detail. The detail, I realised, was just slowing down the story, my kind of story.' I always had a very long way to go to reach his sales stratosphere: the fact that his army, his armies, of readers stretched across, what was it, sixty-eight territories around the world – probably more now (are there more?). However, in that vast conference hotel in Baltimore I was confident that I was dealing with my kind of story, doing it my way, and it was doing OK. I was still bouncing around on the success of my first novel. Things change. Time moves on, of course. I should have listened. Though sometimes, when Julie shrieks at me, when Maggie starts shouting, I switch off. You have to hang on to a little bit of yourself.

'Kids!' I bellow, now marching down the heavily scuffed landing – you wouldn't know the house was decorated top to bottom three or so years ago, shortly after we bought the place. 'Jack, Poppy, up, now.'

Maggie's hurrying the other way along the landing, pushing past me, still in her pyjamas: her thick brunette hair portraying a full eight hours of pillow time. She needs her sleep, all right. But with her job and our kids, and me, it's hardly surprising.

'They're awake,' she says over her shoulder. 'Where have you been?'

'Downstairs, working.'

'Oh,' I hear, as she disappears into the family bathroom, the door shutting firmly behind her, the lock clicking into place.

Oh? But Maggie's not going to be interested in my breakthrough this morning. There have been so many false starts before. Besides, the last thing she wants to be reminded of right now is my crushing deadline – to finish the thing. She's in a rush, we're all in a rush. I glance out of the landing window. Has it suddenly got darker outside?

Two

'I'm on my way.' DCI Britt Hayes replaced the receiver, stared straight ahead. In front of her was the operations room. A couple of officers were sitting at their desks, peering at screens. Someone else was on the phone. Half the desks were empty. Holiday leave and the latest round of cuts seriously depleting the ranks.

She walked across the floor, her heart beginning to thump, more through the caffeine kicking in than any adrenalin. It would be her fourth visit to Kingsmouth in the last two weeks, but her first for a suspected murder. There was never any let-up because it was Christmas time. The opposite in fact. So much for the season of goodwill.

Why they didn't base the county's major crime unit in Kingsmouth, Hayes had no idea. Would have saved an awful lot of petrol, and man-hours, especially seeing how stretched the force was. And it was only going to get worse. More layoffs were in the pipeline. Nobody's job was safe. Nobody ever got a break.

'Off for lunch?' said DS Tom Shreve, coming the other way through the double doors.

'As if,' said Hayes. She couldn't help looking over her shoulder at the tall, lean young detective as he made for his desk. The man was far too cocky for his own good. Slick suit, short dark hair. Stubble. Always chewing gum, even when he was standing outside smoking.

Hayes didn't get chewing gum, or cigarettes. She also hated to taste either on other people. She chose her men, and the odd woman, carefully, or so she thought.

My vice is wine. And food too, I suppose. Scratching my chin, the folds of prickly, loose flesh, I find I haven't shaved today. Something tells me Britt Hayes wouldn't be impressed – even though I have other attributes. I'm not thinking about my storytelling abilities, but the fact that I'm a decent cook, and a generous host (far too generous, given my erratic income, Maggie's always suggesting).

It's too early to think of food, far too early to think of wine. Though I'm flagging, mentally and physically, which means (and I've been waiting for this, perhaps even desperately) it's time to connect.

A while ago I used to have to ration my exposure to email, the Internet, the phone and so on, believing I'd never get anything written if I attended to such matters. Now I limit my exposure to maintain my sense of well-being. If I haven't been ignored, someone will have written something pretty hideous, somewhere. Yet I still can't help looking, I can't help knowing.

My in-box states I have 11,503 messages (I rarely delete emails), though just nine of these are unread, and eight of them have been unread for so long I've forgotten why I never got round to reading them, or indeed who they were from. But I eagerly click on the latest, which I presume arrived in the night.

It's from my American publicist Jo Spear – how I love her name, and how apt, I've always thought, for her job as a publicist for a crime list. She'll go far, though I wish she'd stop calling me Dave.

Hi Dave, she's written. *Delighted to say Cleveland, Pittsburgh, and Cincinnati have come on board. Add these to Newark, Indianapolis, and Buffalo, and it's looking good.*

My US tour is scheduled for the end of next month. Though I'm not feeling as excited as I should.

Still hopeful for Chicago, Atlanta, and Washington DC, her email continues, *and I'll make sure something happens in New York, even if it's just lunch with Kent and some bloggers. Those guys call all the shots right now.*

So that's six dates so far and at least lunch in New York with my American editor and some bloggers. What's not to like? Well, they're probably not the largest libraries or bookstores on the planet, and I know Jo hasn't had an easy time getting this far. But you have to start somewhere, and my American publishers (and how good that sounds) are effectively relaunching me. It was always going to be tough. I need to look on the bright side.

I'm about to call Julie, when I see that Jo's Cc-ed her in. My agent will be pleased, surely, that things are gathering momentum in the States for this one, my most recent book, which was in fact my sixth novel here (though only the third one to be published there). Notoriously it took Rankin something like seven novels to really break through, James almost as many. Though I was lucky with my first, no one ever said, least of all Julie, that it was going to happen overnight.

Actually that's not quite true. Julie did anticipate the success of the first. She did think it was going to do well (she took me on, after all), but she also implied, way back then, that the subsequent books might prove harder to 'cement a following' – odd phrase, I thought, but that's what she said.

That it always took a while, she maintained. However, she was more than prepared for the long haul; why she was in this business, to build careers, something of lasting value – so she used to say. However, she never revealed then that it might take quite so long, or quite so much effort, to *cement* that following. (The problem is that whenever I think of cement, I think of someone being tied to a block of cement and thrown off a bridge and into a river or, worse, being buried alive under a lorry-load of the stuff. I'm not sure I've ever wanted to cement my following; nurture and build it, for sure, love it even, but not cement it.)

Still, onwards and upwards, so I keep telling myself. Plenty of very well-known names have been in my position. Or worse. At least my first novel shifted some copies (it was print-only then). And if it takes cement, it takes cement. And the long haul. Except I've been getting stronger and stronger vibes that perhaps Julie isn't in it for the very long haul. Nor my UK publisher.

That's great news, thanks Jo, D – I reply to all.

What the fuck is she up to? Pittsburgh? What's wrong with Chicago? – comes the almost immediate reply from Julie. I see she hasn't Cc-ed Jo in on this one.

It was a thirty-minute drive from the regional headquarters in Attlebridge to Kingsmouth. Hayes knew every twist and turn like the back of her hand, which was just as well because her mind was elsewhere.

According to the duty doctor, preliminary signs were that the body had been in situ for some time. Possibly up to forty-eight hours.

She couldn't understand how no one had spotted it earlier. It was a well-used stretch of dunes. Dog walkers loved it. Besides, there was a Coastwatch station only a couple of hundred metres away.

Because it was Christmas? Did no one go outside? The weather had been shit, that was for sure. Fog, sleet, the usual Kingsmouth fare. Nevertheless, was the place really that deserted this time of the year? She knew there had to be plenty of people somewhere – the large immigrant communities sheltering from oppression, the recession and the weather.

Then there were the pimps, pushers, conmen and corrupt local officials. Drug abuse, prostitution and related crimes were way off the scale. It was like no one did an honest job in the place.

The days when Kingsmouth was a thriving port and a popular seaside resort were long gone. Unemployment was triple the national average. There was little integration between the immigrant communities and the natives, while the council seemed to make one mistake after another. Vast sums of EU regeneration money had either been wasted or had simply evaporated.

The place had the worst crime figures by far of the whole region. Maybe it wasn't surprising that the body of a naked young woman should go unnoticed.

Once over the River Bure, Hayes' Vauxhall Vectra left the A47 at the North Quay roundabout. As she skirted Priory Plain and made for Marine Parade, boarded-up pubs and shops gave way to boarded-up amusement arcades, cafés and hotels.

Lining what was once known as the Golden Mile was one crumbling façade after another. However, some of the hotels and guesthouses remained open for Local Authority business and the odd resident who had all but slipped off the radar, either by design or neglect.

Britannia Pier, swamped by a foggy drizzle, looked like it needed to be put out of its misery. Hayes thought it would be best if it were allowed to collapse into the North Sea. Despite the heat being blasted into the car – the fan was set to maximum – Hayes shivered in her seat.

She accelerated along Marine Parade as it turned into North Drive, the Caister dunes slowly emerging from the gloom. Another 500 metres or so and she came to a stop by the Coastwatch station and an array of squad cars and white scene-of-crime vans.

A cluster of people were braving the chill, smoking and rubbing their hands together by the gap in the weathered concrete wall, which led onto the dunes. Just to the left of this gap, planted in the sand and defying the elements and abuse, was the Area of Outstanding Natural Beauty sign.

Ages ago someone had crossed out Beauty and written Bollocks above it, using a black aerosol. The graffiti was finally beginning to fade.

There was a neat hole in the O of Outstanding as well, as if someone had used the sign for target practice. It too had been there for ages – rust fringed the circumference. As far as Hayes knew, no one had bothered to investigate, to see whether the bullet had come from a handgun or a high-powered rifle. Ballistics had other priorities.

I like dank, dingy backwaters. Cities and towns that have been forgotten about, deprived and neglected. Perhaps it's appropriate that places like Cleveland, Pittsburgh and Cincinnati want me. I really should be happy with that (even if Julie isn't). Though hopefully she'll be happy with my choice of Kingsmouth as the setting for my new novel.

The idea has been bubbling away for some time, I realise. Indeed, I'm not quite sure why I haven't used it before – being so spectacularly, so picturesquely rundown (or was the last time I visited). Plus it's only twenty miles away – research will be a doddle.

Then again – I glance towards the French window, see no sign of spring today – how come someone hasn't hit upon the town already, if it's that perfect for my aims? Maybe there's a crime writer out there, one of my many, many rivals, already hard at it. I can think of a number of writers who'd probably be more suited to the task. MacBride, Kelly, Bateman immediately spring to mind. And P James (not James P) again of course – he'd do a good job, having already honed his skills on another English seaside town.

The thing is, and aside from a number of rivals quite possibly having more pertinent talents, originality in my game is harder and harder to come by – almost impossible. Everything's been done before. Every plot exhaustively, minutely played out. Everywhere described. Every character realised. I need to talk to Julie. I should call my publishers. See if they've heard anything on the grapevine, see who's up to what – before it's already too late.

Turning from the screen once more, I glance over to the French windows and, almost like magic, as if someone is looking out for me, as if someone is trying to keep me cheerful and committed, the day has brightened. Clouds are racing and bare branches swaying, while thick shafts of sunlight appear to be stabbing the ground. Hopefully it'll remain dry. I have a mission.

As if on cue, just as I'm mentally going through the shopping list and mapping the most effective route to incorporate the bakery, the butcher's and Waitrose (I keep meaning to go to Sainsbury's, seeing how much cheaper it is, but somehow the car always steers me towards Waitrose), my desk phone goes, the caller identification revealing it's Maggie.

'Hi,' she says, out of breath. 'Just checking you've got everything for tonight.'

'Where are you?' I say.

'On my way to a meeting.'

She's outside. I can hear wind, lots of open space. Faint voices too in the distance. Colleagues? Students?

'Another?' I'm not sure what I mean by this. Why I've even said it.

'Yes,' she says. 'With the Vice Chancellor, sweetheart.'

'Sorry.' I really don't like my tone.

'So have you got everything?'

'No, not yet – I was stuck on a scene. I'm literally just on my way out of the house now.'

'Are you not leaving it a bit late, David?'

'The kids are both at after-school club today – it is Thursday, remember. I've got enough time.'

'Well, I don't think I'm going to be back until at least six – sorry.'

'That's OK, I can manage.' I feel like adding, *I usually do*, but don't.

'They're coming at seven-thirty, you know,' she says.

'And they're always bang on time, aren't they? Look, Maggie, don't worry. Everything will be ready.'

'I'm sure. OK, thanks. Sorry for hassling. I've got to go.'

'Hope the meeting goes well,' I say, already replacing the receiver, pushing my chair back and standing. Thinking, as I gather my wallet and keys and walk into the hall to search for my coat, that Detective Britt Hayes is not going to be married. And she's not going to have children. I don't want those complications. Outside of work she'll be a free agent. If I really am trying to get a series off the ground (as Julie and Peter have been urging – insisting really), I'm going to be stuck with Britt for quite some time: six, seven, eight books' worth (conceivably, hopefully), who knows (there are more than twenty Rebus novels)? I've got to like her (if not love her). She's got to keep me, and everyone else, completely hooked.

Too much baggage is not just boring, but predictable (and unoriginal). Independence has to be one of her key attributes. The ability to do what she wants. To be answerable to no one. The simple fact is she won't have many close friends, and won't be involved in any serious relationships. Casual's her thing. Lucky her!

Where's my coat? There are so many garments crammed on the rack that I can never find the one I need. Shit, I really am running out of time – there's a dinner party to prepare for, kids to pick up, feed and get ready for bed, plus a wife to keep happy. However, leaving the house, looking down the street for the car, I feel pleased with the way things are shaping up – in Kingsmouth. And yes, in America too.

Yet I also can't help feeling that experience doesn't seem to count for much. The doubts just get worse. The fear of failure seems to become ever more present, if failure hasn't actually become a reality (Julie and I try not to talk sales figures any more).

I realise I'd like to have a word with that guy I cornered at Bouchercon, all those years ago. I was probably too cocky then, too sure of myself (being flush with debut success) to pay enough attention to exactly what he was saying. I should have asked him so many more questions. Surely, with his sales record, he's the man with the answers. Perhaps I'll bump into him again, at another festival, not that I've been asked to Bouchercon this year (despite Jo's attempts).

Though there are always the UK crime festivals – perhaps he'll be coming over for a rare appearance, popping up in Bristol or Reading or Harrogate, to tell us how the fame hasn't affected him one little bit, how he's as prolific and as keen for success as ever, et cetera (I can almost hear him).

Not that I've been invited to any of the UK festivals this year, either. But this might change, should I (and I hardly dare to articulate the idea) win the Crime Thriller of the Year, the big one, which is voted for by the public, the people who really count. I'm in the frame. Yes, I am. Should hear any moment whether I've made it onto the shortlist.

Even the world's best-selling crime and thriller author doesn't win all the awards. How does he handle himself when things don't always go his way? How does he get back on track? Can he spot the weaknesses before it's too late? Surely. I'd love him to have a quick skim of my current project. See whether I've already generated enough drive and action, enough sympathy for the victim. Who the hell is, or rather was, that poor young woman? In my business one must never forget the victim.

Or where you've parked your car. Where is my bloody car? Looking over my shoulder (as ever), I realise I've walked right past it – our gun-metal grey, now rather old Volvo estate. Those Swedes, those Scandinavians, don't just know how to build cars, but crime plots too, of course.

Julie joked recently that I might do better if I adopted a Scandinavian-sounding name and pretended I came from, say, Sweden or Norway. 'Blood looks great in the snow,' she said, 'that's why it works for them. At least try setting your next one in winter.'

Freezing fog isn't quite an Arctic white-out. Still, maybe at least I should make my victim Swedish. The name Kristine, spelt with a K, suddenly comes to me. Though is Kristine a Swedish name? The Swedish spelling of the name? Or the Norwegian, or Danish, or Icelandic (though I'm not entirely sure Iceland is technically Scandinavian)?

However, I guess I'm resistant (as ever, I'm afraid, Julie, Peter) to jumping on a bandwagon. I'd just rather Kristine came from somewhere less charted, less explored, less fabled; frankly, less developed. And a country with much more real crime and corruption, more economic and social depravity. The sort of place that would give Kristine plenty of reasons to want to escape.

It suddenly seems so obvious, and with a name like Kristine too (no?): Eastern Europe is where she has to have been born. And not just anywhere in that part of the world, but Latvia. Latvia! Not because it's so awful and corrupt – it's not Albania, or the Ukraine (from what I've gathered) – but because I happen to have a special connection to Latvia. I like the Latvians (the ones I've met anyway), and more importantly they seem to like me – at least they buy my books. It's one of the few continental European territories that I, or rather Julie, have sold foreign rights to. The Latvians have three of my novels, including the latest, which someone is even turning into a stage play (they do that a lot there apparently). It's going to be performed (if all goes to plan) in Riga, at the Dailes Theatre, which is meant to be one of the biggest and most prestigious in the country.

So it'll not be hard to summon up plenty of feeling for Kristine's terrible plight, her short life, to work on her background, her vulnerability (because she's a Latvian and I like Latvians). Though obviously I'll need to be careful about portraying Latvia, Riga particularly, as somewhere worse than Kingsmouth. While I might be wary about jumping on any old bandwagon, I certainly don't want to alienate my foreign readers (or, I suppose, my local ones – except everyone knows the truth about Kingsmouth).

From an impoverished background, and a dysfunctional family perhaps, she's just going to have to have fallen in with the wrong crowd (of Russians maybe).

Bugger! With the diesel engine soundly ticking over, with warm air already beginning to trickle into the cabin (these Volvos, those Scandinavians), with my hand on the automatic gearstick (for some reason the automatic was cheaper than the manual), with the road clear ahead and behind, I was about to squeeze the button, hook into Drive and pull out, but I don't. Releasing the gearstick, I realise I have to go back to the house – I've forgotten my notebook. I switch off the engine. Climb out of the car, almost bumping into a young man wearing a long trench coat.

'Sorry,' I say.

But he doesn't stop, or turn around, and if anything increases his loping pace up the pavement, seemingly pulling his coat tighter around him.

More were arriving. There was quite a crowd now. Cordons were in place. Cars, vans were spilled all over the road. People were ferrying equipment. Others were pulling on protective clothing. He had the perfect view. It was like watching television.

He stepped back and let the curtain fall into place. Much was bothering him, not least the fact that it had taken them so long to discover the body. He felt strangely guilty that he hadn't done something more, that he hadn't alerted the police – that would have been a first. But he couldn't risk it.

Besides, he still couldn't help wondering whether he was meant to discover the body. Someone might have spotted him, be able to identify him. And then there were his and Baz's prints in the sand.

People – locals – knew he went that way every day, if not twice a day, with his dog. Was someone really trying to set him up? His cover blown?

He walked over to the bedside table, opened the top drawer, looked at the watch. He had a feeling he wasn't meant to have stumbled upon this. Had a feeling too that it might prove useful.

Hayes stepped into the crowded tent. She took one look at the emaciated body lying on the bare ground in the centre – the young woman's badly dyed blonde hair, the dark, chipped nail varnish on her hands, the faint bruises on her arms – and had a pretty good idea what she was dealing with.

She was well aware of the size and perniciousness of the sex industry in Kingsmouth. Its cultural make-up, its infrastructure and hierarchies. Which gangs ruled which streets and which massage parlours. The terrible, brutal injustice that this young woman must have been subjected to. How she would have been controlled, terrorised, abused. And then murdered.

Hayes knew also that there would be many, many people responsible; that to dismantle one operation, let alone all of them, would be impossible.

She was well aware of the walls of silence that existed among these gangs. How no one would miss the woman, let alone admit to even knowing her. Who knew where she really came from, or what exactly had happened to her?

There would be little evidence and no witnesses. Or so Hayes thought, staring at the almost blue skin covering the oddly twisted body.

She turned to her side, looked at the lead crime-scene officer, a man named Buchan, in his white overalls, said, 'Anything?'

'We were waiting for you,' he said, 'before we moved the body.'

'I can't understand why she's in that position, why her arms and legs are twisted like that,' said Hayes. 'Seems like someone arranged her, post-mortem.'

'That's what I was thinking,' Buchan said.

'Where's Colony?'

'She hasn't been called,' said Buchan. 'The duty doctor didn't think it was necessary.'

'Since when has the duty doctor been in charge of a homicide?' Hayes was livid.

'Maybe he didn't think it was a homicide.'

'So she decided to go for a skinny-dip, this time of year? Lost her clothes on the way back? Who the hell do we employ? I don't want the body touched until Colony gets here.'

'Julie, sorry, can I call you back? I'm on my way to the butcher's and I've parked illegally.'

'You can try,' she says, ending the call before me.

I beep the car locked and walk straight into the butcher's, the smell of raw meat hitting me like a blast of North Sea air.

The older guy – red cheeks, mop of thick brown hair, lots of untoned upper body – is behind the counter today. Catching my eye, he smiles, says, 'Hello, Mr Slavitt, what can I get for you today?'

Despite coming here for the last three years or so, indeed ever since we moved to this part of the world, I still don't know his name, and not for the first time I feel embarrassed by the fact. It pays to remember names. I look at the counter, the cuts of meat on display, dotted with sprigs of bright-green parsley and rosemary, feeling it's far too late to ask him.

'We've got some lovely wild duck in, Mr Slavitt,' says the butcher. 'Last of the season.'

Shopkeepers especially are so friendly and courteous in this town – city technically – that it's almost old-fashioned, and such a relief from the aggression and hassle that stalked our life in South London. We do love it here: the children particularly, with all the wide-open space and emphasis on their well-being. The Green Party has a majority in the city council. There are a number of independent, organic grocery stores. People seem to have plenty of time on their hands, though working parents, and particularly full-time working mothers, are often frowned upon – so Maggie is always saying. Part of the reason might be because there just isn't that much work about, and those with secure, professional jobs such as Maggie's are rare. Naturally people are jealous. Maggie's senior position at the university, which enabled the move here, and my rather specialist (though not exactly rare) line of work were always going to be met with a certain suspicion – so we now realise. It took us a while to be accepted.

Nevertheless Maggie probably found it easier to assimilate than I did. She has a large cohort of like-minded academics to fraternise with. I have the full-time mums whom I meet on the school run, the odd doleful dad and then Maggie's colleagues, whom I invariably end up having to cook for and entertain. And while they are happy enough to eat my food and drink my wine (I'm catering for three of them tonight), I've always suspected they are less than impressed with my work. It might be the most popular genre in the world, but I suppose I can't expect everyone to get it. For some the very notion of popularity is a dirty concept.

They're definitely not having the duck tonight, however lovely it is. I smile at the butcher. 'I was thinking more on the lines of some lamb.'

'Leg, shoulder? It's very good value at the moment.' He nods in the direction of the lamb, in the far left of the counter, rubs his chunky hands together, his fingers like sausages (of course). 'I could always bone and roll a shoulder for you – you've had that before, haven't you?'

'You know what – that would be great. Thanks.' I think I intended to make a beef stew, or rather that's what Maggie implied I could make, for her friends. She thinks stews are quick and easy, and cheap.

Not the way I like to do it. I use an Italian recipe: a little olive oil, a bottle of half-decent wine, some peas, carrots, celery, surprisingly no onions, or garlic, and large chunks of well-aged fillet. Aside from the expense, it's pretty time-consuming to prepare. Plus I'm almost certain Michael and Liz and Ashish, who are coming, have had it before, more than once. But it's the amount of time that goes into preparing the dish that bothers me most. Time that I don't have right now – now I'm on something of a creative roll.

'A good chunk,' I say, thinking of the butcher's fat fingers again. Thinking how friendly and helpful he is. I bet he repays favours, is generous with his time and effort, his hospitality – unlike Michael and Liz, or Ashish.

Sighing quietly to myself and looking over my shoulder and through the shop's large front windows, through the reversed lettering announcing special offers, and out at the wet cold street, at the cars and trucks trundling past, I suddenly feel cross with myself. I don't like being mean about people, and I certainly don't like being inhospitable. So what if we have to entertain Maggie's colleagues again? I like cooking, I like entertaining, I like people. Besides, I spend enough time on my own. 'You need to get out more,' Maggie's always saying.

Julie too, in her way. 'Don't forget, it's all about engaging with an audience,' she's said. 'Meeting and mingling, whether in person or online.'

Something else is bothering me, and I don't even have to rack my brain before an image comes to me. It's of Maggie leaving the house this morning, looking especially gorgeous and youthful, in her navy Sonia Rykiel jacket, her old moss-green Prada skirt, her brown knee-high boots from Burberry, which I bought her for her fortieth (thinking I was about to clinch a film deal – I got that close). There she goes in my mind, rushing down the path, not so much as glancing over her shoulder: her new, shorter-than-normal hairstyle shining in the early morning gloom.

How could I not want to please her, to make her happy? Maggie works hard. Is highly respected. Very personable and outgoing. She'd do brilliantly in my business, in any business. My lamb dish won't disappoint her colleagues – I wouldn't do that to her. Truth be known, I'm probably better at cooking than writing. I'm sure Michael and Liz and Ashish would attest to that. Actually Liz isn't quite so dismissive of my stuff. Nor Maggie, of course. She's not just outgoing, but very open-minded.

The butcher too? I wonder, as I watch him tie the string around the roll of lamb. Does he read crime? My stuff even? He knows my name and, thinking about it, the local newspaper did do a piece on me when my last book came out.

His fat fingers are exhibiting surprising dexterity. Certainly he shows serious talent for his chosen career. He's now weighing the neatly boned shoulder of lamb and – what about this for a nice touch – clearly I'm not even going to have to pay for the bone. I pay for what I actually take home. Just the meat and, as Maggie might add, the fat – a bargain. What do people actually get when they buy one of my books? A bargain?

'That's twelve pounds forty-nine,' he says. 'Anything else I can do for you today, Mr Slavitt?' He's wrapping the meat in greaseproof paper and putting it into a clear plastic bag, which he seals with blue tape.

Flesh being deboned and stuffed into a plastic bag: now there's an idea I should have incorporated before now. What did Julie say to me the last time we spoke, and after I'd informed her that I was well under way with the new one (as if)? 'This time, David, you've simply got to work a little harder at shocking us from the word go. Look at what's out there nowadays, at what's happening in the first few pages – torture, mutilations, some really hideous scenes. This is what people want. Look at your peers – did you see Jo's latest, and Mark's, and Sharon's particularly? She's just getting better and better. I know you are in contact with these guys. Take a leaf out of their books. Before it's too late and you get dumped for being too tame and not generating nearly enough sales – hey, David?'

I might once have exchanged an email or two with those very successful writers, having cornered them at a launch or a festival and badgered them for their contact details (it's not as if Julie or my publishers have ever been overly keen at releasing the personal details of their authors, to their other authors). But there's only so much traffic you can initiate. Only so much meeting and mingling with people like that before you are dubbed a pain in the arse.

'Card or cash?' the butcher is saying, staring at me quizzically.

'Oh, card. Sorry, I was miles away.' I reach inside my jacket for my wallet, retrieve it, fish out my Visa card, hand it over, saying, 'I'm sorry, but I don't think I know your name.' I shrug, but am pleased with myself for trying at last.

'No reason why you should,' the butcher says. 'It's pretty obvious who you are. I get to swipe your card every time. Anyway, it's Howard, Howard Jones. My mates call me Howie.'

'Well, thanks, Howie,' I say – can I say Howie? – as he hands me back my card and the receipt and then the meat, securely taped into its clear plastic bag: watery blood already pooling at the cold, squashy bottom. Maybe he doesn't read fiction. Not many men do.

'Enjoy your lamb,' he says as I'm exiting.

'Yeah, I'm sure we will, thanks.' I don't turn around.

'Wow!' I say into my smartphone (Maggie has an iPhone – I went for the cheaper option, plus not being one to jump readily on a bandwagon . . .). 'That's amazing.'

'It's a start,' says Julie. 'And just in time, frankly.'

'A start?' I've been shortlisted for the Crime Thriller of the Year, as voted for by the public of course. I can barely breathe.

She rattles off the other contenders.

'I'm in good company, too,' I say. 'This really is something. Thank God!'

'To be honest, David, it's taken me somewhat by surprise also.'

'Thanks, Julie.'

'Pleasure. Let's just hope you win – hey? No one remembers runners-up.'

'Give me a chance.'

'And, David, we also need to have a proper chat about America. I'm not sure Jo Spear is pushing you hard enough. Though this will give her some ammunition.'

'Can we talk about this when I'm at my desk?'

'Talk about backwaters.'

'What?'

'Those forgotten American cities.'

'It's my style, I think. I like backwaters.'

'But a whole tour off the beaten path?'

'It's not that bad, plus there are six stops now. And more to come – come on.'

'Pittsburgh,' she laughs, more snorts actually, 'says it all, doesn't it?'

'I've got to go, Julie, I'll talk to you later.' I'm about to press the End Call button when something urgent occurs to me. 'Hang on, you still there?'

'For you, David, as ever,' she says, sniggering.

'Has Kingsmouth come into your orbit recently?'

'Kingsmouth? That shithole in your part of the world?'

'Never mind where it is, but have you heard of anything being set there? Anyone using it as a backdrop? Anything in the pipeline featuring the place?'

'Nope, don't think so.'

'You sure? No one using it for a new series?'

'David, don't tell. Please.'

I can't discern whether Julie's quietly excited or bloody worried. I don't want to know which. 'I've got to go,' I say. 'Speak soon.' I stab the red End Call button, determined to enjoy my moment of shortlisting glory

Recognition comes in the end, if you work hard enough, and long enough. And have the talent.

Having typed in Crime Thriller of the Year, it takes me seconds to find the current year and a list of sites featuring the shortlist announcement. It's the blogs and e-zines I'm looking for – the comments.

I click onto Shots, find the brief item, then already a few comments below it. Oh!

Amazed to see David Slavitt among this crew. Hasn't written a decent book since sometime in last century. – The Hammett.

Didn't know Slavitt was still writing. – Penny M.

Didn't know he ever could write. – Mark.

Too cruel. He's a fine prose stylist. Great on character and place. And his plots always feel authentic. – Mrs Peacock.

Too authentic for me – they're boring. Or the only one I've read was. The guy shouldn't be writing crime. – Christa X.

The crime is apparently he still is writing crime, and being rewarded for it. – J.

That's why I've been trying to avoid this shit – bloody hell, even now – and get on with what matters.

Three

Howie Jones stepped out of the shower, found the small, thin towel, dried himself as best he could. Throwing the towel on the single bed, he looked at his hands closely – an old habit. He reached for his clothes. Baz was fast asleep on a rug at the foot of the bed, snoring away. He'd never had a dog that had snored quite so loudly. But he'd never had a Boxer before.

About to wake the dog Jones had second thoughts. He walked over to the window, pulled back the curtains and peered out.

Up by the Coastwatch station there were fewer vehicles, but the tape and tent were still there, flapping in the stiff breeze. A couple of figures could be seen on the dunes.

He brought his gaze closer, and looked down. His room was in the corner of the building and had two windows, providing views of Marine Parade and the Kingsmouth seafront and a side street, Victoria Road. It was why he'd specified this one.

The side street was deserted. He knew the parked cars by heart, scruffy Fords, an old Merc, an ancient Nissan, a couple of Fiats, a Hyundai. There was nothing he hadn't seen before, except a midnight-blue Audi A6 – sports trim. Someone was sitting in the driver's seat.

Grabbing his coat, his phone and kicking Baz awake, Jones hurriedly made for the door.

But by the time he'd stepped onto the pavement, Baz by his heel, and had walked the twenty metres or so to turn the corner into Victoria Road, the Audi had gone.

'That's enough, Maggie,' Michael is saying, 'stop deflecting. What's he really like?'

'Intense,' Maggie says.

'He has got extraordinary eyes,' says Ashish. 'Don't think much of his dress sense, however. He wears this huge trench coat, lots of black and these massive steel-toe-capped boots. Has lots of wispy facial hair too.'

'That doesn't surprise me,' says Liz. 'He'd have to be pretty strange and intense, given his subject. Obsessive anyway. What is it exactly: Proust and unconscious desire? That right?'

'I think so,' says Michael. 'Maggie – he's your guy?'

'Hasn't that been done a hundred times already?' says Ashish. Adding quickly, 'It's not his first PhD, is it?'

'No idea,' says Liz. 'Not my school – I'm just the low-rent sociologist. You lot in Lit should know. But a multiple PhD-er? I'm always wary of them. Multiple MA-ers are bad enough. Beware the serial student.'

'He's got a new angle,' says Maggie.

'If you say so,' says Ashish. 'Though I doubt it will be very revelatory. Those Proustians are always rehashing old ideas, somnolently, one after the other.'

'Steady on,' says Maggie. 'That's a bit unfair.'

'Still, he must be very bright,' says Liz. 'There must be some rewards to supervising him.'

'From what I've heard – though I'm not sure it's got to do with his brain,' laughs Ashish. 'Maybe he's the type that women like to mother. But what would I know?'

'To be honest,' says Maggie, 'he's a pain in the arse. I've never had a postgrad who's quite so needy and persistent. And incompetent. He's taking up far too much of my time. He won't upgrade.'

'Really?' says Ashish. 'Why am I not surprised?'

'You certainly seem to attract them, don't you, Maggie,' says Michael.

'It's just my area,' says Maggie, 'I guess. More fool me.'

I don't mean to be hearing this. And I don't quite know why I'm hovering here, just outside the kitchen, by the door to the toilet, within clear earshot.

Having checked on Jack, who'd been coughing loudly, and then having quickly slipped into my study to jot something down, I was on my way back to the kitchen – not, I suppose, exactly hurrying, because blimey I was getting a little bored with all the shop talk (pleased actually that Jack had provided the initial excuse for me to escape the dinner) – when Michael's voice stopped me in my tracks. '. . . *What's he really like?*'

Michael has always fancied Maggie. And I can definitely detect a jealous tone to his voice tonight. Actually, I've heard him use that tone with her before (also in front of his long-suffering wife Liz).

Maggie's fully aware that Michael fancies her. Aware too, as is everyone in this city, that Michael is an atrocious flirt and completely lecherous – those poor students of his – and quite probably an adulterer. Not that I care particularly, because Maggie most certainly doesn't fancy Michael. It would be impossible (given his absurdly sculpted beard, his strangely thinning hair, bad breath, grand age and general out-of-touch demeanour), as she's more than made clear, on more than one occasion.

'Jack OK?' says Maggie quickly (warily?), as I step back into the kitchen.

'He'll be all right, if he can get to sleep. Bad cough.' I look around the table. It's almost an antique and can fit eight at a push, so there's plenty of space for the five of us, except that Michael seems to have shifted his chair closer to Maggie's. He, Maggie and Ashish are now up one end, with Liz nearer the other end.

As usual Michael's glass is empty, Ashish is on mineral water, Maggie is taking her time over a glass of white wine and Liz appears to have made little headway with her red. Before sitting, I reach over for the bottle, a 2009 Château Calon, which I managed to find lurking at the bottom of the almost-empty wine rack under the stairs, fill Michael's glass, and my own.

'That was lovely lamb,' says Liz.

'Thanks. Does anyone want any more?' I don't tell them that they really have Howie Jones to thank. I suppose I need to thank him too now, for providing me with not just a name for my character, but a shape.

'I couldn't,' says Liz. 'I'm stuffed.' She starts patting her large stomach.

The others appear not to have heard. 'Well, I'm going to,' I say, and walk over to the counter by the cooker, pick up the carving knife – an old Sabatier that I find impossible to get sharp – and slice myself some more meat, spoon on some of the salty, lemony sauce, thickening now as the fat begins to solidify, then return to my seat, which creaks rather alarmingly as I sit. Some of the chairs, an odd assortment of almost-antiques too, are getting very wobbly indeed.

'Are you working on a new book, David?' says Liz brightly, obviously now being excluded from the conversation going on at the other end of the table.

'I think so,' I laugh.

'What's it this time?' Michael says, suddenly lifting his near-bald head – a vivid mess of colours and sheen – and looking straight at me, a smile beginning to spread across his pointy little face, with that ridiculously sculpted beard. He quickly takes a slurp of wine, finishing his very recently replenished glass. 'A serial killer preying on whom?' he says, swallowing. 'Old grannies? Young girls? Little boys?'

'Prostitutes, actually,' I say, before taking a long sip of wine myself. 'Well, maybe anyway.'

'Now that has been done,' says Ashish, looking up and my way too, frowning slightly, 'a hundred times before.'

While Michael has far too little hair, of the wrong colour, Ashish has a full head of wonderfully thick, very dark shoulder-length hair. A few too many acne scars sadly spoil his rich complexion. Though he's a handsome and pretty stylish fellow all right – never short of a boyfriend apparently, not that we ever get to meet them. Maggie is always saying he's surprisingly secretive about his love life, doesn't like to be gossiped about at work, even though he's not averse to gossiping about everyone else.

'Sorry, I don't mean to be rude, David,' Ashish continues, 'but something of an obvious target also, no?'

'Everything's been done before,' says Maggie. 'But as David will tell you,' she smiles at me, with her lovely mouth and perfect teeth (all natural), 'it's how you tell it. How he tells it. The characters and dialogue and suspense you create. That's the skill. That's how to keep it fresh, and up to date, sort of. Isn't it, David? It doesn't have to be new all the time. Just good and entertaining.'

I wish I could articulate my aims – what I do – so clearly. I'm suddenly wishing also that Maggie would go online in my support, add a few well-considered (and deserved?) comments. She has always had a pretty good grasp of the main issues, and has always been brilliantly supportive of my work. But of course it's her job, one way or another, to articulate literary intent. Literary? 'I've always thought Maggie could do my job for me,' I say.

'Hardly,' she says. 'Not to award-winning standards.' She winks at me.

I cough, look away. Maggie wanted us to have champagne this evening, but I said I didn't want her to mention the fact that I'd been shortlisted for the Crime Thriller of the Year, in case I didn't win.

'There's not a lot Maggie couldn't do,' Ashish is saying, shaking his head, or rather tossing his mane over the collar of his dark-green, satiny shirt. To have hair like that!

'I can't believe, syntactically, that it can be, or should be, all that complicated and original, each time – the amount you or your chums churn out, David,' says Michael. 'Surely anything too sophisticated or innovative would pass over most of your readers' heads. Aren't they just after blood and guts? Some gratuitous violence? A bit like pornography, I suppose. A quick fix.'

'You know all about that,' mutters Liz.

'Expectations change,' says Maggie. 'Though crime fiction probably has got more violent.'

'Definitely,' I say.

'See,' says Michael. 'And to feed this fix you have to create ever more graphic scenes and images.'

Weirdly Michael's beginning to sound a bit like Julie on a bad day. I can hear her saying, again, 'Don't shy away from what's out there, David.' The last book Julie told me to read came with the strapline: *A professional torturer whose methods know no bounds*.

'That's just it,' Ashish chips in, while tossing his hair back again, but with more vigour, a definite waspish note of jollity in his voice too, 'ever more shocking and inventive descriptions of murder and mutilation. The language, like the plots, being twisted and twisted,' he laughs some more, 'to accommodate what might once have been described as indescribable. You know how, after an atrocity, you are always hearing people say "Words can't describe such evil". Well, perhaps David, and his lot, are describing that so-called evil.'

No, I'm not, again – nowhere near (not yet anyway). But Ashish wouldn't know. He's never read any of my books.

'Making it the everyday,' he continues, 'what we should expect – there's a danger there, I suppose. But nothing is indescribable.'

It's one thing to get direction and pressure from Julie, and Peter too, occasionally and brutally, as is his way. But from Ashish, Michael, these academics? I look at Maggie, seeking support or just a friendly, conspiratorial smile, but she's looking at Michael.

'I hate the word evil,' Michael's now saying. 'Bound up as it is with a wholly outdated religiosity.' He taps his empty glass. 'Actually I should rephrase that – with an ignorantly appropriated religious fundamentalism. It's basically lazy, prejudicial shit. The Nobel laureate Mario Vargas Llosa said, of course, referring to people who commonly used the term, that it was mental laziness that turned people into idiots.'

'Actually, I don't think David's books are even trying to be that gory or graphic,' says Liz, turning to me, her round cheeks smothered with something greasy and lilac-tinted; though it could be the lighting, our new energy-saving bulbs.

Thanks, Liz, I don't say – I'm not sure I want to be reminded of the fact. Liz is an odd fish. Deeply unattractive like her husband, but in an entirely different way. While he's so thin and angular, she's so round and plump. Yet they're on something of a physical par, Maggie's always saying, meaning that they are equally unattractive.

'You'd know, I suppose,' says Michael, catching my eye and attempting to smile – those thin lips, encased in that ridiculously maintained facial hair – 'there's always one of David's books on the stack by your bed.'

Is he trying to pay a compliment?

He reaches across for the wine bottle, starts helping himself and not anyone else. 'The stuff Liz reads at night – well, it shocks me. It's not the violence so much as the quality of the prose. Does it give you nightmares, darling?'

'David,' says Liz, 'he's never read one of your books. I don't think he's ever read a thriller.'

'I've skimmed a few,' Michael says. 'Enough. Anyway I'm not talking about David's books specifically, obviously,' he says. 'But that fellow Dan whatsit, and that other one who doesn't even write all his own books, and that Essex woman and her gangster stuff.'

'You're surprisingly well informed,' says Maggie.

'I am married to Liz,' says Michael, smirking again. 'It's unavoidable.'

'Well,' says Ashish, 'as we all know, there's a vast market for them.' He takes a sip of his mineral water. 'Lovely food, as ever, David.'

'Thanks,' I say, thinking it might be unavoidable to incorporate Michael (or rather someone modelled on him – it would be a shame not to use his very particular features) in my current work. It's not that he'd recognise himself, as he won't be reading it. But Liz might, I suppose. Though would she care if she spotted him on the page? She might find it funny – depending on what happens to him, what role he plays.

'Who's for some dessert?' I start clearing the plates, taking Michael's, then Ashish's.

'Yes, please,' says Liz. 'I can always find a little room for some pud.'

Stepping across to the sink, I'm suddenly bothered by something Ashish said a little earlier, about obvious targets. Shortlisting or not, as I very well know, I've got to dramatically raise my game.

'Detective, I thought you should see this,' said the forensic pathologist, Dr Michelle Colony, through her mask. They were in the cold, brightly lit lab, attached to the regional operations and communications centre.

'How was that missed?' said Hayes, as the pathologist held up a big plastic evidence bag containing a large knife. The blade smudged with dry blood.

'You're not going to like this,' said Colony. 'It was inserted so deeply there was no obvious trace around her labia. And rigor mortis meant that it wasn't until I performed the autopsy back here that it became clear. The officers who bagged her didn't have a clue.'

'But you were on the scene,' said Hayes. 'I don't understand. Why didn't you spot anything? There must have been some blood, tearing.'

'As I said, it had been pushed a long way in,' said Colony.

Hayes shivered in the crisp, purple chill of the lab. 'Well, let's hope it's smothered in DNA. What is it? A small carving knife?'

Colony was in her early thirties, a decade younger than Hayes. She was bright, attractive, had a decent sense of humour. Hayes had no idea why such a person would want to be a forensic pathologist. But then she often wondered why anyone would want to be a detective.

'Yes,' said Colony studying it, 'a Sabatier, but pretty old, and blunt too. Which might partly explain a lack of blood.'

'Partly?' Hayes stepped back from the gurney.

'I don't think she was alive when the knife was inserted into her vagina,' said Colony.

'That's not how she died?'

'No, definitely not.'

'So how did she die?' said Hayes.

'Too early to tell, I'm afraid, Britt. Though you knew I was going to say that.' Colony smiled. 'I need the toxicology results to be sure.'

Colony put the knife down and moved round the gurney so that she was facing the corpse. Feeling steadier, Hayes moved closer. The corpse's legs had been parted, but she averted her eyes.

'She was drugged first?' asked Hayes.

'I believe so. The thing is, the knife was not used in a particularly frenzied way. The internal trauma is limited.'

'Nevertheless we're talking posthumous mutilation, right?' said Hayes.

'As I said, I can't be certain yet, and it depends what you mean by mutilation, but it appears something like that,' said Colony.

'Any other sign of force? I noticed a few faint bruises.'

'She definitely wasn't strangled, if that's what you mean. In fact there are no other serious marks on her body. There's a fair amount of bruising for sure, some odd patterns; most is old, however, and nothing that could have proved fatal.'

'So she must have been drugged,' said Hayes.

'One way or another,' said Colony. 'She could have OD'd.'

'Any track marks?' said Hayes.

'No track marks, but that doesn't mean she wasn't a user. She was very thin, malnourished. Bad skin, under the make-up. Bad gums.'

'Look at it this way,' said Hayes, 'unconscious, she could have been stripped, if she wasn't naked already, and then dumped in the dunes. Which might mean we're not looking at murder.'

'I guess,' said Colony.

'But why would someone ram a knife up her vagina, if she were already dead?'

Colony, looking intently at Hayes, shrugged. 'I can only do my bit, as quickly as possible, then it's up to you, I'm afraid,' she said.

'Thanks,' said Hayes.

The bedroom is very dark, with just a faint frame of street light leaking around the curtains. The windows are firmly shut and doing what they can (for their age and condition) to block any freezing draught. Despite not fully succeeding (by any stretch), there's a rather cloying, roast-meat smell.

Maggie's on her side of the bed, the duvet tucked tightly around her. Walking quietly to my side, nearest the window, I hear her stir. Placing my glass of water on the bedside table, I somehow dislodge a book, can't grab it in time in the dimness and it falls to the floor with a thump.

'Where have you been?' she says, shifting under the covers, sounding as if she hasn't been asleep.

'Finishing tidying up.'

'I thought we'd done that.'

It really does feel incredibly stuffy in the bedroom (despite the ever-present draught), probably because the heating has been on later than normal. 'Mostly,' I say. 'And I just had to note something down.'

'Oh, of course, the new novel.'

'I hope you're not going to start sounding like Michael.'

'Please,' says Maggie. 'You can give me more credit than that. You know how proud I am of you. How supportive.'

'Sorry. Yes, of course I know you are. And I really appreciate it – more than you could ever know.'

'I'm just very tired. Shattered.' She fidgets, grabbing more duvet. 'It's work – it's really getting to me at the moment.'

'All that time you're spending helping ungrateful research students can't help,' I say. Though I'm not sure why I said *ungrateful*.

'That, yeah, but there's talk of more cuts within the administrative staff; it just heaps more pressure on the academics.'

'I can see that – must be awful.' I pick up the book and place it carefully (my eyes more used to the dimness now) on my bedside table, thinking: poor Maggie, poor university, being starved of cash by a government totally disinterested in any form of state-funded education. I didn't have much of a formal education, and there was a time when I thought I'd done all right regardless. But I'm no longer so sure. I could do with some proper qualifications, a back-up.

Besides, with two rapidly growing children and a wife who's an academic, I want a generous commitment from my government. Education, education, education, as someone once said, a long time ago now.

I wouldn't mind if Michael was axed, though. Sighing to myself, I know this is not a good line to go down. I know very little about Michael's particular world, his area of study – Modernist poetry, some obscure thread, featuring lots of Italians, I believe, or is it Latin Americans? – just as he knows virtually nothing of mine.

Is his world as competitive, as thick with rivalry? Do academics also stoop at nothing for their own artistic and commercial gain?

Having put on my pyjama bottoms and an old T-shirt (my sleeping gear) as quietly as I could, I still feel hot, the room unbearably stuffy (despite that bloody draught). Has Maggie dropped back off? I'd dearly love to open the window properly, get a real blast. Everything needs freshening up, if not shaking up.

Stepping over the rickety floorboards, quiet as a I can (though it's not easy), I gently part the curtains, release the knackered brass catch, put my hands on the middle of the frame, get ready to slide the top half down, when I see someone across the street. Looking at me.

There's a man in a long, dark trench coat just to the side of the front path leading to the house opposite. His back is against the hedge, and he's still looking straight up at me. I can see his eyes. Then I can't.

He's turned and is walking quickly away down the road, adjusting the collar, seemingly sinking further into the heavy-looking garment.

Four

'I'm afraid he's with a new author,' she says. Zoe, I'm sure her name is.

I've spoken to her so many times I should know. But we've never been formally introduced and it's sort of hard to meet someone on the phone, especially when you've been badgering them for a while (I did meet her predecessor, in person, however). Plus I don't always want Zoe to know it's me – the difficult, needy author who's always ringing, always asking to speak to Peter, and failing.

However, I'm sure she does know exactly who's on the other end right now. I can almost see the faces she must be pulling for the benefit of her colleagues (the editorial assistants sit in pods, gossiping, while the editors and publishers have their own cubicles and offices – from distant memory).

'Do you know when he'll be free?' I ask.

'I think they are then going for lunch. He's meant to be in a meeting from three-thirty. You could try him nearer five. Five-thirty might be more realistic.'

'What time's he leaving for the evening?' I know what she's going to say.

'It depends whether he's got an event,' she says. 'I'm pretty sure something's going on tonight.'

'Well, could you tell him I rang, please? I have been trying for a while. It's quite important.' Right now I do want Peter to know that I would like to speak to him. Frankly I think he could have rung me when he found out I'd been shortlisted for the Crime Thriller of the Year – the event itself is now just days away; I don't even know whether he's going.

OK, I got a brief email when it was announced (or shortly after), but that's not the same as a call. Plus I want to reassure him that the new novel is up and running, that I'm not going to be too far behind schedule – indeed, that plans can be made for its publication next year, as per the contract.

I want to slip in news about my forthcoming American tour too. Though this will have little immediate commercial impact on the UK side of things, it has to look good, if I'm being taken seriously in the US, again. Indeed, I want to stress upon him that all is looking good. I shouldn't need to be doing this of course. It should be obvious. However, what I think is obvious and what Peter thinks is obvious do not always tally.

'Sure. I'll tell him,' she says. I can almost hear her yawning.

'It's David by the way, David Slavitt.'

'Yes, I know,' she says.

Replacing the receiver, I turn back to my screen and a page on the university's website detailing current literature research students. Quite a few people are listed. Though I can't find any males doing anything on Proust specifically. Or the unconscious. Or desire. That said, I probably don't know what to look for. How, critically, it would be couched. The language these people use is almost foreign to me. And there are no photos anyway.

I reach for the phone again, dial Maggie's office number. But it rings out to answerphone. I don't leave a message. Or try her mobile. But can't help thinking there are only so many meetings she can go to. She's an academic, not an administrator.

'I said leave her in an obvious place, out in the open.' Adrian Fonda had his mobile clamped to his ear, the newspaper open on the desk in front of him. 'Make it look as if she just wandered off,' he added.

'I did,' said Kesteris, faintly, in his thick accent.

'You seen the news?'

'Yes.'

'So what the fuck was she doing without her clothes on?' Fonda was struggling to keep his voice down.

'I don't know.'

'What the fuck do you mean, you don't know?' He should end the call – have this conversation elsewhere, even if the place was deserted because of the Christmas break.

'I left her in the dunes, in the clothes she was wearing when we found her – honestly, my friend. I did exactly what you asked me to do. She was still alive. I promise you.'

'How then do you explain the fact that she was found completely naked – so it only says all over the fucking news?'

'I don't know,' said Kesteris, 'perhaps she wanted to go for a swim.'

'In her state? In the middle of winter? The police are talking about a sexual motive, about disturbing details they can't go into. The news is full of it: some sexual predator, some psychopath on the loose, is what that lot of troublemakers are making out.'

'My friend, I'm telling you the truth. It's nothing to do with me. I drove her to the front, beyond the Coastwatch station. Carried her from the car. Left her where you told me to. Everything was shut up. It was dark. It was Christmas Eve. No one could have seen anything. I promise you. It's nothing to do with me what then happened to her. I don't understand it. When I last saw her she was in her clothes. And she was still alive – just.'

'You're lying,' said Fonda.

'Adrian, my friend, I'm telling the truth, I promise you.' His voice wasn't so faint any more. But that accent was grating on Fonda.

'If you're trying to set me up, I'll kill you,' Fonda said.

'Adrian, we're working together for many years. You don't trust me now?'

'Where the fuck are you?' said Fonda.

'Out of town.'

'I bet you are. Well, I want you back here. Now! We need to get to the bottom of this. Someone's fucking me around.'

There, the first ring of the bell. Followed very quickly by another, and another, and the usual scuffling by the front door.

'Dad?' I can hear, even from my study. It's Jack, shouting. I look at my screen, then at the door to the study, before returning to my screen.

Julie, or rather Julie's assistant Mel, had emailed me a link to a new author's site. *'Julie thought you'd be interested in this,'* Mel had written. The author, a German, or actually a Croatian who writes in German, has, it seems, with his first novel become, almost overnight, an international best-seller. It wasn't the pithy one-word title of this novel that especially struck me, but the very brief description of it on the site's home page – the opening gambit. A nameless man drags a nameless woman into an apartment building and nails her to the wall. It doesn't say whether she's alive or dead, or which bits of her are nailed. I'll have to read the book.

I hear the key being put into the front door, hear the front door opening and Jack and Poppy and Emily piling in.

'Hi,' I hear Emily shouting. She has a very loud voice. A loud way of being. Seems to be making sure that her gap year doesn't go unnoticed. Now there's rattling on my door – Jack or Poppy, though probably Jack – trying to get in.

'Hang on,' I shout, leaving my desk and marching across to the door and pulling it open, to see Poppy's lovely face looking up at me.

'I'm hungry,' she says.

'Hi, darling,' I say. 'Hi, Emily.'

Emily is down the hall, picking up Jack's coat, Jack as usual having just shrugged it off onto the floor.

'Hi,' she says.

'Poppy,' I say, 'Emily will get you something to eat. I've got to work.'

'Mum said we could have pancakes,' says Poppy.

'Really?'

'Can you make them, please?'

'No, sweetheart, I've got to work.' I'm trying to edge back into my study.

'But Emily doesn't know how,' Poppy says.

I look at Emily, who, having hung up Jack's coat, smiles.

'I can try,' she says.

I don't think I want her to try. She has problems warming up baked beans.

'You'll have to wait,' I say to Poppy.

'But Mum said,' says Poppy.

'When?'

'Just now. We saw her walking back from school.'

'What?'

'Maggie was cycling into town,' says Emily. 'She was in bit of a rush, but said if the kids were good they could have pancakes. It's Pancake Day.'

'Oh. Where was Maggie going exactly?' I ask Emily.

'I don't know. She was heading into town,' says Emily.

Maggie didn't tell me she was going into town this afternoon.

'She might have been with someone,' says Emily. 'I'm not sure.'

'What do you mean? Who?'

'I don't know really. There were some people – one person anyway – who stopped when she did. Though he wasn't on a bike. He was walking. But I think Maggie knew him. Perhaps it was a coincidence. He looked like a student, I guess.'

'Dad,' says Jack, joining Emily and Poppy, 'Mum said we can have pancakes.'

'So I hear, but, guys, I have to work. You'll have to wait until your mother gets back. Emily can make you some toast.'

'That's not the same,' says Jack.

'Come on,' says Emily, placing her hands on Jack's shoulders and steering him towards the kitchen, 'your dad has to work.'

Firmly shutting my study door, I can't help wondering about how you nail someone to a wall so that they actually hang there. I guess Jesus was nailed to a cross, but a wall seems harder somehow, at least harder for a nail to get purchase on. It would be easier, I reckon, to screw someone to a wall. Though would you have to put in a Rawlplug first? DIY was never my thing. Maybe that's part of the problem. I need to think not just more imaginatively, but more practically.

Where the fuck was Maggie going? And with whom?

Fonda stabbed at the red End Call button on his phone. Dropped the cheap Nokia into his pocket. Buttoned his suit jacket, checked himself in the small mirror on the back of his door, traced the sharp outline of his beard with his fingers, then grabbed his coat and headed out of his office into the empty corridor.

He'd fling the pay-as-you-go into the river. He was getting through a device a week at the moment.

That fucking Latvian! He should never have trusted him. A bullet in the back of his head would be too good for him. What he deserved was a slow, painful death.

It could be arranged.

Taking note is one thing – in my line that's being sharp and observant, et cetera. Interrogation is another (not to mention paranoia). Marriages, like all good working relationships, have to be built around trust. I'm not going to ask her, this time (if I can help it). Besides, I need to concentrate while I can. A lot is coming up. I'm going to be busier than ever. I don't need further, unnecessary distractions.

'I'm onto it, mate,' the man across the aisle is saying far too loudly into his BlackBerry, with more than a hint of an Essex accent.

Funny how life imitates art, I can't help thinking. Or rather how, if you look for something hard enough, you can find it. Funny too how time consolidates and chunks disappear. Is this life-editing?

He's my age, perhaps a bit younger, a bit slimmer too – much slimmer actually. He's wearing a dark suit, with faint blue stripes, and wide lapels. He also has on a white shirt with an embossed pattern: the top two buttons undone. I look away, thinking he probably doesn't treat the women in his life very well. I wouldn't want to get on the wrong side of him, either. Some people just exude menace.

'How many fucking times?' he's now saying.

The train's late. The train's always late. We're idling somewhere, still at least an hour from London, Colchester to come first, then Chelmsford, then Stratford. My laptop's open in front of me, my beloved MacBook Pro, which is a godsend on occasions like this – or it would be, if the other passengers weren't so distracting. But they always are. Just what did I expect? Peace and quiet?

There's a new housing estate out of the window on my right, on the outskirts of Colchester; I'm pretty sure that's where we are. These oddly tall, detached houses – half brick, half clad in brightly painted clapboard, with strikingly small windows – have been arranged, though much too close together, in seemingly random patterns, no doubt to diminish the effect of uniformity, of claustrophobia. Built here, on the cheap, on a former green-field site – three-four-bedroom executive homes, in prime commuter belt – with numerous people on the make (I'm thinking of the grants and tax-breaks, the cuts and backhanders, not just the sales), including of course at least someone from the council planning department. How these applications get pushed through in the first place.

While Fonda had plenty of legitimate power as head of Kingsmouth's planning department, and was being touted as the next council leader, it was his other activities that had generated both the lifestyle and his air of invincibility.

Perhaps it was because of the season, the season of goodwill, but for once he'd been looking forward to getting home, to his large, detached house across the River Yare in Gorleston. And to spending the evening with Tanya and their son River – so named because of the view.

If River had been a girl they were going to call her Hope: the dilapidated docks and redundant power station of Kingsmouth sprawling away beyond the water. Hope for some – for those who knew where to look – but not for many.

Now he'd have to make other plans.

'No way. You're kidding, right?' the man across the aisle is now saying. 'You lucky fucker.'

Retrieving my phone from my suit jacket pocket, I call Maggie. It goes straight to answerphone. 'Hello, darling,' I say, loudly. 'I'm on the train, not moving. Hope it doesn't get in too late – then again, I can't say I'm exactly looking forward to this evening, especially without you. I'm not going to win. I can just feel it.' I pause for a second, look out of the window; can't spot a living person in any of the new-builds. 'Everything all right? I'll call you when I get to London, before the event.'

Maggie's going to Birmingham early tomorrow for a conference, and I won't be back home until God knows when tonight. I would have stayed in London, had she not been off first thing in the morning – she's a plenary conference, and couldn't get out of it, really. So I'll be needed to get the kids to school (again), plus I just didn't feel like staying in town, without Maggie. Not that I relish the late train back from London. I'll have had too much to drink and will only be able to sit there in an uncomfortable slumber: unable to read, unable to work, unable to sleep properly. It'll be a terrible waste of time. As this evening will be also, no doubt.

I'm nervous. First major prize I've been up for in years. It used to be held in the autumn, a big swanky dinner at a posh London hotel, and on telly too, but it's still a major deal, even if the dinner has been replaced by drinks and canapés, and the venue shifted to the South Bank.

Maggie would have come with me of course, had she not been going to this conference in Birmingham – she was asked ages ago. It's the most important international event in her field. Happens every two years. And of course she is a plenary. I understand. I do.

We could have arranged childcare, used Emily, I'm sure, and she could have gone straight to Birmingham from London, tomorrow morning, but she couldn't face all the rushing around and the late night. Said she needed to be fresh, on top form, and was too busy at work today anyway – even if she had been fully prepared, which she wasn't – with another round of meetings. It was just very bad timing, she said, more than once. 'It's OK,' I replied, more than once as well.

And in a way I'd rather she didn't see me lose to, well, I reckon it will be the guy I lost to all those years ago, when I was last up for an award; it was with my first novel. Can't believe we're both in the running this time.

Not everyone is saying it's my turn; I've stopped looking at the comments on the Internet about it, since I spotted the word 'fraud' on *CrimeTime*. Someone had actually bothered to log on, find the site, find the item, find the trail and post the comment: *David Slavitt is a fraud*.

Fortunately Julie believes it is my turn. Finally she seems to be getting excited. Peter's not as excited or, of course, as excitable as Julie anyway, but he knows, as he informed me on the phone just this morning when I eventually got hold of him, how many sales of my latest book – and my backlist – a win would represent; how it could well push me into Sainsbury's, possibly even Tesco.

'The thing is,' the man across the aisle is saying, 'you don't have the goods. Never have had.' He's on a new conversation – with, by the sounds of it, not such a lucky fucker.

As I tap a key on my laptop, the screen flickers to life, as too does the train, which begins to gather speed, noisily and shakily, as we pass more of the new housing development. Here most of the properties appear a long way from being finished. Plastic sheeting is flapping in the wind. Dusk is gathering fast all around.

'I'm joking, mate,' he's saying. 'Calm down.'

How can I work? And now my phone seems to be going. I quickly press the green button. 'Hello?'

'Looking smart?' she says straight away.

'What do you think?'

'I did ask you to make an effort. You might not think it's the point, but tonight's as good a platform as any to start repositioning you.'

'I think I look OK. I'm wearing a suit.'

'That's what I'm worried about. Plus, you sound a bit nervous, David. It's your big night, you should be excited.'

'Julie, I'm forty-two, I don't get excited, not any more,' I lie.

'Well, don't be too nervous.'

'With everything that's riding on this?'

'It will be all right,' she says, coughing.

'Where are you? Sounds like you are outside.'

'I'm having a ciggy – celebratory. In your honour.'

'Bit premature, no?'

'I just heard from someone who's already at the Festival Hall that you're ahead in the public vote. Pretty amazing, if I say so myself.' She coughs some more.

'Can't hear you very well, Julie,' I say, trying to keep my voice down, noticing that the man across the aisle is staring at me. Don't tell me he's annoyed that I'm on the phone.

'What's more, the PR people have been onto Mel for more information about you,' she says. 'And the publicity lot over at Peter's have been kept hard at it, apparently.'

'Peter didn't mention anything like that when I spoke to him this morning.'

'You know what he's like. It's almost in the bag, my boy. I can smell it this time.'

He's still looking at me. I turn away, trying to focus on what's happening outside the window – the dark countryside slipping by, behind my reflection: my chubby cheeks, not going anywhere. Perhaps I should start exercising, lose some weight and help that repositioning. Go to the gym maybe; Maggie now goes (when she's got a moment, which is meant to be like never), says it's doing wonders for her bum. And her energy levels. 'You're cracking up, Julie.'

'Don't be late,' she says, clearly.

Pushing aside my laptop and reaching for my notepad and pen, I write *Kristine* at the top of a fresh page. Circle it. The title? Sitting back in the ancient seat (courtesy of the oldest rolling stock still in use in the country), I close my eyes for a few moments. *Kristine?* It reminds me of something, a novel, I think. Opening my eyes and leaning forward, I take a sip of my Innocent smoothie: a purple one, thick with pips.

Kristine – the name, such a title, is reminding me of something Scandinavian and landmark anyway. But would such an echo, if I'm on the right track, be a good thing? I suppose it depends how landmark, how classic. Anyway, so what if I'm not the most original crime writer around. As Julie once said to me, 'We're not paying you to be original, you're being paid to entertain.'

Plus the guy I'm up against tonight has been churning out the same stuff for years, piling on one twisted torture scene after another. Though the public don't seem to mind. They clearly love his stuff.

Though do they still love it more than mine?

Has the train stopped again? Yes, it's stopped, and the guy across the aisle is stabbing at his BlackBerry, putting it to his ear. I'm now trying to picture him with a beard, like Michael's, and thinning hair and glasses, but the same clothes, the same build, the same accent and air of menace.

Not wanting to look at this character again – he clearly thinks I've been staring at him, and no doubt wigging in on his telephone conversations (as if I had any option otherwise) – and not wanting to catch another eyeful of my chubby cheeks, I retrieve my phone and call Maggie again. Once more it goes straight to answerphone. I don't leave another message, but putting the phone away, I can't help seeing myself again, against the almost-black, still backdrop of somewhere in rural Essex. I hate wearing suits. And the waistband of my fine, once new-wool, dark-blue trousers (I got married in this suit) is awfully tight. Far too many dinners – mostly cooked by me.

Certainly, sitting here on my fat arse, in a stalled train, isn't doing anything for my figure, or my health. For a moment or two I think about writing a tweet: something on the lines of public transport letting everyone down, again, while ruthlessly contributing to the country's obesity problem. The ever-revolving pool of publicists at my publishers are always trying to get me to tweet more, be more visible, more social-media-savvy.

However, I always feel that whatever I try to say, however funny I try to be, these tweets must sound like nothing other than rather desperate self-promotion. I just don't have the knack, or the confidence. Unlike my old rival that I'm up against tonight – he fires them off at an extraordinary rate, so I've been made aware.

Avoiding looking at my reflection in the train window, and across the aisle to yet another adversary, avoiding also the compulsion to call Maggie yet again, I'm overwhelmed by the feeling that I'm simply not engaging with my audience (to anything like the required level for a potentially award-winning crime writer). I'm overwhelmed too by the feeling that I'm not entertaining enough anyway. I probably don't have enough to say, definitely not in short, pithy asides.

Voice isn't the only thing. Confidence and commitment are also part of the package. Putting on a front in this game seems to be more vital than ever. What do I have to do to really stand out? To stop being regarded as a fraud?

The smoothie suddenly decides to repeat on me. I struggle to swallow it back down.

What do I have to do to hang on to Maggie, and save my marriage?

Has she lost sight of my conviction? Or has she just grown bored too? Sick of looking for something that's not there.

Come on, the British public, and all (all?) my fans, keep voting, get voting, I need you now more than ever.

'Looking like a winner,' says Julie, as I walk over. She's at a small table, at the far end of the bar, by the vast windows: seemingly the whole of London stretching into the night behind her. Lights dancing on the river.

'Nice view,' I say, struck by how large, how sophisticated, how metropolitan London seems – the sense of occasion, also, now that I'm here, beginning truly to dawn on me. I'm even more nervous, and excited. 'Haven't been to the South Bank for years.'

'I don't think it's at its best,' says Julie. 'Could do with a revamp, if you ask me.'

She tilts her head towards me, making it easier for me to kiss her cheeks. She smells expensive, as ever – Coco Eau de Parfum, I reckon. And cigarettes. Appears to be wearing a Chanel jacket too.

'But it makes a change from the Grosvenor House,' she says. 'Crime writers and dinner jackets don't go. Though I guess the organisers are on a tighter budget, especially now they've lost that TV deal. Shame your big moment won't be televised.'

'Let's hope it is a big moment.'

'David, everything's pointing your way. Champagne?'

Blimey! A bottle is sitting in one of those metal buckets on a stand by the side of the table. 'Why not,' I say lifting the bottle out and filling the spare, empty glass in front of me. 'Sorry,' I add, realising Julie's glass could do with a refill. As I'm topping up Julie's a very pretty waitress appears, obviously feeling awkward that I've had to pour the champagne myself, especially as the bar, strangely, is not full. 'Don't worry,' I say to her, 'I was gasping.'

'Can I get you anything else?' the waitress says.

'No, we're fine, I think,' I say, smiling at Julie, 'aren't we?'

'Just fine,' says Julie. 'We can fill up on cheap canapés when we get into the hall.' She takes a long sip of her champagne. 'I'm sorry you've got to rush straight back home after the event. We could have made a night of it. Gone on for a proper dinner at least. I probably owe you one.'

'Probably,' I say, looking around the bar. 'It seems rather quiet in here. Sure we've got the right night?' We're in the bar restaurant at the top of the Festival Hall. It was once called the People's Palace, I seem to remember – not sure what it's called now. The event is on the lower ground floor, at the back of the building. Doors opened ten minutes ago, though the actual awards bit is not scheduled to start for another hour and a half. I really don't want to have to stand around chatting for too long – to people who either lie about having read my work, or lie about the current, staggering success of their own work. Or, worse, have to stand around not having anyone to chat to.

'I guess people are going straight there,' says Julie, 'so they can get stuck into the free fizz.'

'And the nibbles,' I say.

'That's why Peter's meeting us there, I suppose,' says Julie, grinning.

'You know what he's like,' I say. 'He doesn't seem to part with his cash, or his time happily. Not when it comes to me anyway. Though can you blame him, in this market?'

'David, crime's still bucking the trend – you know that.' Julie takes another long sip of her champagne, finishing that glass.

This time the waitress gets there in time to refill it, topping up mine also, not that I'd drunk much. If I'm going to win I certainly don't want to make some rambling, drunken acceptance speech – or bang on about how I think Shakespeare was the first true British crime writer, as I've heard before. Speaking in public is not one of my favourite things to do, which is why, just before the train arrived at Liverpool Street, I jotted down a few sentences and made a list of who I had to thank – though the most important person is not going to be there anyway.

'That's as may be, Julie,' I say, 'but all this supposed growth is not exactly impacting on me and my books.'

'OK, it's still tough, and becoming even more focused in a way, but let's see what happens tonight,' she says, leaning over the small table and slapping my thigh. 'Hopefully we'll be in a good position to make our mark and exploit what we can.' She looks at her watch, which, as I've noticed before, is man-size: a great chunk of glinting stainless-steel. 'While I've got you to myself for just a little bit longer,' she continues, 'tell me how the new one's going.'

'Good, good,' I say, before taking a long sip of champagne, then quickly look beyond Julie, to the London night sky: the Embankment thick with cars, the Savoy beautifully lit. And over to the right, the City, dominated by Tower 42, the Gherkin, and the Barbican. It makes me think of power and money, success, greed and corruption. And sex. Plus death, too, of course. But I've done with London. Don't think I was tough enough. My last London-based thriller, *The Showman*, was about a wannabe serial killer working at Canary Wharf. The *Metro* review said it '*throttles itself in a monotonous cycle of implied violence*'. Needless to say, the sales were poor.

'I should bloody well hope so,' says Julie, sharply bringing me back to the present. 'It's meant to be done by June. Isn't it?'

'I don't want to think about that – too much pressure.'

'For an autumn release, you're cutting it fine. I imagine they wanted proofs well before Harrogate. Are you going this year, by the way?'

'I don't know. I'd love to, of course, even if the last time I went I happened to be the least-popular author on the panel, as I'm sure you remember.' I smile, grimly, recalling the experience – especially of being in the bookshop afterwards, where I generated a total of five sales and had to sign someone's paperback of my first novel, which they'd brought along in a very knackered plastic bag. The three other panellists had queues stretching out of the room, with people buying their latest works.

Julie knocks back a lengthy draw of champagne, says, wiping her mouth, 'Maybe pressure's what you need. That bit of urgency. It might rub off on your plot.'

'Thanks a lot.'

'Seriously, a word of caution, though,' she says. 'You win this award, you'll be a lot busier. Think of the appearances, signings, festivals – Harrogate will be a dead cert – and then of course the foreign tours, and not just American backwaters. Will you be able to cope with that as well?' She cackles, in delight.

'Perhaps it would be better if I don't win, then.'

'David – win this and I'll press for a Crime Writers' Association lifetime achievement award. I'm on the committee, remember.'

'A lifetime achievement? I'm only forty-two.'

'But you've written so much.'

'And made so little money.' I can hear a phone ringing.

'That's not entirely my fault.' Julie smiles. Keeps smiling. 'The thing is success breeds success.'

'Is that your phone, Julie?'

'Oh yes.' She fumbles in her bag – Chanel also, I reckon, the style showing its age, but also its class, like Julie. Pulls out her BlackBerry. 'Missed it, damn!' She thumbs the roller-ball. 'It was Mel. Wondering where we are, I expect.' She puts the phone to her ear, listens to her voicemail.

'We've still got plenty of time, haven't we?' I say, mostly to myself. Looking around and behind me, I realise that the bar has filled up considerably. Though I don't recognise anyone from the world of publishing. Any authors. Oh yes, I do. By the bar, amid a group of flamboyantly dressed men, is a petite woman with strikingly blonde hair. We once shared a McDonald's. And at the far end of the bar is a tall, broad man with a natty beard. He's in a tan leather jacket and jeans, and is talking to a glamorous brunette in a short black dress. I suddenly remember that his last two novels were number-one best-sellers, and that his protagonist has now made it to the small screen, courtesy of Sky.

I also remember that I'm wearing a suit that is probably years out of fashion and is certainly far too tight.

'She wants us down there in ten minutes,' says Julie, dropping her phone into her bag. 'A couple of journalists would like a quick word with you before the ceremony. You know Barry from *CrimeTime*, don't you? Everyone knows Barry.'

'I hope Mel hasn't been saying things she shouldn't have.'

'Like what?'

'Like I've won, before they've made the announcement.'

'At least she's down there, working on your behalf. I hope your publicists are pulling their weight.'

'I'm not sure they're getting a lot of direction from Peter,' I say. 'He doesn't seem to be taking it that seriously. It's been bloody hard to get hold of him, as ever. Wouldn't surprise me if he doesn't come at all.'

'He'll be here. He doesn't want to piss me off – he's desperately trying to land one of my authors.'

'Who? What makes them so interesting?'

'If I told you who it was, you'd have a pretty good idea.'

'Don't then – I don't want to feel more insignificant.' We seem to have run out of champagne, just when I feel an overwhelming desire for another glass. Maybe I could get Julie to make the acceptance speech for me – if it comes to that. People obviously want to hear what she has to say. Besides, she could make use of her acting skills.

'I don't know what's got into you this evening, David. Is everything all right at home? With Maggie?'

Those big eyes won't let me go. Julie has long stopped making passes at me, though she still shows an interest in my marriage. Looking away, I notice that the woman I once had a McDonald's with seems to be observing us keenly. I smile at her, and half-raise my hand in a wave, but don't give her a chance to ignore me. Quickly turning back to Julie, I say, 'Absolutely fine, thank you very much.' Her antenna's up all right. The old actress is no fool.

'Good, I'm glad to hear it,' she says, studying the empty champagne bottle, as if another few drops might have materialised from the heavily perfumed air. Realising they haven't, she continues, 'So, on to more violent subjects then. Do you want to give me a quick summary of your new plot and, hopefully, these new series characters that are going to get you out of this hole?' She now looks around – for the waitress? 'I suppose we don't have time for another glass,' she says.

'No, Julie, I don't think we do. Let's go.' I straighten my jacket, reach for my bag. Stand.

'Hang on a minute.' It's almost a roar – those years of voice-coaching. 'Sit back down.'

As I sit, letting go of my bag, she pats me on the knee. My mind is suddenly blank, my eyes caught again, not by two of the most successful crime writers in the country enjoying cocktails at the bar with glamorous chums, but by that ever dramatic London skyline. I should never have abandoned the capital, should never have been so weak and oblique. The provinces just don't provide the exoticism, the scope and definitely not the full spectrum of depravity.

'Title, even?'

Slowly something seeps back into my brain: that desolate stretch of dunes, the body lying in the marram. Seemingly a million miles from here. 'I suppose I was thinking of, well, *Kristine*. That's the name of the first victim.'

'Oh,' says Julie. 'Oh,' she repeats, slowly, quietly, unenthusiastically. 'Not the most exciting title I've ever heard.'

'I knew you were going to say that. But there are very successful precedents for using simple, one-word, one-name even, titles.'

'Well, if Peter doesn't think it's right, he'll change it anyway.' She smiles. 'So she's the first victim of . . . a serial killer?'

'Do I have to reveal any more, already? It'll ruin the surprise when you get to read it.'

'If I get to read it.'

'Come on, Julie, I'm working flat out. Trust me. All right, I will tell you that one of the main characters is a tough, sexy female detective – she's head of the regional Serious Crime Unit.'

'Christ, don't make her too good to be true,' says Julie. 'Give her some flaws at least. But I'm bored of alcoholics, women with tunnel vision and, of course, young, tattooed computer hackers.' Julie looks behind her for a split-second, refocuses on me. 'Sex, though, is coming back, big time. Can you make her addicted to sex, to casual sex? What do these people do? Dogging, is it?' She pauses, a grim smile spreading across her finely made-up face. 'Just giving you some ideas here.'

'Thanks. Thanks, Julie.' Grabbing my bag once more, I stand, determinedly. 'Let's go.'

'OK,' she says, slowly standing as well and straightening her jacket and skirt and gathering her things, assembling all that Chanel, all that front. 'Into the fire.'

As we weave through the now-crowded bar – but already minus those two hot authors and their suitably fashionable entourages – Julie says loudly, behind me, 'So where's it set, this . . . what's it called again?'

'*Kristine*, and I thought I told you, Kingsmouth – somewhere like that anyway. Not sure how specific I'm going to be.'

'Oh yes, you did mention something about Kingsmouth on the phone. I hoped you weren't being serious.'

'I was, I am. What's wrong with it?'

'A little out of the way,' she says, pushing through the exit. 'I mean, it's not like you'll have much of a captive audience. Do people there even read?'

'Julie, come on.' Suddenly we're on a wide, airy concourse. We pause to get our bearings.

'Sorry, David – only joking,' she says. 'I suppose Mankell did set his Wallander books in that dumpy little Swedish coastal town.'

'Kingsmouth's much more deprived than Ystad, believe me.' I can feel my phone vibrating in my jacket pocket.

'Well, that could be something,' she says. 'Don't hold back then, this time.'

'What do you mean this time?' Retrieving my phone, I see it's Maggie, on her mobile.

'David, if this place is that shitty,' says Julie, 'just make sure you do it full justice. And make the characters behave in an equally extreme fashion. It's all about extremes right now. I don't want any of that implied nonsense. Make it clear.'

Turning my attention to my phone, I say, 'Maggie?'

'David darling, hi. I just wanted to say good luck,' says Maggie, faintly. It sounds like she's outside, again. Seems to be wind and traffic noise in the background.

'Thanks, sweetheart. Where are you?'

'Oh, still at work. Getting everything ready. It's been a horrible day.'

'Who's got the kids?'

'I asked Emily to stay on for a couple of hours. She didn't mind.'

'Oh, OK. Hope they're all right.'

'Of course they are. So, good luck then. I'm sure you'll win. You more than deserve to this time.'

'We'll see. I'm sorry you're not here.'

'So am I. Bad timing.'

'Yeah.'

'Julie will look after you, I'm sure.'

'She's right beside me.' She's not quite. She's stepping away, beckoning me down the corridor, towards the main staircase, with much theatrical urgency to her actions, which I'm not sure goes brilliantly with the Chanel. Though I suppose it's all sort of extreme. How, I realise, Julie always is.

'Send her my love. Shit!' Maggie says.

'What?'

'I've just stepped into a puddle, and done something to my ankle. Bugger – that hurts. The potholes round here. Oh God, my tights are now splattered in muddy water too.'

'I thought you were still at work?'

'I am, or I was. I'm heading to the car park.' There's the sound of rustling, and then, faintly, Maggie saying, 'Don't worry, Alex, I'm fine.'

'What? Maggie?'

'I've just bumped into someone – a student.'

'Who?'

'Just a student. It doesn't matter.'

Julie's gesticulating is becoming painful to watch. 'Oh, right,' I say. 'Look, I've got to go.'

'Me too,' Maggie says.

'Love you,' I whisper, which is not something I normally say, then press the End Call button, and let the phone drop into my pocket and jog towards Julie. 'I'm going to have to have a pee before this thing.'

'You need to watch your prostate,' Julie says.

'I'm not that old, Julie. Jesus!'

'You are in this game,' she says – without laughing.

Hayes let the damp towel fall to the floor, and waited as the mist cleared in the full-length mirror. Then, turning slowly on the spot, she took in her long legs, the gentle curve of her bottom, her flat stomach, her small breasts. She was still in pretty good shape, considering she never had time to go to the gym. She never had time to eat properly, either.

Naked, she walked into her bedroom and over to the chest of drawers. Opening the top drawer, she fished out a red thong with black edging and a black bra with red trim.

Once in her underwear, but not having stepped into the short black dress she'd decided on for the night and which was hanging on the handle of the small, built-in wardrobe, she suddenly sat on the corner of the bed, put her head in her hands. Tiredness overwhelmed her. The investigation was stalling already, while the press and her bosses were piling on the pressure.

She knew she should be getting some sleep. At the most, firing up her laptop and going through the reports once more. Instead she was going out, and she was going to stay out until she got what she wanted. There would be no stopping her.

She stood, grabbed her dress off its hanger. Paused. What the hell was she playing at – again?

She put on the dress, hooked it over her shoulders, stretched her arms through before smoothing it down over her hips.

But maybe that was part of it. She didn't want to know what she was playing at. Rational thought didn't come into it. It was about losing control, forgetting for a few brief moments who she was.

That was when she had always felt most truly alive. Perhaps it was the proximity to death, to wasted lives, that did this to her. Why she was feeling the urge most keenly right now.

Five

The phone remained silent. There was no Audi or anything else unusual that he could see, out on the street. No one was knocking on his door.

And Howie Jones wasn't going to spend another evening in this bare room, with just Baz for company and the North Sea ringing in his ears. Besides, he'd always worked to the maxim that you don't wait for trouble to come to you. Was why he believed he'd survived, for so long.

Where he was coming from, it paid to be one step ahead. But he was worried that he'd already been too slow. That, while trying to distance himself from the past, he'd taken his eye off the mark. Someone was circling, and it seemed they didn't mind that he knew.

The idea that he could just slink away, turning his back – who had he been kidding? However much care he'd taken, you could never completely guard against chance, against coincidence, of being spotted in the wrong place at the wrong time. Of history catching up.

Plus he hadn't always helped himself. He was only human. He laughed quietly at the thought – always the weakness.

He wasn't taking Baz with him tonight. Where he was going, dogs weren't allowed.

*   *   *

Another one's pinged in. They're still coming. Days later.

Great to see you the other night, David, and see you looking so good too. Sorry you didn't win. But here's to next time! All Best, M.

M? Was he embarrassed to add the rest of the letters to his name? Or does he assume we're on first-initial-only terms, given the regularity of our exchanges? Because we're not. I can't remember the last time we did have an email conversation.

This is getting ridiculous. I wonder whether I'd have got so many emails had I won. It's almost as if people – people in my industry, my so-called rivals, indeed – are enjoying reminding me of the outcome of the awards. Enjoying sticking the knife in.

They all knew why they were there, but what got Hayes was how long it always took anyone to make a move. Though, as ever, she wasn't going to be the first. She hung back, in a corner by the fruit machine, sipping her white-wine spritzer.

Finally she had warmed up. Circulation had returned to her fingers. She took another sip, thinking it seemed emptier than usual. Thinking she should have stayed at home with the reports instead. There must have been plenty she had missed.

'Hi,' came a man's voice, right beside her.

She turned to see that a large, well-built man – sandy-coloured hair, greying by the time it got to his sideburns, piercing blue eyes, two-day stubble – had seemingly materialised from nowhere. He was standing a little too close.

'Hi,' she said. 'I didn't see you come in. I would have noticed.' She stepped backwards.

'You were looking in the wrong direction,' he said. 'I've been watching you. I came in the rear.'

'Do you always sneak up on people?'

'I don't want to make any mistakes,' he said. 'You could have been with someone.'

'How do you know I'm not?'

'As I said, I've been watching you.'

'For how long?'

'Do you want a drink?'

'I have one, thanks,' she said. She held up her glass. It was half full.

'Why don't you finish it and let's go somewhere else,' he said.

'You always this quick?'

'When I'm certain.' He smiled, and that did it.

'Sure,' she said, putting the glass to her lips.

'Come on, Jack, hurry up.' Where the hell is he? Poppy as usual is waiting patiently by the front door, shoes on, coat buttoned up. The woolly hat her maternal grandmother knitted, badly, loyally, sitting on her mounds of dark curly hair.

'Dad,' Poppy says, 'I don't want to be late! Why is he always late?'

'Jack? He takes after me,' I say, mounting the stairs. 'Jack, hurry up,' I shout.

'OK,' he says, emerging from his bedroom. 'I'm coming. I just need to find my cards. I can't find them anywhere.'

'We really don't have time. What cards?'

'You know, my Match Attax.'

'But you haven't played with them for ages.'

'So. Everyone is, now. You should see Billy's. And Joel's. Joel's got all the shiny ones. Can I get some more, today?'

'Come on.' I grab him gently by the shoulders and steer him towards the stairs. 'We really haven't got time for this.'

'But I need them. I need them, Dad.'

'Jack, we're late. Poppy's waiting.'

'Please,' says Jack.

'Dad,' shouts Poppy. 'Hurry up.'

She gets this sense of urgency and sharp time-keeping from her mother. Her mother's never late. Except, as I manhandle Jack down the stairs, I can't help thinking that actually that's not always right. Not any more. Hasn't been for some time in fact. Maggie's late right now, for instance, by days.

She should have been back from Birmingham on Saturday. It's now Monday. And the children are in danger of being late for school – not because I'm especially disorganised, but because they sense something's up. They know their mother should be here, and they know that I'm not totally happy about the fact that she's not.

It was fine, her staying in Birmingham on Saturday night – she'd always implied that might be a necessity. But Sunday night too? The trains on the Sunday, apparently, were effectively out of service. There were engineering works on two of the lines, and she couldn't face taking a series of buses. After such a hectic, stressful conference, she was utterly exhausted, so she said. And I didn't blame her – then. I loathe buses.

But I'm not so happy about it now.

Maggie never used to be so spontaneous, or rather so flaky, about her arrangements. She never used to be quite so short with me on the phone, either.

I've finally got them out of the house, and it's much colder than I thought it would be. The usual late-winter dampness having been replaced by a nearly clear sky and a strong, bone-chilling breeze. As I take my children's hands, worried that they are not wearing enough clothes – neither has gloves – my eyes fall across the street, are drawn there in fact, to where I saw that man in a trench coat, a number of nights ago. I've realised I've seen him at other times and other places recently as well. In our street. On the main road. Near Jack and Poppy's school.

He's watching us, I've decided. Except that, despite the fact that I keep glancing out of the window – at all hours – I haven't seen him for a few days. Since Maggie's been away.

'Dad, you're holding my hand too tight,' says Jack.

My concentration has gone. It's not just Maggie, thinking about what she's up to (and with whom). The reality of what the Crime Thriller of the Year result means seems to be almost as distracting. I need to channel my energy, my anxiety, more efficiently, more productively. It can be done. It's been done before. There's no choice now anyway.

'Dad,' says Jack, 'let go.'

'Sorry.' I release my son's hand, and Poppy's, but hang on to the collars of their coats. We're now on the main road and, though Poppy is nine and Jack seven, although they are pretty sensible kids, I've always been terrified they'll step out and be knocked over.

Mostly people drive cautiously in this town, but there's always the odd idiot. And Audi drivers, I've started noticing (if I haven't always known), are especially bad.

Nearing the school, up a long hill of small terraced houses, I start to recognise other parents, some hurrying after their children, others dragging their offspring by any available limb or piece of H&M fabric. We're very late and I'm barely able to acknowledge anyone, except Clare. Oh, God, Clare: her short, mauve-coloured hair glinting in the harsh, low sunlight. Clare's son Billy is in Jack's class. Clare and Billy seem to be waiting for us at the junction ahead. I force a smile.

'There's Billy,' says Jack. 'I told you I needed my Match Attax.' Billy's a big lad, bigger than Jack (possibly technically obese – like me). He's good at football and especially good at playing on his Wii, apparently. Which is why Jack's obsessed with getting a Wii himself. Though if there's one thing (just one thing?) his mother and I completely agree on, it's not letting him have a Wii. Jack rushes ahead; first time he's got a move-on this morning.

'I hate him,' says Poppy.

'Who?' I ask.

'Billy.'

'I can't say I like his mother much,' I whisper. Poppy takes my hand as we approach.

'Hello, Clare,' I say, making a show of looking at my watch, trying to impress upon her that I'm really not going to slow down, let alone stop and chat for her benefit. 'Bit late, aren't we?'

'Unlike you to be in such a rush,' Clare says, wheezing slightly, attempting to fall into step. Her BMI must be even more out of kilter than mine.

I used to think she took a shine to me because of my own weight issue, that she saw some solidarity in our fatness, our greediness. To begin with she was always asking me if I wanted a quick coffee in the nearby organic café, The Green Grocer, after drop-off. She loved their flapjacks – thought I might too. I didn't. Though I guess they were a much healthier option than anything I've encountered at her house.

Yes, Jack, Poppy and I have been persuaded to go back for tea and brownies, after school – on more than one occasion. Plus I've been hauled in off the street, when I've called by her house to pick up Jack after he's been there on a play-date.

Why I continue to let him go round there and enact battles on the Wii, with various motion-control accessories, while, incongruously if you ask me, Clare pours over her alchemy texts (she's training to be a homeopath, or is it a herbalist?), I don't know.

I do actually. And it's got little to do with Jack and Billy's friendship – you can't choose your children's friends for them, any more than you can choose your spouse's colleagues or students. It's because Clare is a huge fan of crime fiction. She's quite a fan of my work (so she says). And just as you can't choose your children's friends or your spouse's colleagues, or especially her postgraduate students, so you can't choose your fans.

'Sorry that idiot won last week,' Clare's saying.

So she's heard. So everyone's heard – of course. 'Well, he's won before,' I say, now really trying to hurry ahead.

'You're better than him, David. Come on' – she taps my arm, pulls me back – 'your books are much more considered. OK, they might not be so violent, but I think that's a good thing. You're a real writer, you know that. You're not just out to shock.'

Clare actually seems to have devoured everything I've ever written. She's probably my most dedicated fan. And of course I should love her, as I should love all my readers, though up close, in person, it's not always possible to feel quite so loving. Maybe I just don't have that knack. 'Well,' I say, faking a weary sigh, 'it was down to a public vote in the end. I did what I could.'

'They don't know what's good for them,' she says, 'the public.'

'Dad,' Poppy is saying, pulling my arm, 'we're going to be even more late.'

Turning right at the junction, we all stumble forward towards the large primary school, now in view: the concrete playground ringed by Portakabins, all looking particularly shabby in the piercing late-winter sun.

'I read this book last week,' Clare is saying – she never stops talking – 'that featured a killer who'd made this device, the size of a small apple, which contained a load of needles, and he'd ram this thing into the mouths of his victims, while they were alive. The catch was that if they tried to remove it, it would effectively explode, the needles shooting out at all angles, whereupon the victims (all women by the way) would quickly die, drowning in their own blood. I mean, who wants to read that sort of stuff?'

'Lots of people, frankly, all around the world too,' I say. The book sounds familiar.

'I don't know what's wrong with them. You know what Chandler said, don't you, David?' she says. 'When it comes to mystery writing, brutality is not strength.'

I'm not sure I did I know that. 'Times have changed,' I say. 'Or should that be, tastes have changed?'

Suddenly, thankfully, we're next to the school gates, being stalled by a mass of people and children – Jack and Billy somehow squeezing straight through and rushing ahead, while Poppy still hangs on to my arm. Her classroom is round the back, in part of the original, late-Victorian building, while Jack's current classroom is in a Portakabin.

'Don't underestimate the intelligence of the reading public,' says Clare.

'No. Look, sorry, Clare,' I say, 'I need to deal with these two.' Jack and Poppy are more than capable of getting themselves to their classrooms from the gate (and it seems as if Jack's doing just that this morning anyway), but I always like to see them to the door.

'Yes, of course,' she says. 'Billy? Where's Billy gone?'

'He's over there with Jack.' I spot my son now. He hasn't quite gone inside.

'Oh yes.' She pauses. Looks at me. Says, 'I suppose you haven't got time for a quick coffee, after the bell, have you? We could zip over to The Green Grocer – and have one of their flapjacks. Maybe I can cheer you up.'

'Clare, sorry, I'm pretty frantic at the moment. And I don't need cheering up, honestly – I've got over it. Plus, Maggie's been away for the last four days at a conference. She doesn't get back until today in fact. And I'm sort of behind schedule.'

'Where's she been?'

'Birmingham,' I say, as Poppy gives my arm another yank.

'Dad,' she pleads.

'Oh,' says Clare. 'I could have sworn I saw Maggie yesterday evening, coming out of that pub on Stafford Street. I'd been to my book group.'

'No, can't have been her,' I say, allowing Poppy to lead me away quickly.

'Well, I thought it was a bit odd,' Clare says behind me. 'Peculiar lot who drink in that place. Students mostly, I suppose.'

* * *

I reckon I've always been pretty good at displacement activity.

Walking home, back down and up the streets of squashed terraces, a few other people, women mostly, dispersing among the homes, and with the sun having suddenly shifted behind thick cloud, with more, darker clouds looming to the west, it occurs to me that at least I don't have to go to some bland office and be subjected to all sorts of corporate or institutional bureaucratic nonsense. I'm heading home, to my study, my work – the house empty of children, and my spouse of course – where indeed I'm the boss.

As if.

Not that I'm exactly qualified to do much else. It's surprising really the number of writers I've come across who are as poorly qualified as me (or worse), even the so-called literary ones. And to think I first got into writing because I wanted to be a poet.

The thing is, there are times when it's good to have a big imagination, and times when it's not. Back to that old conundrum: there are things you don't know and don't want to know. But simply, urgently, have to know.

And there's so much – from working out how to create ingenious devices that explode in your mouth, to being fully connected, fully up to speed, with every new facet of social media. OK, James P, my old Baltimore chum, whose international popularity, as far as I can tell, is very far from dropping off, notoriously doesn't do emails. He doesn't even work on a computer.

But he is considerably older than me – a generation away. Nevertheless that still makes me quite old. Too old for this game? Isn't that what Julie implied the other evening?

Too old to be sprinting up this hill, in a cloudburst, that's for sure. I pause, catch my breath, rain dripping off my nose.

Right now, it seems clearer than ever that a Sabatier carving knife, wherever it's been stuck, is not going to be nearly enough. Sorry, Clare. It's what the public want. And they're not stupid.

*　　*　　*

'Where the hell have you been?' said Tanya, as Adrian Fonda walked into the hall, shaking the sleet from his overcoat.

She was standing there, out in the hall, waiting for him. Had on her purple silk dressing gown, over her pink trackie bottoms.

'You don't want to know,' Fonda said, marching straight past her towards the large kitchen-diner.

He put his leather briefcase on the granite-topped island, next to the waste-disposal unit. Thought for a moment about stuffing the whole thing into the waste disposal, with all the incriminating shit it contained.

He was getting sloppy. Talking too much at work, whether it was the holiday season and deserted, or not. Carrying around all this material, these accessories. Besides, he was giving far too much licence to too many people. Like Girts Kesteris for starters. And now the lazy Latvian was too scared to show his face.

But he would, when he realised what had happened to his brother. Bernard Kesteris' head was no longer attached to his body – that can happen when you slip between a supply vessel and the quayside. The idiot shouldn't have been drinking. Should have been more forthcoming too.

'Everyone else is at home with their families, on holiday, but you have to be out working,' Tanya said. 'All hours.'

She'd followed him into the gleaming kitchen and was now leaning against the far wall, next to the fake fireplace. She was tall, taller than Fonda, with long, immaculately dyed and maintained chestnut-coloured hair.

Fonda knew that he couldn't even trust his wife. 'Where's River?'

'In bed. Where did you expect him to be, at this time? Waiting up for you?'

'You're not having another go, are you?'

'It's late. I couldn't understand where you were, that's all. You didn't say you were going to be late. You could have rung.'

'I was out with clients, all right? A new lot want to invest in the outer harbour. Bring in some heavy equipment.'

'Sure. Where was it this time? The Imperial? The Carlton?'

'The casino, if you're that interested.' Fonda walked over to the huge fridge, opened the right-hand door, peered inside – bollocks to eat! He shut the door without extracting anything. 'You know what those Eastern Europeans are like, how they love to gamble.'

'I thought they preferred fucking young girls,' said Tanya.

'You'd know all about that, wouldn't you?'

He then walked over to Tanya, who was still casually – too casually, as far as he was concerted – leaning against the wall. Was she pouting or sulking? He could never tell which.

Taking her chin in his right hand, with Tanya offering no resistance, he began to squeeze gently, staring straight into her eyes. 'Don't forget where you came from.'

He squeezed harder and harder, but she didn't attempt to break free. What was she on tonight?

Finally he let go of her face, turned, walked out of the kitchen, heading for his study. One of these days he was going to shut her up for good – mother of his child or not.

Footsteps coming up the path. The sound of someone scratching around in the porch, of something bumping against the front door – the postman, or a delivery person, perhaps, arriving slowly, noisily, clumsily, to ruin my concentration. I brace myself for the bell. But I'd probably finished that scene anyway.

A key goes into the lock. The front door opens. The time on my screen says 13.09.

'Hello?' says the voice in the hall, Maggie's voice, questioning, wary. Tentative?

'Hi,' I shout, standing, immediately feeling the stiffness in my legs. I don't know how long I've been sitting.

Maggie's pushing open my study door before I'm halfway across the room. 'Hello,' she says, smiling.

'Hi,' I say again, suddenly not sure whether I should kiss her hello. We don't normally when she comes home, but she's been away for a number of days – a couple more than expected. As I lean towards her, reaching for her with my right hand, she abruptly turns and steps back into the hall, my hand left groping thin air.

'I need a shower,' she says, quickly hanging up her coat.

'Wasn't sure what time you were coming back,' I say, following. 'You've done pretty well to get here by now.' I look at my watch, or where my watch should be on my wrist, realising it's on my desk.

'Believe me, I had to leave bloody early this morning. Those cross-country trains, what a nightmare! And that's when they supposedly work properly.'

Maggie, I realise, is not looking her usual polished and stylishly attired self, as she makes to grab her compact wheeled luggage by its worn, chunky handle. Her hair can't have been brushed for some time – or perhaps the wind's just got up – and is slightly greasy-looking too (something she particularly dislikes). Her dark-navy trousers are decidedly crumpled, while her top – a rather delicate and also crumpled shirt-cum-jumper with silky cream sleeves and a fine woollen trunk that's just a touch too large for her – is something I haven't seen before. And, if you ask me, it's not something that quite goes with her snugly fitting (though crumpled) dark trousers. But she has just spent God knows how many hours traversing the country on slow, no doubt overcrowded and vastly expensive diesel trains. Hasn't she?

'Let me,' I say, making for the handle. 'I'll carry it up for you.' We're by the foot of the stairs and I know how heavy her bags always are, being stuffed not just with numerous items of clothing and shoes in particular, but with books and papers and her hefty, years-old university-provided laptop.

'Sure.' She still seems in quite a rush as she takes the stairs two at a time in front of me.

I can't keep up, even though her bag is actually not that heavy (not as heavy as normal?), but it's awkward lifting it up the stairs (the wheels, the solid frame) and there it goes, banging into the banisters, chipping further the already-chipped paint. Why am I in such a rush as well, struggling with the thing, suddenly half out of breath (again)?

Maggie's beautiful rear reaches the landing and swiftly turns and shifts along the corridor, towards our bedroom at the front of the house.

She's already pulling her top over her head as I enter. 'New top?' I say. 'I don't think I've seen that before.'

'No. Yes. I can't remember,' she says, her head emerging.

The bedroom's decidedly warm and stuffy – unsurprising perhaps, given that the heating has been on since early.

'First time I've worn it, I think. Though I did buy some clothes just before I went to Birmingham. I do like to look my best at these things.'

'New bra too?' Now I really don't think I've seen this thin, black lacy number with red trim before. Or have I?

'Jesus, David, I'm trying to get into the shower. What's this: the Spanish Inquisition? I've had people questioning me about this and that all weekend. I really don't need it from you.'

Questioning her about what? Her underwear? Her commitment to her family, her kids? Her husband? The precise nature of her marital status? Is she having an affair, and with a fucking PhD student, or not? I'm not sure whether I'm about to boil into a rage or faint with lame acceptance.

'Sorry,' I say, trying to calm myself, trying to remain rational. 'I was just rather admiring it – your bra.' I don't say anything further as Maggie, looking away, slips out of her trousers, revealing that she's wearing an almost matching red-and-black thong. A fucking thong? She never wears thongs. Says they are the most uncomfortable things imaginable.

And to think that she supposedly traversed the country on slow, shitty trains, wearing a thong.

Still, I keep my mouth shut (because I don't want to know the truth?) as she makes her way out of our bedroom and to the bathroom. I find myself sitting on the bed, her side, feeling the mattress continue to sink deeper and deeper (collapse more like), while hearing the bed frame creak wildly. Or is the noise the shrieking in my head? Work, my marriage – it's all going horribly wrong.

Lying back on the bed I close my eyes, now hearing the deathly quiet of our leafy residential street around lunchtime, on a Monday, and feel not fresh and invigorated, ready for the week ahead, but old and fat and ineffectual, way past it. Plus, I realise, I'm listening for footsteps out on the pavement. For someone walking past, pausing, watching. Or has he scurried home (to where? a bedsit, some horrible student house-share?), having seen Maggie to the door?

We should never have moved from London, from the centre of things.

Why did we move to this provincial dump, where it turns out even the academics are small-minded – or is that high-minded? As for the students . . .

Maggie's suddenly leaning over me, wrapped in a towel, her hair dripping, onto my face. She's kissing me on the cheek, gently on my lips: the taste of toothpaste and Clinique moisturiser instantly hitting the back of my throat.

'Sorry you didn't win last week, sweetheart,' she says. 'Don't let it get to you.' She kisses me again. Says, breaking off, 'And I'm really sorry I wasn't there to support you on the night. I feel awful about it. That conference has got a lot to answer for – it turned out to be a complete nightmare.'

'Just as well you weren't with me in London,' I say, pulling her down, onto me, hugging her tightly, now overwhelmed by the smell of shower gel and conditioner, of clean, freshly moisturised skin. 'It doesn't matter. I was fine. I had Julie to support me.'

'Yes, but you know what?'

'No.' My mouth is right by her ear.

'You're so much more talented than the rest of them who were on that list. Particularly that idiot who won.'

'Well, you would say that.'

'It's true. You're in a different league. Don't ever forget that.'

The thing is, my league feels like a league of one, with about one fan to go with it.

Maggie kisses me yet again, on the lips, and then tries to free herself from my clasp. But I kiss her back, and hang on to her, tight (as if she's all I've got left), moving my left hand up and over the back of her head, through her wet hair, lightly massaging her scalp with my fingers, as she loves, as she used to love, and moving my right hand slowly down her back, sort of walking my hand down until it's dipping into that hollow at the base of her spine. I start massaging her there too, with my whole hand, which I then move lower, up the slight curve of her buttocks – where, or rather when, we both know, a hug and cuddle becomes most definitely something else.

I lay my hand flat across her bottom and gently press her onto me – her crotch on mine. This is the beginning of our type of foreplay, how it's evolved for us. What we do before we do it.

'David, I haven't got time,' she suddenly says, determinedly lifting her head, trying to pull her body free. 'Really, I've got to get into the office.'

An image comes to me of Howie Jones, standing on the beach, enveloped in wind, the smell of the sea. Swamped by a feeling of rejection. He's lonelier than he could ever have imagined. He's lived with betrayal all his life. One way or another he's made a living out of it. But money shouldn't be everything. He knows that, now more than ever.

Maggie's up off the bed and is manically opening drawers, getting out clothes, throwing them on the bed next to me. Stepping into and pulling on these items: her usual attire, stuff I've seen endless times, stuff that suits her better than what she was wearing when she turned up half an hour or so ago, from wherever she had really been.

She's not just rushed, clearly she's also cross. Obviously I've pissed her off. You great oaf, I tell myself, though half-heartedly. A sense of resignation is building, inextricably.

'We can do it later, sweetheart,' she says, as if catching my drift.

The *sweetheart* sounded all right. 'Yeah. I've got work to do as well,' I say. 'I don't know what I was thinking. Sorry. But you're just so gorgeous. I've missed you.'

'Right. I'm off,' she says, walking out of the bedroom.

'You here for supper?'

'Of course. I intend to be back early. I'm dying to see the kids. Have they been OK?'

'No.' I laugh. 'Terrible.' I pause. 'Actually they've been fine, sweet.' I wonder whether Maggie picks up my subtext here: that our children always behave well, better even, when she's not around. 'Jack's getting obsessed with his Match Attax again.'

'Well, he's always obsessed with something.' She's already on the landing, striding away. 'I wonder where he gets that from?'

'Baz, come here, you miserable hound,' shouted Jones, the dog's thick lead hanging around his neck – the dog having lumbered somewhere out of view.

There was a strong, sharp breeze blowing in from the sea, but it wasn't as cold as it had been. It wasn't quite as foggy, either. The giant blades of the wind turbines out on Scratby Sands were clearly visible. They were rotating swiftly.

'Baz,' Jones shouted again, suddenly wondering whether the dog had found another body.

But Baz then emerged and seemed happy to stick with him.

A minute or so on and Jones had cleared the dunes and was out on the pebbly beach, having reached the high-tide mark – a thick line of drying seaweed and stone-washed plastic rubbish. There was a faint smell of rotting fish and tar. Looking back and to his right, Jones could just see the top of the Coastwatch station, its dark-blue and red flag fluttering.

He returned to the first bank of dunes, climbed up for a better view. There were no vehicles near the lookout now, no patrol cars, no crime-scene investigation vans. The tent out on the grassy sand had gone. Nothing was left to suggest anything terrible had ever been discovered near there.

Yet Jones knew the police hadn't given up already. With Baz now looking up at him expectantly, he retrieved the mobile from the outside pocket of his puffa. Dialled the number he'd memorised.

He never wrote anything down. The only thing he hung on to as he switched identities was Baz, and at the back of his mind he was beginning to wonder whether the dog had given him away.

She answered immediately.

'Hello,' Jones said, loudly, suddenly conscious of the wind. 'It's me. Steve. From last night.'

'Steve. Oh, yeah. Hi. How could I forget!'

'This a good time?' She sounded rushed, or embarrassed. Perhaps both.

'You know what, it's not actually. I'm at work. About to go into a meeting.'

'Should I ring you back?'

'I'll ring you – this number good?'

'My mobile? Yeah, that's fine.' Soon as you can, he wanted to add. But didn't.

'OK.'

He didn't like the way she said OK . No hint at all that she was interested in pursuing contact, and suggesting that she just wanted him off the line, whether she had a meeting to go to or not. It was clearly a brush-off.

'You eventually told me what you did, last night,' he said, quickly, wind and sea swirling behind him. 'What you were working on.'

'Did I? What had I been drinking? Sorry. Look, it's probably best you forget about all that.'

'The thing is, I might be able to help you.'

As the man with his dog neared the road, he ducked down in the driver's seat. He counted to sixty, before sitting up to see that they'd crossed the road and were making their way towards the hotels further along Marine Parade.

He put the Prius into gear and began to crawl after them – for once thankful for the car's near-silent engine.

But he hadn't reached the end of the caravan park when another car pulled out of the gloom right in front of him and began crawling up the road, almost as slowly.

It was an Audi, dark blue, sleek, fancy trim. And it too seemed to be following the man with the dog.

Almost immediately he turned the Prius right into Jellicoe Road. He knew exactly who was driving the Audi. But he couldn't understand why Adrian Fonda would be interested in the same person.

Out of the window there's blue sky once more. I can almost see buds on the trees. Spring does finally seem to be just around the corner. While inside the house, for once recently, there's calm – just the faint whirring of my laptop. I'm the only one here, back in charge of my business. Doing what I do best. The emails having all but dried up again. The outside world another place.

However, it's gone two-thirty. I don't have much time left.

I definitely don't now, because the bloody phone is ringing. Not the phone on my desk, my so-called work landline, but the domestic landline. The phone I never answer during the day, during my working hours, though for some reason I feel compelled to do so now. Because actually the outside world is not another place? And I still don't know what's going on in it, with regards to Maggie, and our marriage. The stuff, if you like, that's particularly close to home.

Standing and making my way around my desk, I glance out of the window, towards our small back garden and the collapsing brick-and-flint wall at the end. Someone's running along the path the other side of the wall – clasping something to his head and attempting to crouch below the top. Who the fuck is that? Something familiar about him, his gait.

I rush into the kitchen, not sure whether I'm looking for the handset or making my way to the back door. Confused. Panicked. The phone doesn't sound like it's in the kitchen. It's not, I realise, backing out of the kitchen, into the hall. It's in the downstairs toilet. What the hell is it doing in there, on the ledge by the sink?

'Hello?' I say, frantically lifting it and pressing the green button at the same time. I've managed to answer before the answerphone answers for me. 'Hello?' I repeat, quickly walking back into the kitchen and over to the window. I peer out.

There's the definite sound of a click. Of someone ending the call. Because they weren't expecting me to answer, but Maggie? Because they were after Maggie, thinking she would be here, having just got back from Birmingham. Where the hell did they think I'd be then?

There's no sign of anyone on the other side of the wall, and just as I'm about to unlock the kitchen door and step outside to have a better look, I hear another phone ringing. It's my desk phone, my work landline, and a wave of relief sweeps through me.

Rushing back into my study, I make to pick up the receiver, realising I'm still holding the other handset. Throwing that on the desk, I grab my work phone, stretching the cord and walking round my desk so I can sit. 'Hello,' I struggle to say calmly.

'David?'

'Yeah.'

'It's Julie.'

'Julie, hi.'

'Are you all right? You sound a bit out of breath.'

'I couldn't find the phone,' I say, which is sort of the truth.

'America – remember?'

'Oh, America. What about it?' I settle into my chair, noticing it's now 14:42. I have five minutes at the most, before I need to leave to pick up the kids.

'I've been talking to your American editor,' she says. 'Despite your little setback, they are still behind this tour. OK, he took some persuading, but as promised they are going to pay the air fare, and meet the motel and B&B costs. You'll have to take care of your meals. If you are stuck for petty cash, we can probably help out – at least we can set it against the next tranches you are due from the UK. You've had all your American money already, I think.'

'Motels, B&Bs? Me paying for meals? I don't remember this. I thought they were putting me up in proper hotels, and meeting all the extras.'

'David, they were seriously thinking about pulling the plug. It seems they were banking on you winning the award. And there are a few more dates now than had originally been envisaged. The costs have grown.'

'The last time we spoke about it you weren't exactly full of enthusiasm for what had been lined up – and that was still with the prospect of me winning that blasted award. Shouldn't we just cut back and limit it to, say, three or four stops – seems like the publisher will be more than happy. I'm not sure I can spend all that time over there anyway.'

'Things have changed radically, David,' she says. 'We need to grab every opportunity – everywhere that'll have you. You're going, matey. You're not in a position to be choosy. It's really getting critical now. Do you know how many copies you sold in the UK last week? The week in which you should have triumphed?'

'No, I don't know. And I'd rather you didn't tell me.'

'One hundred and thirty-eight,' she says, 'despite all the publicity leading up to the award ceremony. You didn't even make the top one hundred last week, of all weeks. But at least Jo Spear and her crew have agreed to shoot some new video when you're over there too, and try to upgrade your digital profile in the States. Good of them, really.'

'It's in their interest,' I say.

'Sure,' says Julie, 'but you can't count on favours for ever in this business.'

I'm sick of this conversation already and let my gaze wander over my desk. 'By the way, Julie, did you just try to ring me?'

'What do you mean? I have just rung you.'

'No, immediately before, on my other number?'

'No, I don't think I tried your mobile. Unless I'm losing my mind – not impossible, given what I have to contend with.'

'No, I meant the other landline here.'

'I've got two numbers for you, David: the one we're speaking on and your mobile. I didn't know you had another landline – I don't care, either. What I do care about is America.'

I need to dial 1471, before I forget. Before someone else might ring that number. 'Julie, I've got to go. I have to pick up the kids from school.'

'You've got to be joking – I thought you had someone to do that for you.'

'We do, some days. Though not today.'

'For God's sake, David, you've got important work to do right now. America aside, I've been thinking: it's probably not a bad idea if I see some of the new novel before it might be too late. I want to make sure you're on the right track.'

'All right, all right, I'll email something over as soon as I can. I really have to go now.'

'Quite a lot of people are relying on you, David.'

'Including my kids.'

'Why can't Maggie pick them up today?'

'Because she has a full-time job.'

'And you don't?'

'She would pick them up – she does pick them up, when she can – but she's been away, at a conference, and has a load of stuff to catch up on at work.' I presume.

'I don't like what I'm hearing,' says Julie.

'You think I'm happy about it?' I end the call, reach for the other handset. Dial 1471, only to be told that the last telephone number received is unknown.

Can you do that from a mobile? Withhold your number? I should know this stuff.

PART TWO

The Fatal Middle Bit

Six

'Briefing time, everyone,' said Hayes, through gritted teeth. 'Please gather round.'

Scratching my scalp, hard (have I picked up nits again? that blasted school), I realise how tired I am, that I have a headache and about a hundred other things to do aside from write this blasted book.

I haven't been sleeping well anyway, but last night I was kept awake – for hours. Just as I was drifting off to sleep Maggie suddenly climbed on top of me and initiated urgent, passionate sex. Not only did I nearly have a seizure, I couldn't fathom her actions, her intentions – seemingly coming out of the blue. She hasn't behaved in such a fashion for months, for years. Not perhaps since we were first going out together.

'I do love you,' she said afterwards – and this was when it began to get even more troubling – shifting onto her side of the bed and rolling over to face the other way, wrapping herself tightly in the duvet.

'I didn't think that was in doubt,' was my light-hearted, out-of-breath reply.

'Whatever you hear about me,' she then said, 'I do love you.'

'What are you talking about?'

'Oh, I don't know.' She was still facing the other way, but had unrolled herself a little from the duvet. I was sitting up. 'Everyone is a bit on edge at work at the moment,' she continued. 'It's not just the admin staff who are being culled. There's talk of whole programmes going under. So it's natural, I suppose, that people are rather looking out for themselves, and in the process seem quite happy to put others down.'

'What's this got to do with whether you love me or not?' Having regained my breath, my composure – feeling less like I was about to have a heart attack or something – I was more than awake, my antennae up.

Of course I needed to know what Maggie was really going on about. And by then, and once again in the middle of the night, I must have been listening out for the sound of footsteps across the street, the sudden shrill of the phone or the quick bleep signalling a text message arriving on Maggie's mobile, which would be down in the hall, casually left in one of her jacket pockets. Or not, actually. The device having been hidden somewhere – somewhere I couldn't stumble upon it. (I'm sure she's been hiding her phone, in case I felt the urge to check her messages. I never have before, but until recently I never felt the need to.)

'There's a lot of gossip flying about,' she said, groggily, rolling herself even more tightly back into the duvet.

I was sitting further up, all ears, though my heart was beating harder and more uncomfortably again. 'Such as?' I said.

'Oh, I don't know. Plagiarism, cronyism, rumours of compromising relationships.'

'Teachers fucking students, you mean?'

'And each other.'

'Who?'

'Well, not me, if that's what you think.'

'No, it's not. Of course not. But who then? Who are you referring to?'

'David, I really am pretty tired. I was just trying to say don't believe everything you might hear. There's some pretty horrible stuff going around at the moment. Now I need to get to sleep. Night-night.'

Who would I hear it from, this horrible stuff? And how? I don't work there. This was what I didn't say then (lame and timid as ever), but which kept repeating in my mind, and other obvious things like it, as Maggie quickly drifted to sleep. How would I ever know what she was really talking about?

And then my mind started down a different track. I began to wonder, late last night, whether Maggie was preparing the ground for any rumour (however well grounded) that I might inadvertently hear. Was this what she was doing? Making out, from the beginning, that there was absolutely nothing to whatever I might hear. Knowing it would then be so much harder for me to be surprised, and thus really suspicious, if she'd already warned me that there was a load of shit flying around.

But why bring it to my attention, this shit? Why make the situation worse? Why put me even more on edge?

Maggie's too smart, surely, to implicate herself further. She's a doctor of philosophy. Soon to be a professor.

And she loves me. Whatever crap I might hear about her. And I love her. I should have nothing to worry about.

'I don't want to shout,' said Hayes. She felt like someone had driven a nail into her brain. 'So come up close, please.'

Hayes waited for the small team to advance on the smartboard. Photographs were dotted round the edges, arrows running here and there. A jumble of graphics.

The blood-stained knife was blown up in one shot, nearer the middle of the board. There were also numerous photographs of the naked corpse out on the dunes. Hovering quietly in the background, like a terrible stain, was a map of Kingsmouth.

Though the board appeared busy, Hayes knew that it contained little new information.

DS Tom Shreve was suddenly right in her face. 'Hard night?'

She shook her head. 'Some of us were working.' Who was she trying to kid?

'If you say so.'

'Fuck off!' said Hayes, aware of the other officers approaching. Aware Shreve knew more about her than she was remotely happy with. Had he actually been watching her, spying on her? She wouldn't put it past him. 'I don't suppose you've come up with anything?' she said.

'Has this briefing officially started?' he said. 'We don't want to repeat ourselves, do we?'

The arrogance. But Hayes knew that if she got him transferred, there'd be no one to fill his shoes.

She looked about her, at the pathetically depleted ranks – this was meant to be the Serious Crime Unit, serving the whole county, nearly a million people. 'OK, everyone, first things first.' Her head was spinning, painfully. 'We're still awaiting the toxicology results and any definitive answers from the lab. But let's assume for the time being that our victim died somewhere else, and not as a result of the knife wound.'

'Can we be certain then,' said Detective Constable Jo Niven, the youngest officer present, 'that the knife was used – however you want to describe it – after she died?'

'Posthumously,' shrugged Shreve.

'As I said,' said Hayes, 'we can't be certain of anything, at this moment.' Why had she instigated this briefing? What an idiot! Though, in her experience, breakthroughs were more likely to come through persistence than luck. Momentum had to be kept up, the team invigorated. 'But, yes, Jo, it looks as if the knife was used after she'd died,' she continued.

'So someone out there,' said Niven, 'must be pretty bloody twisted.'

'The lab is trying to determine whether she'd been raped,' Hayes said. 'Though the knife has complicated things.' She wished her head was clearer, not feeling like it were crashing. 'Who's looking at the sex offenders' roll call? Anyone new we should know about?'

'Me,' said Shreve. 'I mean, I'm looking at it,' he laughed.

'Well?' said Hayes, nodding his way.

'There are plenty of perverts in Kingsmouth all right,' said Shreve, 'we all know that. But I can't say anyone stands out at the moment, and there are no obvious new recruits worth speaking of. What happened to this person seems on a different scale, to me.' He paused, stuck out his chin. 'Which makes me wonder whether we're going down the right route with this investigation.'

'Someone off the radar, you mean?' said Niven keenly. 'But new to the area?'

'There's always that possibility,' said Shreve, stepping up to the smartboard, as if he were in charge, which is what he was aiming for, Hayes had always thought. 'But I still don't feel that this is where we should be looking.'

'You got a better idea then?' said Hayes. 'We don't even know who she is. No one's been reported missing, despite the extensive news coverage.'

'The time of the year is not helping us,' said Shreve. 'People have got other things on their minds.'

'Than missing their wife, their daughter, their sister, their girlfriend?' said Niven. 'Over Christmas?'

Hayes had noticed before that Niven was prone to be hysterical. She paused, tried to gather her thoughts.

Last time she went on such an evening, ever. She didn't want to think about the escapes she'd had, as it was. Time had to be running out. Though something in the back of her dulled and whooshing mind was making her think she hadn't fully escaped this time.

'Who's checking out the ships?' Hayes said, suddenly and unusually not sure whom she'd detailed to do what. She hadn't remembered that it was DS Shreve who was looking at the local register of sex offenders.

'She didn't come off a ship,' said Shreve, now facing the group. 'Or at least not recently. She was a prostitute. A contact of mine has just given me the nod – he recognised her from her picture in the press. She worked out of a brothel off Victoria Road. She called herself Kristine. Don't know her surname. But she was foreign – Eastern European.'

'That pins it down then,' said Niven, anger and disbelief still in her voice.

Hayes, ignoring Niven, looked at Shreve. As much as she disliked the man and as much as she distrusted him, he did have the habit of suddenly coming up with the goods. His contact book had always been a mystery.

'Thanks for telling us,' she said. Hayes was livid, being put on the spot like this, in front of the whole team. He should have come straight to her with this information. 'I presume it checks out – is that why you haven't revealed this information until now?'

'Give me a chance,' he said. 'I've literally just got off the phone.'

'If that's true,' said Niven, 'I don't understand why no one had reported her missing.'

'You know how tight that community is,' said Shreve. 'Maybe they didn't want us sniffing around.'

'OK,' said Hayes, 'let's get to the bottom of who she is, who she worked for, who her clients were. See if there've been any disagreements, any drug deals gone wrong, any turf wars. Check out the make and type of the knife, where it might have been bought, or stolen. Double-check the sex offenders' register, local and national – we should know about anyone who might have friends or relatives here as well. Work out what new CCTV footage you need and secure it fast. We have to discover where she died; let's try to start there. And anything you get – anything at all – come straight to me.' She couldn't concentrate on this any more.

Hayes quickly walked back to her cubicle. She knew she'd forgotten something important. For a moment it felt like her mind.

Stepping into her office, it half-came to her. Steve, the guy from last night, on the phone: what did he have to tell her?

But with her head now feeling as if it were splitting in two (what the fuck had she consumed?), she was struggling to process any information, let alone what DS Shreve had just revealed – to everyone. She couldn't have duplicity on her team. They were all professionals. Working together, for the same result.

Her private life was her own matter.

For a moment she worried that somehow she might have lost this guy Steve's number. But she couldn't have. He'd just rung her on her mobile, hadn't he? The number would be logged and listed. Where was her phone?

What she needed was half a packet of Nurofen Plus. And a different life. She found her phone in her jacket pocket.

'Boss?' It was Shreve, poking his head into her cubicle.

'You,' she said, quickly replacing the mobile on her desk. 'What do you want now?'

'There's something else,' said Shreve. 'A body was found in the Yare this morning, under the Haven Bridge, snagged on some cables.'

'That's not the first,' Hayes said.

'True,' said Shreve, 'but this one was missing its head.'

'A young woman?' Hayes felt her pulse rising – a sudden shortness of breath. She was under the impression she was in charge of the unit. Everything was meant to go by her. She really was losing her grip.

'No, a man, middle-aged they think. He hadn't been in the water long. His body had been crushed. Foul play wasn't immediately suspected.'

'Why we weren't told about it, then.'

'Seems so,' said Shreve. 'You know what those local coppers are like – never look further than they have to.'

'So what: he got caught between a ship and the dock?' said Hayes. 'Who was he – a drunk having slipped over the edge and losing his head in the process? They don't always lose their heads, as we know, but they can get pretty mangled.'

'Yeah,' said Shreve. 'But the thing is, he had his wallet on him. There was six hundred and twenty pounds in cash. He wasn't a tramp, and even if he were drunk, he was pretty well heeled. That marks him out in that town.'

'It might not have been his wallet,' said Hayes. 'He might have stolen it.'

'We'll soon be able to find out. There was a driving licence in there too, belonging to someone called Bernard Kesteris.'

'Kesteris? That sound Eastern European to you?'

'Sounds familiar anyway.'

The low afternoon sun is pouring into my study, and catching the thick dust on my desk, on my books and paperwork and phone and laptop and old printer. There's dust on my armchair as well, and on the lamp, on the pictures – there are some framed photos of the kids and Maggie, even one of us on our wedding day. We're coming out of the Chelsea Registry Office, on those famous steps, and of course we're both smiling away, and Maggie has her arm around my waist. My mother, her mother and father and brothers and sisters were standing on the pavement when this shot was taken – by one of her brothers, I think.

We picked the Chelsea Registry Office not because we lived particularly near it, but because we thought it was cool. A little rock 'n' roll.

I reach over and wipe some dust away with my finger, but it only seems to make whatever dust is left worse. Even the rug under my chair, I notice – looking away from the photo, from that moment of great joy and hope, and down at the floor – is greying with the stuff. The archaic patterns, no doubt full of ancient tribal symbolism, have become a thick blur of dark colour – like someone's over-tattooed arm, or one of Jack's paintings. No one's very good at craft in this house. Or cleaning.

I can't stand it any longer.

And I'm out of my wretched study and in the hall, opening the cupboard under the stairs and manhandling the Hoover. Or technically it's a Miele; another relic from the time when things were looking up, when we felt it was worth investing in the future.

Attaching the soft, bristly attachment – I have no idea what it's called, technically, but it's the one I use for my shelves and desk top – and extracting the plug from its powerful spring-recoil system (those Germans still know how to make a decent appliance that lasts – even if nothing else does), and searching for the most convenient plug, which happens to be out in the hall and not in my study, I can't help thinking that I really shouldn't be having to do the hoovering anyway.

That I have more important things to be getting on with – I can hear Julie shouting at me. And Peter also, but way in the distance. But not Maggie. She's too busy, too rushed herself, to worry too much about whether I'm hoovering the house instead of working.

Switching on the device, I'm met with a solid whirr. I wish I had the robustness, the reliability, the restrained confidence of a Miele. Confidence and front are so important in this game, as I'm constantly being reminded.

The guy who beat me to the award has always acted and written like he's a Dyson, if you ask me. A lot of power, vivid colouring and cutting-edge technological expertise (when it comes to death and torture), though I for one have always questioned his sustainability, his reliability, not to mention the authenticity. Not that my voice counts for much nowadays.

Confidence, David, I tell myself work on it. Think of James P. I doubt he ever suffers (not that he would ever need to) from a lack of confidence, long having sat pretty on the other side of the Atlantic (where, indeed, I should be heading shortly), in some swanky upstate New York home, when he's not enjoying his Florida mansion.

What on earth can it be like cranking out number one after number one – never doubting your ability, or the commitment of your audience? I guess the fear of failure simply goes away, and with it any sense of rivalry. There'd be no need to be jealous, or envious, of anyone. People – readers, agents and editors anyway – would be certain about you, about what you produced. Work, life, would be so sure, proven. Success breeding success. Sales, money, marriage. And acclaim, from those who count.

However, James P can't have done it all on his own. He must have a phenomenal team behind him. And, I'm sure, a phenomenal partner. Certainly he'd have a cleaner. Teams of them probably.

'What's wrong with the cleaner?' I can hear Julie shout, as I stamp on the switch and start waving the attachment about. Over my desk, the phone, the correspondence I've yet to attend to, the unopened bills – sort of wishing they'd be sucked up. But they don't disappear and I move the thing over to the nearest shelves, thinking: *what's wrong with the cleaner?* Well, I'll tell you, Julie, we don't fucking have one, any more.

We let her go.

Sure, I used to complain about her banging around the house when I was trying to work. About the cost of her too, when she wasn't exactly the most efficient or methodical cleaner we've ever had. 'Why don't you do it yourself?' Maggie finally said, not that long ago. 'You won't be disturbed when you're trying to work, and think of the money we'll save.'

It was Maggie mentioning money that did it. She's right. We do need to save money, cut our expenses. OK, Maggie is on a decent salary, but my earnings have seriously dwindled over the last few years. It's been increasingly hard to justify to myself, let alone Maggie, the time I do spend writing – and not doing the cleaning and childcare or trying to get a proper job. Per hour the cleaner was earning a lot more than me.

And now Brenda has gone I miss her – I miss the odd chats we used to have, even being disturbed in the middle of the day. The way she used to knock on my study door, immediately pop her head in and ask where some appliance or cleaning product was, or which room she should start in, and whether it was all right to use the toilet. 'Excuse me,' she'd say, suddenly appearing, 'can I just use the . . . you know?'

What was I meant to say? No?

We had our laughs, usually in the kitchen after I'd made her a cup of tea. She told me about her ex-husband, whom she described as 'one of those', and how her kids were doing at school (not bad). Once she even brought me a story (seeing as I was a 'proper writer') that her nine-year-old son had written for class.

It was genuinely disturbing, featuring a character, a boy, being chased by friends who then turned into zombies. When the zombies caught him, they ripped off his arms and blood began spurting everywhere. The zombies then started to drink the blood, which was pooling on the ground, gaining strength as they did so. When they were strong enough, or had developed the taste – I can't quite remember how he phrased it – they began devouring the rest of the boy, starting with his legs, then moving on to his vital organs and finally his head. Somehow the boy managed to stay alive, even after his eyes were sucked out.

There was real feeling and drama to the piece. The spelling and punctuation weren't bad, either. I wonder what Julie, or Peter for that matter, would make of it. A nine-year-old author of horror stories might have some marketing cachet. Replace the horror, the zombies, with a child-eating psychopath and he/they really could be on to a winner. As Julie keeps telling me, crime writers are getting younger and younger.

Maybe I could help – ghost it perhaps. Or just nick the idea, take on a new identity and lower my age somewhat.

Approaching the far side of my desk with the vacuum cleaner, I wonder what Brenda's up to now? Whether she realises the asset she has spawned and nurtured. I should make contact. Add that to my list of things to do. More pressingly, I really do have to contact Jo Spear. She needs me to confirm a couple of things.

And I don't want her to go to any more trouble if I'm going to have to cancel the whole tour.

How can I possibly go to the States with all this cleaning to do? Plus the childcare. I'm not even thinking of the writing. Maggie's now so stretched at work she barely has time to go to the gym – as she confessed just this morning. The gym? For fuck's sake! When are we going to make time to have a serious discussion? Get to the bottom of just what she's really been up to, and with whom. I need the truth now. Though will I get that from Maggie? She's always been able to run rings around me mentally. She'll always think of something, some excuse.

What I need to do is catch her out. Use my once-keen observational skills. And I can't do that if I'm 4,000 miles away, talking to a handful (at best, I reckon) of people in a public library in Pittsburgh. Then retiring to some dismal motel, without a proper supper, because I won't be able to afford it.

Seven

'You're not a coward, you tell me,' said Fonda, his mobile clamped to his right ear. 'Then why don't you come back to Kingsmouth? I need you here. You've still got some cleaning up to do. Hey, I thought we were in business together.'

'You killed my brother. How do I know you don't want to kill me?' said Kesteris.

'Hang on a minute,' said Fonda, peering keenly through the windscreen – rain beginning to smear his view. This wasn't quite panning out how he'd thought. 'I had nothing to do with your brother's death,' he continued. 'Tragic accident, from what I've heard. He shouldn't have been drinking, by the quayside. Big ships, those supply vessels.'

'My brother didn't drink. Never.'

'Maybe he was pushed then – I don't know. His line of work, being your brother, he must have had a few enemies.'

Fonda was parked up on the corner of Marine Parade and Salisbury Road: watching, waiting.

'I'll get you for this,' said Kesteris.

'Girts, calm down, will you? Why would I want to harm you, or your brother? We've done all right together, over the years. It's been a profitable partnership. Think about it.' He paused, as a pale-blue Toyota Prius cruised by once again. He didn't get a good view of the driver.

'You think you own the town, and everyone in it?' Kesteris was saying loudly bang in his ear. 'Not me, Fonda. I can help many people – tell them things about you.'

'You're boring me, Girts. You want me to lose my patience?'

'You don't scare me,' said Kesteris, his voice beginning to falter, or perhaps it was the line.

'So you keep saying. Well, prove it then, before it's too late. I'll give you one more chance. I want you to come back here now. Find out exactly what happened to that girl, if you're still telling me you don't know, and deal with it. Otherwise you'll start thinking your brother was lucky.'

Fonda ended the call, flung the mobile on the passenger seat. Looked up, saw who he'd been waiting for. Good timing, he thought.

Once the man and his dog had turned the corner, Fonda quickly opened the driver's door, climbed out and began following on foot.

This was going to be some reunion.

He'd noticed the Audi again and deliberately slowed as he walked past, finally clocking the driver. But once he'd turned into Victoria Road he pulled Baz into an alleyway that ran behind his hotel. They crouched down by the row of commercial bins, Jones gently stroking Baz's jowly cheeks, amid the damp, cold stink.

He'd always hated Fonda. Then he'd always hated everyone whom he'd worked for.

Fonda must have spotted him around town.

Jones was meant to be here for some R&R, seeing how low he could really lie. Kingsmouth was suddenly a very crowded place. And it was the middle of fucking winter. He should have gone to the Canaries.

But something good had happened. And with it, he felt, opportunities might just arise. Fonda could be outmanoeuvred.

He checked the time. Hoped this little interruption wasn't going to delay him too long.

* * *

On my way upstairs I pull my phone from my jeans pocket and quickly check for any new text or answerphone messages, or emails for that matter. There's nothing new. I fling the device onto the bed and approach my wardrobe.

Jack and Poppy are in the sitting room, arguing over what film to watch. It's meant to be their treat, because Maggie and I are going out and they've got the horrible (in their view) Emily babysitting them. Frankly I'd much rather be spending the evening with Emily than having dinner at Michael and Liz's. OK, we've finally been asked, but it was all very last-minute. Or at least Maggie only told me about it yesterday.

Where the hell is Maggie? Emily will be here shortly. I was rather hoping Maggie and I would have time to stop at The Mulberry for a glass of something strong in my case, and fizzy in Maggie's, before resigning ourselves to Michael and Liz's random, I expect, hospitality. Doesn't look like that's going to be possible.

Opening the wardrobe, seeing my old, crumpled shirts (Brenda's remit never stretched to ironing, and I'm useless at it) and tatty jackets, and a couple of suits, hanging in no particular order, I can't begin to decide what I'm going to wear (probably because I don't often have to make this decision). A clean shirt? A jacket? But why a jacket? For Michael and Liz? I look down at what I'm wearing: a pair of old jeans, a faded denim shirt, a large, maroon V-necked sweater, this is pretty much what I always wear, unless I'm attending a book event or a festival – or an awards function. I try to laugh, but more of a sigh emerges.

Maybe I've forgotten how to look the part, how to look a player – my pretty low sartorial standards slipping even further.

Is this what Maggie has finally had enough of? And Julie?

My phone beeps and I find myself shutting the wardrobe door and deciding I'll go dressed as I am, before picking up the device. It's a new text message, from Maggie (as I'd been expecting), saying she'll see me there. *Sorry for running late, Mx.*

'Children,' I shout, leaving the bedroom, 'stop arguing.'

How *sorry* is she for running late?

Down in the sitting room Jack has Poppy in a headlock. Though two years younger than her, he's almost her height. I just hope he's not going to be quite so out of shape and scruffy as his father, when he's grown up. It could have a disastrous effect on his love life, his domestic happiness. And his career.

'Jack, leave Poppy alone. Leave her alone,' I shout.

Jack lets go of Poppy and she immediately turns and kicks him in the shin and runs out of the room. As he chases after her I grab him. 'Not that I condone violence Jack, but that does serve you right.'

'What for?' he says, trying to hold back the tears.

'Getting her in a headlock? Bullying her?'

'I don't want to watch *Toy Story*, again. *One*, *Two* or *Three*.'

'Why don't you and Poppy watch telly then? You've only got until nine, as it is. If you two keep arguing about it, you are going to run out of time and you won't be able to watch anything.'

'I hate Emily. She smells.'

'Don't say that. And she most definitely doesn't.'

'Why do you have to go out anyway?' he says.

'That's a good question. Not sure I can answer that. But I don't go out that often.'

'Mum does. She's always out.'

'Well, you'll have to take that up with her.' I ruffle his hair, attempting to cheer him up, then head for the hall.

'Who's Alex?' Jack says behind me.

Halfway out of the room, I stop, look back at him, my big son. 'Alex? I don't know. Why? I don't know anyone called Alex.'

'Mum does,' he says.

'What do you mean?' I walk back over to him, crouch, place my hands firmly on his shoulders. 'What do you mean?' I repeat.

Maybe I'm being a little too strident. But I can't help it. 'Alex who?' I say, finding myself holding his face, gently, with my right hand.

He shakes his head free as if, suddenly, he doesn't know what I'm talking about. He's now resolutely staring at the blank, flat screen of the TV, our rather large Panasonic (bought when we had more disposable income, to help entertain the children when we are out, or when I'm in and trying to work).

'Is he one of her students?' I ask, not expecting an answer. How would Jack know? I'm not entirely sure he knows what his mother or I do (not, of course, that I'm always sure I know what his mother does, or for that matter what I do). 'What's she said about him? How do you know his name? Come on, Jack.' The doorbell is going. Emily. Emily is here.

Jack's out of the sitting room and pounding up the stairs, where he'll try to hide, no doubt. From Emily, from the babysitter. From his mother's indiscretion too?

Don't blame him about that bit. Not at all.

Out in the parking lot Hayes zipped up her leather jacket. It was freezing and she was late. Half an hour already, and a twenty-minute drive still lay ahead. But she'd been called upstairs at the last minute. Bullshitted her way through a progress report.

Reaching her car, she considered texting him. Then thought that if he were as keen to meet as he sounded, he wouldn't mind waiting. Whoever he really was.

The name he'd given her hadn't scored a hit when she'd entered it into the system. Widening the search, there was still nothing that tallied.

He wasn't living in Kingsmouth officially – not under that name. Didn't own a car – at least not officially. Didn't work. No reverse trace on his phone. There was no record of him at all.

But because this wasn't police business, not yet, she had no intention of informing the unit of her plans. Besides, there was something about him that she felt she could trust.

And something about him that she felt she needed, also.

Moving out of the parking lot, she turned on the radio, then almost immediately turned it off. She hated Beyoncé. DS Shreve was always humming Beyoncé. Which reminded her: she still hadn't heard back from him.

He was meant to be checking out his lead on the Victoria Road brothel. Following up, too, on Bernard Kesteris' background – why the name sounded familiar. Shreve, supposedly, was the one with the contacts.

Though this had always worried Hayes more than it had reassured her. Information was a powerful tool. It lent itself to corruption.

Hayes would, of course, have accompanied Shreve herself, rather than send Niven with him, if this other opportunity hadn't arisen. She had a feeling this one couldn't wait, didn't want it to wait, and she definitely didn't want Shreve in the loop.

Best to keep his eyes, his mind, elsewhere. If she could.

'Hello, Liz,' I say, being met with the damp, cloying smell of rice cooking, and then a strong whiff of alcohol on Liz's breath, and some sort of make-up smell too, as I lean in to kiss her on the cheeks. It instantly reminds me of my mother.

'Hello, David, lovely to see you,' she says, smiling gamely enough.

I can hear voices coming from the back of the house.

'Maggie not with you?' Liz says, as I follow her down the hall.

'She's not here? I thought she would be by now. She texted to say she was held up at work and coming straight here.'

We're in the kitchen before Liz says, quietly, 'Not yet.'

Michael's already looking at me strangely: his shiny pink head and bright facial hair leaping out from the far end of the room. He walks forward, from the knocked-through dining-room bit, extending a hand, a sly smile beginning to creep across his tight little face.

'Hello, David,' he says, 'good of you to come. Where's your lovely wife then?'

'She'll be here shortly,' I say, smiling, looking around and clocking the two other people present. I don't recognise them, but now remember Maggie saying something about why Liz and Michael were having us over, at the last minute: because they suddenly had a visiting lecturer to entertain, an old friend of Michael's, but someone in Maggie's field. Michael thought Maggie should meet him, and he her.

'She's too conscientious, that woman of yours,' says Michael. 'Let me introduce you to Oliver and Katya.'

We walk towards the couple: a tall, thin man, with the longest, fluffiest grey beard I've ever seen, and an attractive, much younger woman. She's petite, blonde and stylishly attired, in tight designer jeans and a black V-necked sweater.

'This is David Slavitt,' says Michael, 'Maggie Robertson's husband. David' – he looks at me, that taut smile on his livid face, and then, with an extravagant nod of his head, at his guests – 'Oliver Hillerman and Katya, Katya Marks.'

Michael, I realise (not that I've ever had the opportunity to draw such a conclusion before), is not a natural host. He's awkward and shy, or perhaps this is just the effect I'm having on him. I shake their hands and smile and nod away in as friendly a fashion as I can manage – given the circumstances, given my anxiety.

Katya says, brightly, '*The* David Slavitt?'

'Depends what you mean by the *The*,' I say. We shuffle around so that I'm now standing next to her and Michael's stepped into the heavily bearded guy's orbit.

'The author of *The Watcher*, *The Showman*, and – let me think – *The Torturer*?' Katya says.

She has extraordinarily pale-blue eyes. Honest eyes, I decide, for no other reason than they really are the palest, bluest eyes I've ever seen. Be hard to hide anything behind them, surely.

'*The Tortured*,' I say, then laugh, nervously. I made a mistake there – one of many. *The Torturer* is a much better title than *The Tortured*. No one particularly liked that title, except me. From memory, I think I was too bound up with the idea of making the victims the focus of the story, rather than concentrating on the perpetrator, or those out to catch him. I wonder whether it might just have won the Crime Thriller of the Year, had it been called *The Torturer* – and had I repositioned the perspective. Julie, of course, is always stressing how important a title is. 'You've got to grab people's attention from the moment they set eyes on the thing.' Why the hell didn't I listen to her?

Might have helped had I incorporated a few more torture scenes as well.

'Oh yes, sorry, *The Tortured*,' Katya is saying.

'You've read it?' I ask.

'Well, not *The Tortured* actually, but the other two. I enjoyed them.'

'Oh, OK. Good. There're some others as well.'

'Is that so? I didn't know.'

'No reason why you should have. They haven't all exactly been best-sellers.'

'If they are as good as the ones I've read, they should have been.' She smiles – those lovely clear eyes. 'Though there's no accounting for public taste.' She looks around the room: at her partner, at Mike and Liz. She then shuffles a little closer, says, 'I'm so pleased you're here. Michael never said we'd have this honour – an evening with a real author, a crime writer no less. I thought this was going to be another insufferably boring academic supper.' Those eyes, again. 'Complete with bad food, bad wine' – she's definitely whispering now – 'and bad breath.'

I laugh, loudly, then cover my mouth.

'Not you,' she says. 'But have you noticed how men of a certain age, with beards, always have dreadful breath?'

I'm not sure how to reply to this. She's obviously chosen to be with Oliver, unless he's somehow forced her into a relationship: by bribery, blackmail, torture? Perhaps he has some special sexual hold over her.

Though it would seem unlikely – by my most conservative reckoning, Katya must be half her partner's age.

'The Kiss of Death,' I suddenly say.

'What?' she says.

'I was just thinking, of a plot outline,' I say. 'A man who kills his victims by breathing his terrible breath on them.'

She laughs. 'Something tells me there've been a number of books called that already. I might even have read one.'

'Harder than you think to come up with a decent title,' I say.

'Or plot, I'm sure,' she says. 'You know, what I've always liked about your stuff, the ones I've read, is that they always seem rather believable. You don't go over the top.'

'Thanks,' I say.

'I think I liked the randomness of the violence, the killings. And the fact that we don't often see the actual violence. The implication of such is enough for me. I don't like it when it gets too gory.'

'What do you do? I'm presuming you're not an academic.' I need a drink. We all need a drink.

'Hang about, I haven't finished yet,' she says, quickly glancing over her shoulder, at Oliver and Michael. 'Didn't Chandler go on about this? He understood the randomness of most violence – the sudden, personal fury.'

Chandler, again. 'Look, I just try to write entertaining crime stories. Yeah, I've always loved Chandler, who doesn't? But tastes change. I'm sure I've changed over the years.'

She smiles, then frowns, says, 'So what are you working on now?'

While Michael has been talking to Oliver (and not getting anyone a drink), he has been checking us out. A man with such a seriously wandering eye, of course Michael's interested in Katya and, I guess, her reaction to me. He probably had no idea Katya could possibly be interested, even impressed by, my (Chandler-esque!) work. He does look a bit put out. I should be enjoying this. But I can't.

Perhaps Michael's reaction has got more to do with Maggie. The fact that I arrived without her. Maybe he's wondering where she is, almost as much as I am.

'Excuse me a sec,' I say to Katya, pulling my mobile from my pocket, 'I've just got to make a quick call.' I back out of the room, mouthing *Sorry*, as a look of bemusement drifts into those wonderful clear-blue eyes. Is she flirting with me? I'm not used to this sort of thing. I don't know quite how to react – which is perhaps why I've never been great at author events.

I continue on through the kitchen, where Liz is making quite a performance in front of the cooker (while, by the smell of it, overcooking the rice and God knows what else) and out into the hall. I put the phone to my ear just in time to hear Maggie's mobile go straight to answerphone. Dropping the phone back into my pocket, I head for the toilet, needing not a pee, but to take a look in a mirror. I want to see what sort of state I'm in. I need a moment or two to gather my thoughts as well.

'A glass of white wine, please,' Hayes said, as her heart gave a little thump. She wasn't sure whether it was because she wanted to know what information this man had, what he wanted to tell her – or whether she wanted to go to bed with him, again.

Either way, she could feel she was acting against her better judgement. But there was something in his eyes she hadn't picked up on the other night. Something she could not only trust, but a longing too.

Steve walked over to the bar, his broad back encased in a thin brown leather jacket.

Just as he had attracted the attention of the barman she felt her phone vibrating. Retrieving the device, she saw it was DS Shreve. She watched it silently ring out. Then noticed he'd tried to ring a couple of times earlier – when she was driving here, she presumed.

She should have checked before entering the bar, but Shreve had yet to leave a message. She left the phone on silent.

'Here you go,' said Steve, placing the large glass of wine in front of her.

'Thanks,' Hayes said, putting her mobile away.

'Everything all right?' he said.

'Yeah, sure.' She took a sip. The wine was too sweet, and too warm. 'So what did you want to tell me?'

'I'm so sorry I'm late,' Maggie's saying to Liz in the hall, as I emerge from the toilet. 'It was one thing after another, and then the blasted taxi went to the wrong part of the campus, thought I wasn't coming and took someone else. Can you believe that? Wasted twenty minutes waiting for another.'

'Didn't they try to ring you, to say it was there, waiting?' I say, approaching. 'They usually do.'

'Hello, David,' says Maggie.

'We were wondering where you'd got to,' says Liz, looking at me, oddly.

'Me?' I say. 'I thought it was Maggie who'd gone missing.'

As we're walking down the hall, back to the kitchen-cum-dining-room and the others, Maggie turns to me, says, 'You're not cross, are you, sweetheart? I'm sorry we couldn't come together, but it's really not my fault I'm so late.' She smiles.

She's been drinking. I can definitely smell alcohol on her breath. Or she's been kissing someone who's been drinking – the kiss of death.

Before I can think further, Michael is introducing her to Oliver and Katya – Maggie being her usual, overly friendly or, rather, flirty self – and Liz is taking my arm, steering me back towards the cooker, saying, 'David, I need a bit of advice.'

We get to the stove and she points to a large casserole pan on one of the hobs. There's no lid.

'It seems to have rather dried out,' she says.

'What is it?'

'Beef-and-Guinness stew.'

'Sounds lovely.'

'But it's all burnt at the bottom,' she says, poking it with a wooden spoon and revealing that, yes, it is burnt – as far as I can tell from a quick glance – probably beyond repair.

'Smells good,' I say. It really doesn't. It just smells burnt.

'What the hell am I going to do?' She almost whimpers.

'Why don't you just bung in some more Guinness.' I suddenly feel rather sorry for Liz and wonder whether Michael doesn't only bully and endlessly betray her, but actually beat her as well.

'That's the problem. We've run out. Do you think I can put in some red wine?'

I look over my shoulder, at my wife, or my wife's back. She's talking to Oliver and Michael, animatedly. Katya, who's looking my way, appears not to be involved in the conversation. She catches my eye, starts to walk over. 'No, I wouldn't do that,' I say.

'Can I help?' says Katya.

Yes, I think, perhaps you can – more than you might imagine. 'What do you reckon?' I say. 'It needs a little rehydrating.'

'Is that Guinness I can smell?' Katya says.

'Yes,' says Liz. 'How clever of you.'

Damn right!

'Why don't you add some more? That'll do it,' Katya says.

'Liz has run out,' I say.

'Some stock?' says Katya. She gently takes the wooden spoon from Liz, gives the burnt, brown mess a stir. 'But you don't want it too runny anyway.'

'You're just being polite,' says Liz. 'This is why Michael and I never entertain. We're just not very good at it.' She sighs. 'Unlike you, David. Katya, if you ever get the chance, do sample David's cooking. He's a genius in the kitchen. And he's always so calm. That's what I can't understand: how you can cook and remain calm.'

'I think his books are pretty good too,' says Katya, smiling at me.

'How about a drink?' I say, looking away. There's only so much flirting and flattery I think I can take – being so unused to the experience. 'Why don't I find us all a glass of wine? I'm gasping.'

'Oh, my God,' says Liz. 'You don't even have a drink. Michael,' she shouts, 'what the hell are you doing about the drinks?'

Michael doesn't appear to hear her.

'When Maggie's in the room,' says Liz, turning back to her cooking, and sighing again, 'it's like he can't focus on anything else.'

'I don't blame him,' says Katya, 'she's beautiful. Oliver seems pretty captivated by her.'

'Half the campus is,' says Liz, now adding a glass of water to the stew. 'The male half. Fuck – that's far too much water.'

Katya steps in, forcing me to back away. 'No, that's fine. Honestly, Liz, don't worry about it,' she says.

Liz begins to stir furiously, says, 'Bugger it!' Wipes her brow, says, 'They all want to shag her, especially the students. And those PhD students in particular can be very persistent. From what I hear, not everyone's disappointed.'

I look at Liz, the back of her head. She suddenly turns to look at me, those skewed dimples doing their thing. Katya's looking at me too, wide-eyed – that clearest, palest of blues stretching on for ever.

'Oh, shit!' says Liz. She's let go of the wooden spoon. 'That probably sounds worse than I meant it to. I'm a little hassled here.'

She's now reaching for my arm, grabbing it affectionately.

'It's just rumour, gossip, David. Campuses are like that,' she says. 'Wouldn't surprise me if it was something Michael dreamed up in a jealous fit. You know how he adores pretty women.'

Is she saying this to make me feel better? Oddly I don't feel anything, except a sort of numbness. I'm not angry. I'm not even surprised. I look over to Maggie – the two men crowding around her. Katya might have those eyes, and age on her side, but Maggie is the most attractive woman here, by a mile.

'David,' says Katya, laughing (nervously?), 'you must have women falling over you, being a popular author. Besides, a good-looking couple like you and Maggie, I'm not surprised you attract gossip, especially in this environment. University campuses seem to breed gossip like nowhere else – believe me. Oliver's certainly attracted his fair share. Not always unjustly.'

Katya winks. She actually winks at me. What eyes, what a wink!

'You can say that again,' says Liz, turning back to the brown mess.

'Look,' said Jones, 'I might have done things I'm not proud of. But that's in the past. I'm a changed man. Believe me. I came here to escape all that. I wanted the quiet life. Take my dog for walks by the sea. Meet some pretty women.' He winked. Then decided he shouldn't have.

'Why on earth should I believe you?' said Hayes. 'I don't even know what your real name is. You first told me it was Steve. Now you say it's Howie. Could be Santa Claus, for all I know.' She laughed, before quickly looking around the bar.

Was she nervous?

'It's Howie, I promise you,' he said. 'Howard Jones.' He wiped his forehead. It was steaming inside the bar, even though it wasn't packed. Limp Christmas decorations were dotted here and there.

'Howard Jones – I thought he was a pop star, from like ages ago.'

'We've got the same name. People took the piss out of me for years. Has been a bit unfortunate, that.'

'For him, I'm sure. Can't imagine anyone would like to be confused with a professional criminal.'

'Hey, steady on,' he said. 'I've done some stuff that I shouldn't have. But I never robbed anyone. I never harmed an innocent person.'

'Glad to hear it.'

'Look, I rang you, didn't I?' he continued. 'After finding out who you really were. Think about it. Why would I put myself on the line? I know how you lot work. How you gather your information. What resources you have at hand. You think I want to attract attention to myself? Have a load of detectives sniffing around? Why would I do that?'

'Because you want to fuck me – again?'

'Yeah, well, there is that.' He could feel himself smiling. He leaned towards her across the small, round table. 'Why wouldn't I? You're an attractive woman. Still, I should be running a mile. I know how to show a bit of restraint – believe me. But you know what: I think you're different. I feel I can trust you. Never felt that about a copper before.'

'Perhaps I'm not your normal copper – perhaps I am different,' she said, leaning forward a little herself too. 'Though how do I know I can trust you?'

He looked into her eyes – those deep-brown pools exhibiting, if not distrust, then something close to scepticism. Despite knowing she was attracted to him, he knew he was going to have to work a lot harder with this one. Show her he meant business. And quickly.

Even if he hadn't been set up, the last person he wanted chasing around after him was Adrian Fonda.

'Come with me,' Jones said, standing, holding out his hand. 'I want you to see something.'

She stood, but didn't take his hand, or let him take her by the arm.

As they were walking out of the bar she said, 'Does the name Kristine mean anything to you?'

'Katya seemed pretty taken with you,' says Maggie – her voice coming from the dark, out of the blue. As usual she's wrapped herself tightly in as much duvet as possible and is turned well away from me on the far side of the bed. 'She's a very attractive woman.'

'So are you,' I say. I haven't been asleep, not even close. And it isn't indigestion from Liz's indigestible stew that is keeping me awake; no amount of water or stock would have fixed that problem.

'But she's younger – considerably,' says Maggie. 'And she has the most incredible eyes.'

'Yes, I did notice.'

'I bet you did.'

'What's that supposed to mean?'

'You were flirting with each other all night.'

Maggie has turned onto her back. I've turned onto my back. So we're now lying side by side, eyes open (at least mine are), staring at the dark ceiling (full of large shadows, created by the street light seeping round the curtains: these shadows growing in definition as I watch).

I guess we're both contemplating our future, together. Something I never thought I'd have to do. For so long I thought of Maggie as my soulmate – that we'd be with each other through thick and thin, good times and hard times, for ever.

We'd both just emerged from long, tortuous relationships when we met, and it was like we'd stepped into a bright new world. Everything had purpose. Everything clicked. Life was fun. And full of desire – for each other.

'At least someone was bothering to talk to me,' I say. 'On my non-academic level.' How I suddenly hate myself for saying that. I'm no fool. Am I? 'Maggie, why were you so late?'

'So late? What do you mean?'

'Getting to Liz and Michael's.'

'What is this?'

Has she opened her eyes? I daren't sit up and look. I daren't move.

'I was going over some correspondence,' she says, tiredly, 'with the dean, regarding one of my research papers – something I wrote on John Barth, if you must know. Someone is accusing me of plagiarism, really, and threatening legal action. Which is obviously all I need, on top of everything else. And then there was the taxi fuck-up. That damn company – last time I use them. I wasn't that late anyway.'

'You could have cycled. You normally do.' I'm struggling to keep my voice clear. Plagiarism? Legal action? *On top of everything else.*

'It was raining, or about to. I didn't want to mess up my clothes, my hair, as we were going to a dinner party. Just what are you getting at, David?'

'Why did you suddenly stay longer in Birmingham, the other week? Why did you have to stay on the Sunday, when the conference ended on the Saturday?'

'David, you know exactly why. I was exhausted after the conference and the trains weren't running properly, due to engineering work. Why am I even having to explain all this again?'

'Are you sure you were in Birmingham that Sunday night, because someone said they spotted you here, coming out of that pub on Stafford Street?'

A car zips by outside, sounding as if it's going far too fast for our narrow, twisty, ill-lit road (the driver, no doubt over the limit, dashing from some assignation). I wonder who else is out there, lurking, on foot. Watching. Waiting (shifting in and out of the shadows). Waiting to make his presence known – to the right person. Waiting for a signal: some secret code (the language not of espionage, or religious conspiracies, but of illicit passion, of betrayal)

Watching and waiting for his chance – to steal my wife. *On top of everything else.*

I sit up, flinging off my small bit of the duvet. I get out of bed, move over to the curtains, pull them open and peer into the still night. I won't let this happen. I won't let him do this. Whatever it takes.

'This is all completely ridiculous,' says Maggie finally. 'And what the hell are you doing now?'

'Looking,' I say, suddenly conscious that while I'm wearing a T-shirt (very large and misshapen, faded and frayed), for some reason (hope, one last hope?) I'm not wearing my pyjama bottoms. I'm naked from the waist down.

'For what?'

'That's a very good question.' I suddenly feel a lot calmer, that I can breathe. There is definitely no one there. At least the pool of light from the nearest street lamp is revealing no sign of human life. I turn round and face the gloom, the doom.

Maggie's now sitting up, reaching over to switch on her bedside lamp. The bedroom suddenly assumes a warm glow. The furniture and clothes heaped here and there beginning to drift back into place. Like it all fits, except – I can't help feeling, I can't help knowing, for certain – that it doesn't.

'Looking for what, David? For what? It's the middle of the fucking night. I need to get to sleep.'

'Who's Alex?'

'Alex?' she says quietly.

'Yes, Alex. Who the fuck is Alex?'

'You mean Alex, Alex Smith, one of my PhD students? That's the only Alex I know.'

I close the curtains, realising I must have been standing there in full view. 'He wears big trench coats, boots – stuff like that? Hard to miss, on our street.'

'Yeah, I guess you could say that. He's into sci-fi, I think. There seems to be a look. Or perhaps he's an emo; or both. I get confused.'

'Are you having an affair with him?'

She laughs, loudly, cruelly – for quite a long time.

'Don't be ridiculous,' she eventually says, promptly turning off her bedside light, lying back down and wrapping the duvet more firmly around her than ever. 'Goodnight, David,' she says. 'I think we're both a bit exhausted.'

I shuffle back to the bed, sit on my side, the very edge of it. The mattress compresses deeply. 'It's just that Liz implied as much this evening. Honestly. And it all suddenly fitted together.'

There's movement over on Maggie's side of the bed – the duvet being quickly unravelled, that tight little package of lies and betrayal (and possessor of some secret code?). 'Fucking Liz,' Maggie says. 'I wouldn't pay much attention to what she has to say.'

'Why not? She seems to know what she's talking about. She works at your university. OK, she might not be in your department, but Michael is. He tells her stuff too, I'm sure.'

'She's just jealous,' says Maggie. 'It's not my fault Michael's the way he is.'

'What are you getting at?' This sort of makes sense, and doesn't.

'Liz is sick of Michael fancying me, and every other woman on the planet, and she's trying to make me out to be somehow culpable, because I'm that sort of person. Some women are like that. They have to blame other women.'

I don't think Liz was doing that.

'Shagging one of my students?' Maggie continues. 'You think I wouldn't know any better, in this climate?' She clears her throat. 'Even if they are so-called mature and doing a PhD. Honestly, David, this is beyond a joke. I almost feel sorry for you.' She pauses. 'Just the other day I told you there was a load of shit flying around, and not to believe everything you heard.'

Maybe. But why did she have to say *in this climate* – as if in normal times it would be fine for her to shag a student? 'Fine,' I say, 'but when you keep hearing it, from all sorts of people, and seeing things too, it gets a little hard to ignore.'

'David, people see and hear what they want to. You should know that – it's what you do, isn't it? How your books work. Come on, all those plots, where no one ever completely trusts anyone and people are always being murdered for the wrong reasons. Don't tell me they've finally twisted your mind. You poor man.'

The bedroom is freezing. My feet, my hands, feel as if they are going numb. It can only be a matter of time before the circulation falters and gangrene sets in. Perhaps it already has, in my frozen mind, my frozen heart. Perhaps I'm rotting from the inside out.

Though tell me, Maggie – anyone – are there ever right reasons to kill someone? Yeah, maybe.

Spray now seemed to be sweeping in from the North Sea as the squall intensified. The pedestrianised Regent Road was deserted. Fonda sheltered in the doorway of Poundland. Looked at his watch, again. This had better be worth it, he thought.

Directly across the street was the entrance to the Wellington Hotel bar. It didn't appear too crowded, though condensation was clouding the large windows. Christmas decorations could be seen glinting behind the glass.

It was still the holiday season, but the wrong holiday season for this town all right, Fonda reasoned to himself. Not that the place was exactly heaving in summer any more. Those days, those years were long past. Yet someone's ruin was always someone else's gain.

Fonda retrieved his latest mobile from his coat pocket. There was no new message. Wait outside, he'd been told.

Shoving the cheap device back into his pocket, he quickly reversed further into the doorway as two people emerged from the Wellington. A man and a woman.

He had a clear view as they lingered for a moment, zipping their jackets, turning up their collars.

He immediately recognised the man, though it took him longer to realise who the woman was. Bloody hell – what was he doing with her, of all people? Fonda hadn't seen her walk into the place. She must have used the back entrance, having come by car.

But they were leaving on foot, together.

Fonda waited until they were fifty metres or so up the street, where Regent Road hit Marine Parade, before he stepped out onto the pavement, the rain and the wind blasting into his face.

Squinting through the onslaught, he tried to scan ahead. As soon as the two huddled figures turned left and out of view, he increased his pace, only to feel a hand on his shoulder, someone pulling him back.

He spun round, clenching his right fist, ready to swing out. 'Oh, it's you,' he said, trying to make himself heard above the weather. 'Wondered where you'd got to. But next time, hey, don't fucking sneak up on me like that.'

'Sorry – didn't want to take any chances. I couldn't be spotted,' the other man said. 'You know him?'

'Sort of.'

'Thought so. Who is he then?'

'Someone who did some work for me a long while ago, in a different town. He was good. Ruthless. Discreet. But he had one weakness.'

'Yeah?'

'Women.'

'So what's he doing here?'

Fonda laughed, but the sound of the sea drowned him out. 'I don't know,' he raised his voice. 'Haven't managed to ask him yet. But I don't like it, especially with this other stuff that's going down.'

'The hooker? Or are you talking about the guy we fished out of the Yare, minus his head?'

'Have you established a link?'

'We're working on it. Thought you might be able to help. Can we get out of the rain, talk somewhere a little dryer and quieter?'

'No, mate – I've got to be somewhere,' said Fonda, turning back.

'Hang about a minute. You owe me. You could at least tell me what you think she's doing with him.'

'How the fuck do I know. She's your boss.'

Sleep was a long way off. As was any form of peace. Fonda continued to pace the billiard room.

He was annoyed that he'd been given the slip more than once, had probably lost that element of surprise – but he supposed he was dealing with a professional.

Though just what the fuck the man was now doing with the head of the region's major crime unit he had no idea. And Shreve was not proving to be anything like as useful as he should have been, given what he was being paid.

OK, Shreve had tipped him off about the Wellington Hotel cosy-up. But the detective would have to be put to better use – whether that required arm-twisting or not.

Fonda grabbed the white ball, flung it across the baize, watched it rebound around the table. The thudding echoing in the large room.

At least Girts Kesteris had promised to meet him tomorrow.

Eight

'Yes?'

'David? It's Julie. What the hell are you up to?'

'I'm sorry?' I can't hear her very well. The reception's not great. Or perhaps I'm going deaf. Old age rapidly advancing; to go cap in hand with my faltering career, my collapsing marriage: the steady, but inevitable decline of my professional and personal lives.

'What the fuck are you up to?' shouts Julie.

Oh, I don't like her tone at all. She's never this cross, this aggressive. 'I'm on campus, at the university – Maggie's university. Why?'

'What are you doing there?'

In the rain, under a sky of the thickest, darkest grey, with the stained, tatty 1960s concrete of the buildings only enhancing the enormous, freezing gloom, I am wondering too. 'I'm on my way to the library,' I say.

'That's not what I meant,' says Julie, 'you idiot. What the hell are you doing in the UK?'

Sheltering round a corner, against a particularly weathered slab of sodden concrete, I contemplate ending the call – it's not as if I haven't been doing a lot of that recently, when I've actually answered the thing. 'Working,' I say, suddenly rather pleased with myself.

'Working?' She's almost screaming.

'Yes, they have a great library here, with a big local-history section.

I'm doing some research,' I say, which was my intention, though not quite here. I'd planned to drive to Kingsmouth today and finally do that groundwork, but somehow I ended up at Maggie's university.

'David, why aren't you in the States? You were meant to get on a plane, yesterday. Your American publisher is not very pleased, neither is your British agent. In fact, I'm fucking livid. And that poor Jo Spear – she's been in tears apparently.'

'I thought you said she'd been doing a shit job anyway – taking ages to secure those slots in hopeless backwaters?'

'You hardly helped the situation, by not winning that bloody award.'

'And then I was practically meant to pay for everything when I was there. I hate B&Bs, and what was I meant to eat?'

'Less – wouldn't have done you any harm.' She pauses, comes back on. 'David, perhaps you don't realise quite how much work has gone into this. Besides, you were extremely fortunate that they still wanted to have you over there. Most of my authors would give their right arm for such an opportunity.'

'It was bollocks from the start, and you know it.'

'It was a chance, David, your last actually, to get your name about and grab some sales in the States. And you've blown it.'

'Sales? Most of those events were to be in public libraries.'

'And weren't you set to meet various reviewers and bloggers?' continues Julie. 'Those people count. What's Jo going to say to them? More importantly, what are they going to say now? Nothing probably. Which is the worst possible scenario. Even worse than a sniffy review on an amateur site. You will be completely ignored.'

'Julie,' I say, slumping against the cold, hard, wet concrete, 'do you want me to finish my new novel or not?'

'To be brutally frank, David, that depends,' Julie is saying, and despite the weather and my crappy phone I seem to be able to hear all too clearly. 'Of course I want you to meet your deadline and be something of a bankable prospect, here, in the States and all around the fucking world for that matter. Of course I want your new novel to be a massive success – but from what you've told me about it, I have serious reservations. And I'm also concerned – more than ever – about your commitment to your brand. It all requires so much more effort than you appear to understand at the moment. You've let a lot of people down, David.'

I've let myself down too, I could say. Most definitely I shouldn't be lurking around corners on Maggie's campus, still trying to catch her out, given everything she's said and done to reassure me that she's not having an affair. Why can't I believe her? Has my mind become so seriously confused, professionally and personally (as Maggie would have it), that it's skewed out of all proportion? Oh, where is Maggie right now, and with whom? Because she wasn't in her office a few moments ago, despite telling me this morning that was exactly where she was going to be, all day, working on her response to the plagiarism accusation.

'Julie, sorry, I just couldn't take the time out,' I say. 'I'm at a really crucial stage. It's all coming together. I simply couldn't disrupt the flow.'

'You do have a laptop, don't you, David? Most of our authors think nothing of working while on tour. Indeed, they have to, given their schedules – and their commitment. All you were required to do was fly to the States for a few days.'

Shit! There's Ashish, bundled up in a massive overcoat and with an enormous scarf wound around his head and shoulders but it's him all right, that nose, those dark, scandal-hungry eyes – coming my way, fast. I turn towards the wall in my semi-crouch, feeling Ashish sweep past despite the squalling, wintry wind. Why the hell hadn't I gone straight to Kingsmouth? Why the hell am I continuing this conversation with Julie, cowering beside a slab of damp concrete?

Because my sanity, and my livelihood, depends upon it.

'David, something tells me you're not being completely up front with me.' Julie's voice is still somehow penetrating the weather, and my embarrassment. 'Can you just tell me what's really troubling you? Is everything really all right at home? Are you having problems with Maggie?'

What does Julie know? Has she heard anything? Different worlds, but none of them are that large. There are always odd coincidences, odd associations. Gossip, innuendo, scandal, whatever you want to call it, travels fast and light, permeable to all boundaries, all borders, certainly in this digital age (which clearly, apart from everything else, I'm so useless, so backward, at manipulating).

Ashish – younger, more digital-savvy no doubt, aside from being a legendary gossip – where the hell's he gone now? Where was he heading?

'David,' I can hear Julie saying, clearly, 'you still there? I was asking you about Maggie. You are not splitting up, are you?'

'No, of course not,' I say. 'Nothing's wrong with Maggie – with us. Far from it.' Perhaps Julie's heard about the plagiarism accusation, rather than the infidelity. 'Look, I have to go.' I do, I really do, because out of the corner of my eye I can see Ashish coming back my way, through the squall, through all the shit. Why? I too should have donned a pashmina, if indeed that's what he's actually wearing. Hidden myself behind metres of luxurious, warm cashmere.

'I'm coming down to the sticks to see you,' Julie says (she's still there, still hanging on, still believing in me?). 'You need sorting out.'

'Fine, bye.' I drop my phone into my jacket pocket, straighten up and set off at a trot towards the car park, far too aware of Ashish just behind me.

'David?' he calls.

Volvo for Life reads the message on the back of the tax-disc holder. Yet it's death I'm contemplating. Audi for Death? I'm sure I read recently that Audi drivers are the most aggressive on the road. But the most murderous? I need another death, urgently – to appease Julie at least.

What's more, I feel this death needs to be on the page – as it happens, so to speak. I need to get blood on my hands. As ever, I've been shying away from the key moments, the graphic descriptions (and I guess spending too much time on emotion, if not desire – but Jones and Hayes, well, they've got a thing going on). Nevertheless, of course I realise readers want more nowadays, more blood and gore – I think I want more too. Balls, David, balls! You have them, somewhere.

The rain seems to be turning to sleet. I start the engine, wait for the fan to kick in, the warm air to flow. Thinking, thinking hard . . . when I see *him* – walking across the road, away from the Humanities block. Same big trench coat and boots. Long greasy hair and a wispy attempt at a beard. A grin on his face: of satisfaction, relief? What is Maggie thinking?

As he strides up the pavement, ignoring the bus stop and the weather, I put the car into Drive, and begin creeping out of the car park. He's just the other side of a row of thin, straggly bushes, quite unaware of me. For now.

He thought of that moment again – when he came across her, in the dunes. Her beautiful body so callously dumped. He was going to make them pay. Of course he was going to make them pay: one person in particular.

He'd been working on this for so long. Planning. Putting everything into place. Watching. Then he'd moved, first slipping her the drugs in that horrible bedroom, and then . . . it'd worked like a dream. Almost.

He thought again of the moment after he'd removed her clothes and parted her legs, the moment when he retrieved the knife from the inside pocket of his anorak, carefully taking it out of its plastic bag with his gloved hands and then pushing it into her. Death had already made her harder and stiffer than he'd thought possible, and it wasn't easy, and took more than an instant to penetrate her with the kitchen implement.

Especially as he was breathing so fast and shaking too – with the cold, the excitement, the panic. But he kept thinking of Adrian Fonda, and what he'd done not just to him and his colleagues, but to all those who'd had the misfortune of coming into his orbit. The misery, the horror he'd left in his wake.

Fonda thought that he would always get away with it, that he was beyond the law, and he probably was. But he was not invincible. And he had seriously misjudged one of his legitimate employees.

Alex Smith had never been a fool. Quiet maybe. Bookish even. The guy working in community housing, North Denes area, whom no one could ever remember the name of. But he was every bit as calculating and ruthless as the swaggering head of planning and regeneration – if he wanted to be. If he had to be.

You could only be overlooked for so long – if, at the bottom of your heart, you had ambition, and the brains, and a flexible morality.

The knife had gone in up to the hilt, the initial resistance quickly giving way. And then he'd pushed it in even further. Women's bodies, he thought now, seemed so soft on the inside.

He would like to be able to concentrate on this, on this memory, while the rest of his plan worked itself out in the brutally clever way he'd expected. However, he'd been careless. He'd made a mistake. And it seemed he wasn't the only person who'd discovered this.

Smith thought he could handle the man with the dog, who obviously had his own reasons for not going to the police with some evidence from what had suddenly become a major crime scene.

Though Fonda's interest in the same man was troubling him deeply. Was there anything Fonda didn't have a handle on?

Smith was naked, on his bed, in the dark. He scratched at his left wrist, where his watch should have been. He scratched harder and harder until he could feel the skin begin to bruise and split.

I leave the house yet again today, rushing a bit now, shift the car into Drive, quickly pull out, flick on the wipers and gather speed along our wonky road, thinking that perhaps all is not lost – hey, Julie, et al.

Driving has always helped me think. So I go over some stuff. Try to remember exactly what's just happened, where I am, which will obviously help me plot the next course of action. I really can't afford to make any more mistakes. Not now.

'Hayes,' said Hayes, negotiating a roundabout, plenty already on her mind.

'It's Colony,' said Dr Michelle Colony.

'About time,' said Hayes.

'Sorry, Britt,' she said, 'I've been twisting every arm out there to get these results back. Believe me.'

'Oh, I do,' said Hayes, accelerating along the dual-carriageway. 'I'm only surprised you found any arms to twist.'

'There weren't many.' She laughed. 'We've got another round of cuts scheduled next month, haven't we? You lot might have to be doing these tests yourself by the summer.'

Would probably make things an awful lot quicker, thought Hayes. 'What have you got then, Michelle?'

'Acetomorphine, twelve parts per hundred. Decent stuff, too. Though if she was a regular user, it's questionable whether such a hit would be instantly fatal. It didn't stop her heart anyway.'

Hayes exhaled heavily. Overtook a sugar-beet lorry.

'What killed her was hypothermia,' said Colony.

'OK,' said Hayes, thinking back to last night and what Howie Jones, if that really was his name, had shown her. 'How's this for a scenario – naked and unconscious, she was dumped out in the open, in the dunes, where she quickly perished due to the cold.'

'Possible,' said Colony. 'Except you're forgetting one thing.'

'The knife? I'm still trying to get my head around it. Whoever dumped her then, for whatever reason, decided to sexually assault her with the knife.'

'But she was dead when the knife was used. I'm certain of that now. And had been for a short while, at least.'

'No one would stand there waiting for her to die, before doing that to her, surely,' said Hayes. 'I need to have another word with the profiler.'

'The lividity is interesting. I'll send the report down. But there are some faint marks on her wrists and ankles. Hadn't noticed them before. Looks like she was bound at some point.'

'Shortly before she died?'

'No, don't think so.'

Hayes was approaching the turn-off to the city bypass. She indicated left.

'However, there are also some abrasions on her arms and legs that were definitely inflicted after she died. The corpse was moved around a bit.'

Thinking again of the evidence Jones had shown her, something clicked. 'What if she wasn't naked when she was dumped there, but someone then came across her, stripped her, did what they did with the knife, repositioned her body and took away her clothes?'

'Sounds a bit elaborate,' said Colony, 'but it would fit. Though don't forget that the body had been there for at least forty-eight hours before we got to it. Time is not on our side.'

'What about the DNA analysis on the knife?' said Hayes.

'You are going to have to wait until Friday at least before we get anywhere with that. Though, for what it's worth, the knife was well kept, the blade pretty sharp.'

'But it wasn't new?'

'No, not according to Forensics.'

Merging onto the A47, Hayes thanked Colony and ended the call.

In her pocket, wrapped in a wad of Kleenex, was the wristwatch – a gentleman's Seiko on a metal bracelet – that Jones had found in the dunes, so he'd said, a short way from the body.

He'd shown her the very spot, that morning, the rain finally having cleared, the wind having eased too. Though it was still bitter as hell.

It wasn't far from where the body had been located. She'd clearly remembered the dunes, the clumps of marram, the lie of the soft land, where the SOC tent had been erected, how Kristine's body had been positioned. The watch would have been found when the area was raked by uniform, but of course Howie Jones had got there first.

Jones had said he'd come across the body early in the morning, Christmas morning that was, when it wasn't yet fully light.

She still couldn't understand how no one then came across the body for another day or so. The place was usually swarming with dog walkers. The weather had been no worse than usual.

She had already decided not to tell the team about the watch, and at least to get it checked by the lab first. With a number of investigations on her plate, she could push it through without too many questions being asked.

Even if it was going to be increasingly difficult keeping Howie Jones out of the picture. But that was exactly what she was intending to do.

How could she begin to explain that even though Jones hadn't reported a suspicious death and had knowingly withheld evidence from a major crime scene – aside from the fact that he readily used aliases and admitted to a long past of criminal activity – she was prepared to believe him, to trust him? How could she begin to explain her relationship with him?

She'd already slept with him, twice. And knew she was going to sleep with him again. Once was normally her limit.

Besides, who knew what DNA might be on the watch. Who knew whom to trust. She'd stick with instinct for now. Even if it were being driven by desire.

Stopping at the lights, just in time, I pull my phone from my pocket, stab the green Answer button without seeing who's calling and put the device to my ear. 'Hello,' I shout, leaning forward and checking the light is still on red, worrying a little and again about the rhetorical nature of my prose – but what can I do? To be human is to be uncertain, no?

'Mr Slavitt?' It's a female voice. Stern. Concerned?

'Yes?'

'This is Avenue Primary.' A woman's voice.

'Is everything all right? Jack, Poppy?' My heart begins to thump wildly.

'Yes, they're absolutely fine, Mr Slavitt. In fact they are sitting in my office, right here, waiting for someone to pick them up.'

I look at my watch. The car behind beeps. 'Oh, shit! Sorry. I'm on my way. Will be there in twenty minutes.' The car behind beeps again, as I fling my phone onto the passenger seat and speed off, looking in my mirror and clocking the fact that it's an Audi (naturally).

But as I drive right around the roundabout and back towards the city, the way I've just come, with the sky suddenly darkening, or perhaps that's my imagination (though it is late, later in the afternoon than it should be), I realise, easing my foot on the accelerator, that I haven't forgotten to pick up the kids. And neither has Emily. Maggie has.

It's not Maggie's turn today. It's never Maggie's turn on a Wednesday. It's either Emily's or mine. But Maggie said she wanted to pick them up today. She insisted upon it. Saying, as she rushed around getting ready this morning (choosing her clothes, attending to her new hairstyle, applying her make-up, with the utmost care of course), that with all her troubles at work – I laughed out loud at this – she hadn't been paying enough attention to the children recently (who has?) and that she wanted to spend some quality time with them, this afternoon. I can't believe she used that word, that phrase. *Quality time.*

As if that would be possible anyway. The kids are always exhausted and fractious after school, and hungry. And what is quality time? Who really has quality time with anyone? Maggie and Alex?

Isn't that the whole point of having an affair: to snatch the odd moment of giddy relief, to satiate that sense of sudden, overwhelming desire? The ultimate escape from the everyday. Plus the novelty. The sheer excitement, helped, too, by the fear of being caught, which of course (in my professional world anyway) is so closely aligned with joy, or entertainment anyway.

The city is rapidly approaching, or rather enveloping. The dual-carriageway threads into one lane (and a bus lane); the main road (which effectively leads all the way to and from London: oh, the irony, the pathos) now not exactly sandwiched between grand, detached houses – set well back from the road, and sheltered by huge trees (oaks and beeches and planes predominantly) and mature shrubs – but swiftly, coincidentally almost, passing them by.

It's an impressive route into a fine, provincial city, by any stretch. There was plenty of money here once. There's still plenty of space and greenery and a certain amount of understated grandeur, if not exactly in-your-face extravagance (which is why we liked it, why we immediately felt comfortable, that we'd fit in – though just look how comfortable we've got, how comfortable Maggie's got anyway).

Slowing as the traffic builds towards the roundabout marking the city's inner ring road, I can immediately recall the excitement (and trepidation) Maggie and I felt when we visited here, having made the decision to move. At least this was after Maggie had accepted the job, and we came to look for a house – with all our supposed London cash and swagger, our cultural savvy, relative youth and adorable young children.

But I don't think we were particularly complacent. We weren't after further affirmation of our – cultural? – worth. We just wanted to slip into an easier, simpler, quieter, gentler kind of life. One that contained less stress, and less need to constantly prove our stock. That's what we were after, I think. That's what we thought we were going to get. And then we came upon our house, on that well-located side road, with its hill and bends and abundant foliage, and an obvious sense of privacy. It all made so much sense.

Who knew then that we would be spied on, that the world wouldn't let us go quietly. Who knew then that the peace, the calm, would be shattered by a PhD student – and the rest.

Fuck! I have turned into our road, when of course I should have continued on the main arterial route for another two streets (even though it's all conveniently within the inner ring road: 'Location, location,' Maggie said, laughing, when we made an offer), and then taken a left, and on to Poppy and Jack's ('outstanding' – Ofsted) primary school. To retrieve them from the school office, and an angry teacher, because their mother has inexplicably failed to do what she had promised to do only a few hours earlier. Why?

Where the hell is she now? I don't stop, or even slow, as I pass our house (in darkness and surrounded by near-darkness – he must have had a splendid view of our bedroom window from the far side of the street), but continue towards my children, our children, who must be feeling pretty lonely and let down; though maybe not. Not Jack anyway. He'll think it's a bit of a laugh. Not being collected from school. A chance to soak up some extra attention. He likes the unexpected, any sense of drama – already knows he can't rely, 110 per cent, on his parents.

This is all I need, as I accelerate up another side road, packed with two-storey terraced houses (most with interior lights ablaze – full of warmth and life, full of happy families). I should be in Kingsmouth, researching. I should have been there hours ago, indeed weeks ago, when I first hit upon this (stupid?) idea of a man stumbling upon a naked corpse (of a young woman, disturbingly and posthumously mutilated, not that he or anyone else knew that then) early one Christmas morning, in an Area of Outstanding Natural Beauty . . .

Instead, well, I only have my wife to blame, for dragging me away from the more practical aspects of my work in progress. Though no doubt she'll blame me, for failing to pick up our kids from school – when she'd promised so stridently otherwise. She said it was going to be the highlight of her day. The *highlight*.

Pulling up right outside the school gates, bang in the middle of the yellow no-parking zigzags (feeling more like an Audi driver than a Volvo driver), I reach for my mobile, thinking I'll just try Maggie before I go in to get our kids. I don't want them to hear me berating their beloved mother. Of course her mobile rings out to answerphone, as does her desk phone. The school would have tried her first anyway. They always try her first when they need to contact us (urgently or otherwise), despite the fact that I take the kids to school and pick them up so much more often than Maggie. Nevertheless Maggie is the primary school's primary point of contact, the person they believe is ultimately responsible for, and in charge of, our children – being the mother.

Climbing out of the car and heading through the gates, I suddenly wonder not about the latent sexism of the teaching and administrative staff of this provincial school, or where Maggie actually is right now, whether indeed she's OK and hasn't had some terrible accident, but about what will happen to the kids should Maggie and I split up, should we be forced to split up (and then the attitude that the school will have towards me and my responsibilities). Do they treat single dads differently? Could I ever become the primary point of contact?

I find myself having to catch my breath. Despite all that has happened (and hasn't happened) over the last few days and weeks with regard to her affair, with regard to Alex Smith, I haven't once thought about separation, divorce, daily life without Maggie (and/or the children) until now. It's not what I want, of course. Not remotely. I want to be with Maggie and the kids. Even if it means jacking in a day's research. Research has never really been my favourite thing.

Perhaps I'm in the wrong job, always have been. But times change, of course. Needs must.

'Mr Slavitt, you have to press the green button.'

Turning round, I don't see anyone.

'Not the blue button.' The voice is coming from the intercom panel. How do they know my name? How do they know I'm here, already? Then I see the little square window, behind which sits a round security-camera lens (why have I not noticed this before, such high-tech security at such a low-tech, public institution?). When I press the right button, the door suddenly opens and I enter the hall (which is in part of the old, original school building), and am immediately engulfed by that relentless, timeless school smell (a sort of sweet, musty, bleachy tang). My shoes squeak (or am I just imagining it?) on the worn lino as I make my way to the admin office, feeling ashamed, careless, guilty, with something else suddenly troubling me too. Something I'm struggling to latch onto – think, think, think – as I look about the chipped and tatty walls, brightened by children's wonderfully naïve artworks.

The little square window, the tiny CCTV camera – of course! Call myself a crime writer?

I haven't made enough of this. The fact that Hayes and her team would have immediately trawled through all the CCTV footage they could locate, especially of the Kingsmouth seafront. Only to discover that not one working camera (well, it's a very depressed and neglected area – even more so in the middle of winter – all but abandoned by the authorities and left to its own devious devices; not really an Area of Outstanding Natural Beauty, not any more) captured anywhere near that spot in the dunes (of course – the perpetrator was no fool) or anyone of interest heading to or from that way.

But things are missed. Things are always missed. And anyway there's no point being overtly reactive in this business, is there? You have to move on, keep moving forward, while exercising a little restraint – if possible.

'Dad,' says Poppy, suddenly by my side.

Jack's with her, but he quickly looks away, neither smiling nor saying anything. Next to him, coming forward, in her voluminous jumper and trousers, her grey hair pulled tightly back, is the head teacher, Mrs Naughton. Naughty Naughton, as she's known, but who's never exactly been a barrel of laughs, as far as I'm aware, and who certainly doesn't look too happy now. And rather than greet her, rather than begin apologising profusely, on behalf of my wayward wife, I can't help but look away, suddenly wondering what the university's CCTV cameras have picked up today (they'll be working all right, despite the ongoing cuts). I wonder what else they might have caught over the last few weeks. Could I get access to that footage? Sneak into the Porter's Lodge? Would I really want access, more confirmation? When I already know the truth. When it's already far too late.

'Where the hell is she?'

'Sorry, Mr Slavitt?' says Mrs Naughton.

'Sorry,' I say, realising I was speaking aloud. 'Children, have you got all your things?'

'Yes, Dad,' says Poppy, clutching her book-bag and lunchbox.

'Jack?' Jack looks up, shrugs, shifts my way a little. He seems to be carrying all his things too, but he still doesn't open his mouth.

'OK, guys, let's go,' I say, stepping away from Nasty Naughton (seems a more appropriate tag), trying to shepherd my children with my large hands; trying to protect them, I suppose.

'Very sorry about this,' I say, looking straight at the head teacher and smiling in a pathetic, defeated kind of way. 'A communication fuck-up with their mother.'

The second I turn and we start to walk back down that squeaky, stinking corridor, I curse myself for saying *fuck-up* – words are just slipping out. If it came to sole custody, would I be declared an unfit father? Because I'm unreliable? Because my language is unsuitable for minors? Because, professionally, I deal in violent acts?

Not as violent as they could have been. Not as violent as they should have been.

Emerging into cold fresh air and swiftly exiting the grounds, I'm suddenly aware of someone rushing across the road out of the dark towards us.

'Mummy,' says Jack.

'Hello, darlings,' says Maggie, bending down to embrace Jack, gathering in Poppy. 'Everyone OK?' she says, between smothering her children with kisses.

'Oh, fine,' I say, but I'm not sure she hears me. I'm not sure she was asking me anyway.

'Dad was late,' says Jack. 'We had to sit in Mrs Naughton's office.'

'Oh, you poor things,' says Maggie. 'Naughty Naughton's office – can't have been much fun. Silly old Dad for being so late.'

Straightening, she looks at me now, tries to smile, but really it's nothing more than a grimace. She hates me, I'm suddenly certain of it. I don't blame her.

'What happened?' she says. She doesn't look particularly dishevelled or bedraggled, or in any kind of shock. Clearly she hasn't had an accident, or some kind of mental breakdown. Her coat is neatly belted, her hair in place. Her work make-up is still on. Everything about her is sort of normal, except the scowl, the loathing (though that's becoming normal).

'What happened?' I say. 'Sorry, Maggie, I'm not with you. I get a call from the school about twenty minutes ago saying why haven't we picked up our children – I was right in the middle of doing some crucial research as well.'

'That would make a change, darling,' Maggie says.

'So of course I drop everything and rush here.'

'That's funny,' says Maggie, 'because I get a call from the school saying the same thing, except I was actually in a meeting, a faculty meeting, and the secretary has to barge her way in, broadcasting the fact that our children haven't been picked up from school. Can you imagine how embarrassing that was, in front of – well, I don't even need to tell you who was there. What do you think they think of me now? Someone who can't even organise childcare for her own children? And this on top of that other little problem I'm having at work right now – in case you've forgotten.'

'Perhaps we should continue this conversation later,' I say, looking at my children, who can't bear to look at me (do they hate me too?), wondering just which other little problem at work she's referring to. 'But for the record—'

'For the record. Oh God, David, here we go.'

'Maggie, you were meant to pick up the kids today. You said at breakfast, quite clearly, that that was what you wanted to do.'

'No, I didn't,' she says. 'Actually that's not quite true.'

I've beeped the car unlocked and the children are clambering into the back – desperate to get home? Maggie's walking round to the passenger seat, obviously having taken a taxi here (though really from where?). 'You said, I can remember quite clearly, that you wanted to spend some quality time with the kids. Quality time, you actually said that.' I'd laugh, if I could. Instead I ease myself behind the steering wheel, the driver's seat feeling somehow closer than normal. Maggie elegantly but stiffly slips into the passenger seat, patting the creases out of her once-expensive mac as she does so.

'Sure, I'm sure I said that,' she says calmly. 'But I was referring to tomorrow, to Thursday. I said I'd pick them up after school tomorrow. How could I have picked them up today, when I knew I had an important faculty meeting this afternoon? We always have these meetings on Wednesdays.'

'You didn't, Maggie. You said today. You said you were going to pick them up today, this afternoon. I shouldn't even be in this country. I should be in America.'

She sighs, shakes her head. I pull out.

'You've gone mad,' she says, as I quickly make a right onto Avenue Road.

Maybe I didn't look carefully enough, or maybe I wasn't quick enough – there's a car suddenly, immediately behind us. Coming from it is a loud, long, aggressive hoot.

I stamp on the accelerator, but the car behind not only keeps up, but continues to hoot and flash its lights, the driver weaving it around the narrow, residential road – which during certain times of the day (though of course not quite now) is packed with young cyclists and pedestrians: kids going to and from school – as if he wants to overtake.

Fuck it! I brake, hard.

'See,' Maggie says, clutching the sides of her seat, 'you are mad.'

'Probably,' I say.

There's silence for a few moments. The children are appalled, no doubt, by their father's behaviour today (who wouldn't be?), by the fact that I just put them in serious physical danger. There is something very wrong with me all right. Though is it madness?

The car behind – it's an Audi of course, another Audi, a dark metallic colour this time – swerves out, slows parallel to us. I look away, down at the steering wheel, at my lap, and the Audi then roars ahead. Perhaps realising I'm carrying too precious a cargo to embark upon some form of properly violent act.

'By the way,' Maggie says, her voice penetrating that suddenly dreadful quiet, 'Ashish says he saw you on campus today, lurking by a wall not far from the cafeteria, which obviously sounded a bit odd to me – you know what Ashish is like. But he said he could swear it was you. He said he even called out your name, but you ran off. Please tell me it wasn't you.'

If only I knew when to act and when to restrain myself also.

Nine

As soon as I hear the email ping in I find myself turning away from what I'm reading, what I'm trying to digest, and taking a look.

David. Oh God, here we go. I knew I shouldn't have – but I was between a rock and a hard place. *The cancellation of your tour has generated a little more attention than we expected. Thought you'd be interested in the links below. Cheers, Jo.*

I try one of the links, follow the stream, the few comments – there are two actually. One of them particularly grabs my attention:

> *So pleased I'm getting my money back on David Slavitt's 'novel'* The Tortured *– seeing as he now won't be here to sign it (as was promised by my favourite bookstore in the world). Never has a title of a book been more apt for the reader.*
> *Lauren, Pittsburgh.*

At least they have a sense of humour, in Pittsburgh. Nevertheless, I don't try the other links, and reluctantly return my attention to something else that was (pointedly) thrust my way.

And just get this: I'm trying to, very hard.

A police officer returns to her car to find a woman slumped over the door (it's not clear whether the door is open or not, though presumably it would have to be if someone's slumped over it, otherwise they'd slide off, particularly in the state she's in – wait – though the police officer surely would have shut and locked the door, when she left the car some time before; unless the officer had a very low-slung sporty model, I suppose, but that would be unlikely, given police pay). Anyway, this woman – middle-aged, well kept, wearing expensive clothes and jewellery – is bleeding profusely, fatally. Blood is pouring from her throat, which has been slashed, and from her stomach, which has been ripped open. Her guts are actually spilling out.

The police officer and the fatally wounded woman do then fall to the ground, with the police officer (a newish recruit, a budding detective indeed – with lots of personal issues, of course) trying to stem the flow, from the neck and the stomach, and comfort the woman as best she can, and call for an ambulance and back-up too.

Oh, and they're in the middle of a sink estate, in London (of course), South London, and it's dark and threatening. The police officer (she shouldn't have been there, at that time, on her own – more of which will come out later, I can just see) does not know whether the attacker is still close by. As the woman's life quickly ebbs away, so the tension builds, until the shocked and scared detective, herself splattered in blood, is left staring at the dead woman and remembering, somehow, that the average female body contains five litres of blood. She just never considered quite what it would look like when it was all spilling out.

Thanks. Thanks, Julie, for bringing me this gift – in the form of an elaborately produced proof of a new thriller from her newest client (who also happens to be published by my publisher).

Having finally arrived in a considerable fluster (the train was packed and late – big surprise – and there were no waiting taxis at the station), Julie's gone for a walk to calm down. So she said. She's actually gone to buy some fags, while I'm meant to digest (take on board?) the stunning (her word) intro from her latest protégée. Apparently this is the publishers' – my UK publishers' – big fiction debut for the coming autumn (now that I've been relegated to the spring, next spring, in theory).

What am I meant to make of it? Well, there's obviously much more blood (litres of the stuff) right from the start, than my current effort. Plus, and I suppose significantly, the victim is still alive, albeit just, at the beginning. Actually it reminds me of that novel where the young woman had an exploding device rammed into her mouth (see, invariably it is always women – young, old – who always come off worst). We get to *see* someone die. I suppose Julie is trying to tell me that I need not just to incorporate more blood, but to describe someone dying, and gruesomely, in the first few pages, if I have any chance of reclaiming an autumn publishing slot. If I have any chance of getting the thing published at all (in this country, let alone America).

However – not that I've yet had a moment to tell Julie – I have recently been thinking about having someone die, in front of our very eyes. I now feel better equipped to describe it, because frankly, given the circumstances, I'm racked with morbid thoughts. It's a fine line in my world, of course, between imagination and experience. I'm just waiting for the right moment (again). Patience, Julie, please – though I'm not at all sure she has any left for me.

Flicking on through this proof, and this is why I try not to read any of my rivals' work (let alone debuts by the latest new big thing, with, clearly, their fingers on the pulse – albeit a rapidly weakening pulse in this case), I begin to get more of a measure of this young, inexperienced female detective, who's called Nicky Blunt (for the moment anyway, though I believe I can see a twist coming here; why does everything have to be so predictably unpredictable nowadays?). I move over to my reading chair, in the corner of my study, quite short of breath. I wonder, if I was fitter, whether I'd be able to work faster, kill more people – sort my fucking life out.

Where is Julie? How long does it take to walk to the bottom of the road, turn right, carry on for fifty metres or so to the Co-op, buy a couple of packets of cigarettes, stuff them into your Chanel bag and totter back here?

This young detective constable, this Nicky Blunt figure is (I really can't believe this bit, and what indeed Julie must have been telling this author – and indeed all her authors? – to incorporate) into casual (is that really the right word?) sex. She likes to pick up men in various seedy North London bars and have quick, no-strings-attached sex with them. Oh God, just like my Britt Hayes. Well, almost – Britt's cruising ground being not Camden, but Kingsmouth.

And like Britt (and Maggie?), Nicky Blunt finds it's never quite so simple. Desires, attachments, compromises and of course complications build. She should know better. They should all know better. We're only human.

Standing, I fling the proof across the room, just as the doorbell goes. Julie's back, no doubt having smoked a couple of fags on the way up the hill: the harbinger of bad news, more bad news, plucking up her courage.

At least this Nicky Blunt novel (which obviously will be the next big thing – given Julie's and the publishers' enthusiasm and commitment, and it is pretty well written), called intriguingly *Now You*, is not set in Kingsmouth. I still think that someone's out there, at this very minute, putting the finishing touches to their gruesomely violent tale set in that town. I can almost see it – coming as it will with an infinitely more exciting and enticing title than *Kristine*. Something like *Psycho*, but obviously not that. *Weirdo*, perhaps.

'Steep hill,' says Julie, wheezing: a thick waft of fag smell coming into the house with her, and perfume – Chanel, I guess. 'I thought Norfolk was meant to be flat.'

No, that's just me, I could reply. Tired, deflated, worn out. I actually feel like getting down on my knees and praying for some higher guidance. At least for James P's email address. Though notoriously he doesn't communicate electronically. He doesn't do email. What would he say anyway? 'Pace, pace, pace, David. Keep it up, old boy.' Would that be it? Is he still sticking to that line?

But there've been recent developments of course. Do I need to remind myself already?

'Are you all right, David?' says Julie. 'You're standing there as if . . . as if you've seen a ghost.'

'Sorry, I was miles away. You know how it is – trying to crack on with the writing. Every moment I get. It's hard to pull yourself out of it sometimes.'

'Well, I'm sorry for disturbing you, David,' says Julie, pushing past me, heading for the kitchen. She's only been here once before, but she's the sort of person who instantly knows their way around, making themselves at home. 'Coffee, I think I need a coffee. Do I have to do it myself?'

'I think I can manage that,' I say, passing my study and following her into the kitchen.

'Oh yes, I forgot, you're the domesticated one. The house-husband. That's what Peter calls you anyway. Or is it hen-pecked?'

'You've been talking to Peter recently, have you?' It's getting dark outside, or perhaps it's about to rain. The large kitchen windows, which we've never thought of getting blinds for (preferring the uncluttered view, and thinking, I suppose, that we've got nothing to hide), now only add to the sense of cold and gloom, and sheer, naked exposure.

'Yes, obviously. He's as worried as I am.'

Though the children are at after-school club today and Emily's then collecting them, it won't be long before they are home. Julie and I obviously need to get this stuff out of the way before Poppy and Jack come barging in, immediately demanding to be fed and watered and entertained.

'You and Peter,' I say searching for the cafetière, 'really have nothing to worry about. Not any more. You wait and see. I'm a little late, that's all.' Try to think positively. Things have moved on. Action has been taken. What more could you do, in the circumstances?

'That isn't all,' says Julie. 'And you know it.'

'OK, I didn't win the Crime Thriller of the Year. Big deal. At least I came close.'

'At least? You didn't go to the States, David. That's a very big deal. And it doesn't take a genius to deduce that this new novel of yours, this *Kristine*, is not exactly going to get the blood pumping – for want of a better expression.'

'Julie, you haven't even read a page of it yet.' Are we out of coffee? I've just been to the supermarket, and the butcher's (only to find that Howard Jones wasn't there), sourcing Julie's dinner. Looks like I'll now have to go to the local Co-op myself. Though I could do with some air, with getting out of here, already. Perhaps I'll take up smoking, and then take my time making it back home. Maybe I won't come back. Make good my escape while I can.

'By the sounds of it, I'm not sure I want to.'

'Things have changed, Julie – it's getting meaner, meatier. OK, it still might not have as brutal and bloody a beginning as the one you've just given me, but it gets there. There'll be plenty of lethal surprises.'

'You've been working that fast?'

'Why do you think I didn't go to the States?' I say, slamming a cupboard shut – in triumph.

'Not sure you're off the hook there,' says Julie.

'We seem to be out of coffee, sorry.'

'Wine then, how about a glass of wine? Today seems to have gone on for ever already. You really live a long way away, don't you? That awful fucking train.' Julie puts her handbag (the Chanel) on the table, pulls out a chair, sits and practically falls forward onto the table. Now that's what I call a slump. She hasn't even removed her coat.

'Good idea,' I say, looking at my watch. They'll be back soon. Though not Maggie. Maggie won't be here until suppertime probably – another long, late meeting. Most days now. Same excuse, despite our last few confrontations. I think now she just can't stand being in the same house, same room as me.

'I brought some with me, if you're out of wine as well. It's in my luggage,' says Julie.

'It's all right – I have plenty.' Or did, once, in the cupboard under the stairs. I trudge out of the kitchen, wondering just who I've become. A liar? A monster? Why Maggie might hate me so much. If only she knew the truth.

The light in the cupboard doesn't work and I have to move the vacuum cleaner to get to the rack. I can see at least two bottles. But I know one of them is a Bulgarian rosé that someone once brought round, and which fortunately we've never had to open, and that the other is a Hungarian red, which has never looked great, either.

I should have bought some wine, some of that Co-op claret would be fine, when I went shopping earlier today. Though I was worried, am worried, that I've reached my credit limit. And I really can't bring myself to ask Maggie to transfer some money into my account. Not at the moment.

Maybe Julie will have to get hers. I mean, I am cooking – what more does she expect?

'Time we had a chat,' said Hayes. 'In my office, now.'

She turned, marched across the operations room, knowing that Shreve wouldn't dare not follow.

She closed the door behind him, rattling the flimsy structure. She remained standing, in front of her desk. 'Do you want to tell me what the hell is going on?' She was shouting.

DS Shreve was suddenly looming in front of her, far too close, and she had nowhere to retreat to. But she didn't feel threatened. In fact she felt like slapping his smug face. And not for the first time.

'Like I just said in the briefing,' he whispered aggressively, 'this guy, Girts Kesteris, Bernard Kesteris' brother, ran the Victoria Road joint, and at least three other places in Kingsmouth. We were already sifting through some pretty interesting CCTV footage. He also had links with similar operations in Essex and Bedfordshire. Estimates of how many women he had shipped over here and controlled are around the fifty mark.'

'Jesus' said Hayes, 'with that size of operation, how come he was never picked up, once?'

'He was – just not in this county.'

'That's what makes it worse, Detective, isn't it? Why weren't he and his brother even on the radar? That's what I want to know. It's your beat.'

'Because they were good?' said Shreve. 'Made sure none of their girls ever complained. Made sure no one else did, either. Must have stamped out all opposition before it got too vocal. Something like that. Who knows how many girls, how many bodies, have simply disappeared. There's a lot of fear and silence in that world.'

'Sure – but it still doesn't make sense,' said Hayes. 'That number of people involved, something would have given. Unless they had friends in the right places.' She looked at him, hard. 'You're sweating, Tom.'

'Yeah, well, something has given now all right,' he said. 'Seems like the whole operation is imploding.'

'Why's it taken this long? Why now? You got the Victoria Road tip-off, so you say. And not for the first time you come in here, telling us this and that, as if you're in fucking charge. What's your game? I don't like the way you sneak around. The way you play your cards so close to your chest. Do I need to remind you that I'm your commanding officer?'

'Sorry, Boss – I can't help it if you don't like the way I operate,' he said. 'But believe me, I'm doing what I can for this investigation, this department. Always have.'

'Why then do I get this feeling that you're just not telling us everything? I'll ask you again: why weren't you onto this lot before, these Kesteris brothers? Plus I want to know who's watching their backs. Someone must be. Come on, Tom, are we that out of touch in Kingsmouth?'

'There's only so much I can do. Perhaps you want to talk to the Chief Constable about budgets,' said Shreve. 'Surveillance isn't cheap. Neither is paying informers.'

'And no one isn't expendable, in this force, at this moment in time – that's what he'll tell you.' She fixed Shreve with another cold, hard look.

'My guess is something happened to the girl that wasn't meant to,' Shreve added quickly, staring straight back at her. But he still didn't look remotely rattled.

'Like she died?'

'I am aware of the toxicology results, what the lab's come up with so far,' said Shreve. 'So how about this: she overdoses – wouldn't be the first of them – and they try to get rid of her when she's still alive. Make it look like she went for a walk, got lost and dies. Which would leave only circumstantial; except someone came across her, and decided to have a little fun.'

'Decided to have a little fun? Is that what you call it?' Hayes thought of the watch Howie gave her, and which was now with Forensics – behind everyone's back. Was she testing Shreve, or herself? 'And they just happened to be carrying a sodding great carving knife,' said Hayes, 'saw her, and thought: I know where I want to bury this. That's too random, too weird, too much of a fucking coincidence, even for me.'

'OK,' said Shreve, 'maybe someone had been watching that particular Kesteris hellhole, had a thing about that girl, or any of the girls. Then he's presented with an opportunity, bang on a plate. I don't know – yet.'

'We've been through much of this before. And we're not getting anywhere. It's our job to start coming up with answers,' Hayes said, though more calmly.

'Maybe someone was trying to frame them – and my guess would be Girts. He seemed to be the one in overall charge. Looks like Bernard was the muscle, around here anyway.'

'I prefer the sound of that – and they obviously weren't having a little Latvian turf war between themselves. Those Eastern European families tend to stick together. Perhaps Bernard's death was a warning. But I don't like it when we're so out of the fucking loop, and on the back foot. And now this Girts Kesteris, the one person who might have been able to shed some light . . .'

'You'd have been lucky.'

'. . . had we known more about him, which of course we should have – come on, Tom, call yourself a detective, you should have had an in there – is dead.'

Girts Kesteris' body had been discovered under an hour ago, in a car, on a side road behind the old South Denes oil-storage depot. He'd been shot in the head, at point-blank range, the bullet having entered just below his left eye. Apparently half his brains were spilling out of the exit wound.

That was all wrong too, of course – the victim's identity having been so easily certified. A driving licence was found at the scene, along with a wallet – again. Fingerprints were immediately whirred through HOLMES, the result confirmed.

Which was when Girts Kesteris' past form, in Essex, and Bedfordshire, came to light. There was a charge for rape and one for extortion – though both cases had collapsed before they came to court.

And he still hadn't been on their radar.

There was another odd thing surrounding the discovery of his body. Uniform on the scene thought they smelt traces of an accelerant around the car, probably white spirit. Forensics had yet to determine what exactly.

Had the perpetrator, on the point of setting fire to the vehicle, been disturbed – and if so, by whom?

Hayes had yet to visit the scene and make her own assessment: nothing more was to be touched until she got there; the body to be left in situ.

Then the pathologist would of course be doing her thing, and who knew what would be thrown up regarding the calibre of the weapon, et cetera. But already Hayes didn't hold out too much hope. Whoever was behind all this was no fool.

It was like they were being played with. Continually pointed in the wrong direction.

'Get your coat, Shreve,' she said, knowing she'd already wasted too long. 'You're coming with me. And on the way perhaps you'd like to furnish me with a little more information about your contacts. What I'm beginning to think, you see, is that something very rotten is going on in that town.'

'Nothing new there then,' said Shreve.

Stepping out of her office, with Shreve right behind her, she added, not caring who else heard, 'Let's just hope you don't have blood on your hands.'

Removing my hands from my head, I look up. Maggie's opened my study door and is entering my private space – her trim frame, her sharp hairstyle, slowly coming into focus. I feel like I've been asleep. Though it can't be possible.

'David, sorry to disturb you, but Julie's looking a little bored, and I've got to get the kids to bed. And I'm sort of vaguely worrying about supper. Do I need to stir something?'

'Supper? It's under control. Sorry, I just had to sort something out.' I push my chair back and stand and follow Maggie into the hall and on through to the kitchen, where Julie's sitting at the table, an empty glass of wine in front of her. Jack's sitting opposite her, drawing something ugly on a large piece of paper. Not Julie, I hope. Bright kid that he is, he's not always the most diplomatic.

'Jack, off to bed, now,' I say. 'You can finish that upstairs.'

'In a minute,' he says.

'He's just taking his time,' says Julie, smiling at him, 'like you.'

'More wine, Julie?'

'Thank you,' she says.

Moving over to the fridge, I'm diverted by a burning smell coming from the cooker. I can see that the gas is on too high. Turning it as low as it will go, I then lift the lid off our very old and battered Le Creuset, to find that some pork has stuck to bottom. The whole point about the dish is meant to be its delicacy – loin of pork in a curdled milk-and-lemon sauce. The fact too that the pork can, and should, be eaten pink, or what most people would consider to be underdone. It's fine, apparently, if the pork is well sourced and butchered.

But not fine if it's badly burned. It looks ruined to me. Did someone turn up the heat? Maggie? Julie? Was this deliberate sabotage?

Maliciously or carelessly, or out of genuine concern, it doesn't make that much difference in the end. It looks fucked. 'Fuck!' I mutter, wondering also why I had Girts Kesteris killed off-page. I still seem unable to be that graphic, that to the point. When I'm trying so hard and in all manner of ways.

'Language, Dad,' says Jack, who still hasn't disappeared to his bedroom.

'Interesting observation,' says Julie.

'Bed, Jack,' I say, moving on to the fridge, retrieving a new bottle of white wine – where did this come from? 'Do you want to stick to white, Julie?' We should have seen it of course – the brutality, the ruthlessness, the moment the bullet entered his head – even if the reader didn't know who was pulling the trigger. But at least he's dead, I suppose . . . brain and blood everywhere.

'Sure,' she says.

I refill Julie's glass, pouring myself some.

'Good boy,' I say as Jack finally leaves the room, carrying his drawing and the old shoebox full of pens.

''Night, Jack,' calls Julie.

He doesn't reply.

'He's growing up fast, isn't he?' says Julie. 'And Poppy. It's lovely to see them after so long. They look well. And Maggie, I have to say, despite what she's been going through. She was just telling me about all her problems at work – poor thing.'

Julie looks up at me, though I can't quite read her expression, or don't want to.

'She's still a very attractive woman,' Julie continues (hanging on to that expression I can't read). 'In damn good shape.' She laughs, sort of a phwoar-ry laugh. 'She obviously takes care of herself, and knows how to dress. I'd forgotten. You, however, David, look like you could get out more. Quiet, leafy city like this – you should take advantage. Must be endless opportunities, seeing as you're not on tour at the moment. How do you keep fit? Are you doing any sport at all?'

I laugh, just managing to stop a mouthful of wine spurt all over the place. 'Sport?' I say, swallowing and wiping my lips. 'It's not really my thing. You know that.'

'Well, it should be, David – honestly. You've got to be pretty fit and energised to be at the top of your game nowadays.'

'I thought it was our game.'

'I'm on the touchline,' Julie says, finally looking away and gracefully, yet eagerly sipping her wine. 'Or in the dugout. Not totally sure of the terminology. Anyway, I'm the manager.'

'As if I don't know,' I say. Not wanting to sit across the table from Julie right now, to be put even more in my place, I shuffle back over to the cooker and my ruined food (seemingly one meal after another nowadays). I lift the lid again and, grabbing the wooden spoon, shift some of the burnt meat around, which is exactly what you shouldn't do with this dish. I could add some more milk, I suppose, but God knows what would happen then. I stop stirring and replace the lid.

Looking back towards Julie, I'm suddenly overwhelmed by the unnerving sense that she can read my mind – that she knows me that well. And I also realise (to my shame) that I don't know Julie anything like as well as she knows me. I don't know whether she's happy, at work, or at home. Whether she's still effectively single, or not. She once told me she was too selfish to get married again. But she certainly likes male company. 'Flirting comes naturally to the civilised,' she once said. 'It's how things get done.' And undone, I didn't add. But could now.

Maggie appears in the kitchen. But not how she was.

'Maggie, you didn't have to change,' Julie's saying, 'for my benefit.'

I'm taken aback: Maggie does look fantastic, in her dark-purple tunic dress, with matching fawn-coloured roll-neck sweater and tights underneath. She has on as well her knee-high purple boots (from I can't suddenly remember where, but it would have been expensive – how easily we used to live beyond our means, though on what looked like the promise of still so much more to come).

Maggie smiles at Julie. I look down at my tatty slippers.

'Children asleep already?' I ask. Adding, before she can answer, 'How did you manage that and make yourself look so good?' We've always had this loose arrangement that if I'm cooking dinner, Maggie will put the children to bed, and vice versa. And because Julie was here I don't think there'd been any discussion as to who was assuming what role this evening anyway.

'They're reading, calmly – they're fine,' Maggie says. 'Look, sorry, Julie, David, I know this is awfully rude of me, but I've just got to pop out. I'll be half an hour at the most.'

'Where the hell are you going?' I say, too aggressively probably, because Julie's looking at me, harshly once more.

Maggie's out of the kitchen already, hurrying down the hall, saying over her shoulder, 'I left something at work. Be as quick as I can. Start if you have to.'

'Fine,' I say, hearing the front door open and quickly shut.

Not wanting to catch Julie's eye again, possibly for ever, I turn back to the cooker and the casserole dish containing the burnt pork and some over-curdled, or wrongly curdled (who knows what the correct term is for anything any more), lemon-infused milk. Lifting the lid yet again and hoping vaguely that the dish has somehow cured itself (if cured is quite the right verb) and that I'll be met with a waft of sublime-smelling, lemony pork, I realise I can no longer even see the mess I've created. There's just a brown blur. Or should that be a smudge?

'David, sorry to bring this up now, but I've got to tell you something,' says Julie shortly. 'I think it best if I get this out in the open – certainly before you hear it from anyone else. I would have said something earlier today, but I didn't seem to get the chance. Look, it's bad news, I'm afraid.'

'Do you have to tell me right now?' I wipe my face on the frayed sleeve of my too-tight shirt and then, for want of something better to do, I prod at the blasted meat again. I doubt even Katya would be much help sorting this out. Maybe I hate cooking, and entertaining, as much as I hate my job (whatever that still means). Though I think I hate being a husband even more. I didn't. I loved it. Every moment.

'Yes,' says Julie. 'Then we can all enjoy the evening.'

'Enjoy the evening – right,' I say. 'It's certainly going to be memorable.'

'What was that?' says Julie.

'Nothing.' I'm facing her now, though still muttering – nonsense, I suppose. She's looking at me strangely again, though it's a different sort of look from the one she was expressing moments earlier. This one's softer, more caring. She's the actress. I'm the writer, though I can't seem to accurately, thoroughly, succinctly, aptly, sharply (forget originally) articulate this look, even to myself. Words, like life, do sometimes feel particularly hard to hang on to.

For a moment I think the terrible, high-pitched scream is coming from inside my head, but it's not, it's coming from upstairs: Poppy. Though she's older, Jack certainly has the capacity to wind her up. To hurt her. To torture her. I suppose it's a boy thing, a male thing, this reliance on violence.

I don't think I like men much. Never have.

'Excuse me,' I say to Julie, running out of the kitchen, along the hall and up the stairs, suddenly very short of breath and thinking that perhaps the twist, or trick if you like, still missing from *Kristine* is to do with gender. There are no really mean, let alone psychotically aggressive, murderous women. Because women don't do torture? Not normally – though I can think of one fictional character with a Lecter-like taste for such stuff, from Portland, Oregon. There are always exceptions, of course, but invariably women are the victims.

Though they can still inflict pain all right (by other, less physical means). By God!

'Jack,' I shout, entering Poppy's dim, soft room to find Jack standing on Poppy's bed, as I somehow knew he would be, armed with a handful of Poppy's beloved cuddly toys. 'What the hell are you doing in here?'

'She said she wasn't my real sister. She said I was adopted.'

'Jack, sweetheart, of course Poppy's your real sister. You most definitely weren't adopted. I saw you being born.' I step over to the bed and ruffle his hair and try to lift him off. He's getting heavy too.

'I didn't say that,' says Poppy, emerging from the covers.

'Yes, you did,' says Jack. 'You said Dad wasn't my real dad.'

'No, I didn't,' says Poppy.

'You did.'

'I didn't.'

'Back to your room, Jack,' I say. 'Now. Come on, it's getting late.'

'She did,' he says, as I gently push him out of Poppy's room.

'I didn't,' Poppy calls out.

Everyone lies, some just more than others.

As the rain punched out of the sky Adrian Fonda walked briskly towards Victoria Road. He didn't bother to stop and turn up the collar of his coat, despite the freezing water creeping down the back of his neck. He was in too much of a hurry.

It was one in the morning and Victoria Road was dead. There was just the sound of the incessant rain.

Only one house showed any sign of life – a red glow seeping round a curtain shrouding an upstairs window.

Walking quickly along the short path to the front door, he was about to tap on the door when he heard someone shout his name. He turned and, coming towards him, from across the road, was the tall, athletic figure of Tom Shreve, the hood up on the detective's parka.

Fonda realised he had been expecting as much.

'Adrian,' Shreve said, 'we need another word.'

'Way past your bedtime, isn't it, Tom?' said Fonda. He still had the Smith & Wesson in his coat pocket. His right hand was gripping the handle, his index finger slipping the safety catch off.

'I'm not saying Peter's abandoning you in any shape or form,' says Julie. 'While his list will be a fraction of the size it was, they're doubling – tripling – the effort they are going to put into the books they will be publishing.'

'So it's not really bad news then?' I say, hanging on to an almost empty glass of red wine, as if this is somehow anchoring me to the table (to the here and now; to exactly what I'm hearing) and stopping me from giving up completely and simply slumping to the floor. A great fat waste of vengeful space. All purpose gone, now that the children have learned to lie with impunity. Now I know exactly what I am and am not capable of.

Food's been toyed with. Much more wine's been drunk and still Maggie's not back.

'No, you're right. In a way it's good news.' Julie takes a sip. 'Except that they can no longer guarantee your slot next spring. They're tearing up the old contracts and starting again. Not normal business practice, I know, and there's already been quite a stink in the trade press about it. But there's little we can do, except hope they'll still take you. Hence it's more crucial than ever that what we do submit is spot-on. And the sooner we can do that, the better.'

Another sip passes her lips. 'It's probably not too late to start again, you know.' She pauses once more, goes to take another sip, but she's already finished what was in her glass. She pretends to swallow something nevertheless (ever the actress). 'I'd rather we get it right than use up any credit we might have with the wrong project.'

'But you still haven't even read a page,' I just manage to make myself say.

'Well, the thing is, David, you haven't exactly sold it to me so far. Or to Peter, obviously. And what little you've told me today has done nothing to reassure me that you're back on track.'

'Oh, just wait, Julie, will you, please.' I'm not sure I can take much more of this. It can't possibly be worth it.

'But that's just it,' says Julie, quite brightly (perhaps she's relieved, a get-out clause opening up), 'time's fast running out. That advance proof I brought you – that's what people want. That's where you should be aiming.'

'So you keep telling me. OK.'

'Come on, shock me, David. Shock us all. I still think you can do it. I wouldn't be here if I didn't.'

Fine, I'm thinking. If that's how you want it, I might just be able to please you. And sort of on cue, I hear not another scream, but the front door. A key being inserted into the lock. The door opening.

This is the best and the worst thing I've heard all evening, and exactly what I realise I've been listening out for – all along. It's nearly ten. Maggie's been gone for well over an hour and a half. She's missed dinner, though I can't blame her; the food was as disgusting as it looked. I let go of my glass, my anchor, and make myself sit up.

Maggie rushes into the kitchen, still wearing her coat. 'Julie, David, I'm so sorry. I've ruined the evening.' Her hair's plastered to her head and is still dripping. That fancy cut washed clean away.

'Nonsense,' says Julie. 'David and I had plenty of boring old work stuff to discuss. You're drenched, poor thing.'

'It's pissing down,' Maggie says.

'Why were you so long?' I say.

'Let me just dry my hair,' Maggie says, leaving the room.

Ten

Hayes woke with a start. Though she sat up slowly, silently, desperate not to make a noise. She listened hard, craning her neck. But when the sound of her heart thumping finally died down, all she could hear was the rain, another steady beat.

Nevertheless she switched on the bedside light, before lying back down and closing her eyes.

She often slept with the light on. However, she knew she would have trouble going back to sleep tonight.

Some time later she was not surprised when Kristine's face appeared, as if from nowhere. But this wasn't the face of a corpse. This was the face of an attractive young woman, full of life. Everything ahead of her.

Victims often came to Hayes like this – struggling to be heard, in the dead of night. Especially when an investigation was slipping out of control. As if Hayes needed reminding that justice was still a very long way off.

There were people out there of course who needed, who deserved, closure. Even if they hadn't yet been identified. Kristine's friends and family were still proving frustratingly elusive, even with the help of Europol. While her former colleagues at the Victoria Road brothel were clearly still too terrified to say anything useful.

But, Hayes thought, everyone had someone who loved them, didn't they? Someone who cared about them. Everyone came from somewhere. No one was truly alone in this world – were they?

Plus, and more urgently, Hayes had a strong feeling that there was plenty of unfinished business behind these deaths. More blood would flow.

Quietly lifting back the covers, she climbed out of bed. She could hear something now all right. Someone was moving about downstairs.

'Well, that was a great success,' says Maggie, turning over and grabbing more of the duvet, and then tucking it tightly around her.

Snug as a bug in a rug, I think, for some reason. Actually she's just created a barrier, another barrier. Indeed, the final barrier – so it feels.

'You really need to keep Julie on your side,' she's saying, her voice somewhat muffled. 'The way you behaved tonight, I wouldn't be surprised if she dropped you. Why would she need the hassle of working with someone who can be so unreasonable, so unpleasant?'

'You can be very self-righteous, can't you? You think your behaviour's reasonable?'

'Stop deflecting the issue, David, please. We're talking about you, not me.' Maggie's brainy, resilient head must have found more air, a clear passage, because her voice is no longer muffled.

'Well, I've had enough of me for today. And I thought everyone else had.' I shut my eyes, shutting out the world. Of course people only ever see and hear what they want to. And then twist it.

'David,' says Maggie, 'pull yourself together and stop being so negative. Everyone still believes in you, including me. You just need to believe in others a little more.'

It's no good. I open my eyes. 'What are you referring to?'

'Stop having a go, stop accusing me,' she says. 'I know what you think. But you are wrong. Very wrong.'

Funny too, I can't help thinking, how people go on the attack when they should be on the defence. It's Maggie all over. Me as well, probably.

But at least I wasn't so blatant. I wasn't the one who tore off into the night, saying I would only be twenty minutes or so, and then came back nearly two hours later. Belief? Right!

Maggie's still said practically nothing about where she really went, or why she took so long. *Stop having a go, stop accusing me*? I've barely started. I mean, where the hell did she go this evening? Where could she have gone? Just what did she hope to find? What did she hope to achieve now? What the hell was she thinking?

What was I thinking?

However, I'm not sure now's quite the right moment to press her, despite actually not wanting to know the truth, and despite the fact she's lying next to me possibly, probably, for the very last time, because I hear someone. Not downstairs in the house (our once-lovely home, our very own castle), but walking up the path just outside – hard shoes on old paving.

Even though I'm lying under the covers (what little I've managed to gather over me, my great bulk) I feel that I might faint, or rather pass out (is there a difference?).

It's like everything is suddenly inside out, the wrong way round. Or rather in the wrong place. The wrong reality. Who's really orchestrating this? Who's the perpetrator and who's the victim? What the fuck is going on?

There's more than one person outside. I can hear two people, at least. A car door shutting as well. Or perhaps I've already heard that. More than one car door slamming now. A certain urgency to the movement – the manoeuvre.

Someone's knocking on the door. Hard. What's wrong with the bell?

'Who on earth is that?' says Maggie, sitting bolt upright.

'I'll get it,' I say, leaping out of bed.

'What time is it?' says Maggie.

'Christ knows,' I say, switching on the bedside light and fumbling for my watch. 'Nearly midnight.'

There is another loud knock on the door. I try to peer round the curtains and down at the path, but the porch is obscuring whoever's there. Maggie's out of bed too now and retrieving her dressing gown from the back of the door. But once she's put it on and fastened the belt, she retreats to sit on the bed.

'You go,' she says, her voice a little breathless – for her. 'I'll stay up here, in case the children wake.'

'OK,' I say as I open our bedroom door, grab my own dressing gown and hurry along the landing, pulling it on.

There's yet another knock before I reach the hall. Turning on the hall light and then the porch light for good measure, I finally hesitate by the front door: my heart thumping away, my fists clenched, while perspiration, I can feel, is beginning to prickle my brow. This must be what I've been waiting for – the real confrontation.

'Hello?' I say, one hand on the handle, the other on the lock, but not opening the door. I don't think my voice was very loud or clear. 'Hello?' I try again. My mind suddenly overwhelmed by something I recently read, the obvious notion that clichés exist because there's something true about them.

Suddenly I'm sweating, profusely, and my heart's still thumping away, because I know exactly what's coming next. Of course I do.

'Police,' says a male voice, loudly, firmly. 'Open the door.'

Quickly looking over my shoulder and crouching a little, I can see Maggie's feet at the top of the stairs, pointing my way, her unslippered toes. For a second or two I wonder what's going through her mind, and then I open the door.

'Mr Slavitt?' a tall, young man in a dark coat says. He has no obvious accent.

'Yes,' I say, still clasping the door, which is little more than ajar.

He steps forward, placing, I think (though I don't want to look), his foot in the way, in case I were suddenly to shut it. He's with a woman, short, trim, older, in a dark but fashionably cut anorak, with the hood up.

She has an attractive face, I can't help thinking, as she pulls back her hood. Though I also can't help noticing how tired she looks, how lined her face.

'Can we come in?' she says, pulling from an exterior pocket and then holding in front of her an identity card in what looks like a leather, windowed sleeve. There's the image of a badge to the side of her photo, with the word CONSTABULARY sticking out most prominently above a coat of arms. 'I'm Detective Superintendent Dora Lupton. This is Detective Sergeant Grant Ellis.'

Behind them, where our short front path meets the pavement, I can see at least two more people – in uniform.

'Who is it?' calls Maggie behind me.

'Yes,' I say, 'of course.' Only when I've fully opened the door and stepped back to let them in does it occur to me that legally they are not allowed to enter, if I don't want them to, unless they have a warrant, for an arrest or a search. Do they have a warrant? They are certainly acting like they have one.

'Who is it?' calls Maggie again, as if she hasn't already worked that out.

'The police,' I say, looking up the stairs, but her feet have disappeared. She's disappeared. Turning back to the detectives, I say, 'Can we go into the kitchen? The children are asleep upstairs. And we've got a guest staying.'

'Sure,' says Lupton. She smells of cigarettes.

'Is Mrs Slavitt here?' the male detective, Grant Ellis, says, as we walk through to the back of the house. He smells of chewing gum.

'Yes,' I say, switching on the lights. 'She was a moment ago, anyway.' I try to laugh. The kitchen still smells of burnt pork. 'But I wouldn't call her Mrs Slavitt. It's Dr Robertson. She's never used my name – don't blame her.' I try to laugh again, shrugging. Though neither detective is remotely amused. I can hear other male adult voices in the hall now. Can see uniforms, down the hall. They've entered, uninvited.

'Should I get her?' says Ellis to his superior officer.

'Let's deal with Mr Slavitt first,' says Lupton.

My back is pressed against the worktop. The kitchen is not seeming at all snug and homely. I glance over at my once-beloved range-cooker, the rack of Sabatier knives next to it. Who am I kidding?

'Mr Slavitt,' Detective Superintendent Lupton says, looking me straight in the eye, 'we are arresting you under suspicion of murder. You will be taken to the station for questioning. You do not have to say anything, but it may harm your defence if you do not mention, when questioned, something which you later rely on in court. Anything you do say may be given in evidence.'

And I'm thinking: this is not quite what I was expecting. When did they change the exact wording of the rights? It should be *that* you rely on in court anyway. Not *which*. But, 'What?' is all I can say. I have nowhere to retreat, cornered by these two arresting detectives – uniformed back-up in the hall. Some more outside the kitchen in the rear garden, for all I know. A warrant seems quite superfluous now (as ever?).

The Ellis fellow has pulled a pair of thick, steel handcuffs from his coat pocket. They glint in the warm light from the halogens.

'I really don't think they're necessary,' I say, looking down at my tatty dressing gown, my pyjama trousers, my fat, bare feet, which used to be a size eleven, for decades, though I can't fit into any shoes under a size twelve any more.

'Let him put some clothes on,' says Lupton. 'But go with him. I need to find Mrs Slavitt.'

'Dr Robertson,' I say, as we all move out of the kitchen, me sandwiched between the two detectives.

The hall is now stuffed with people: a couple of uniforms; two other detectives, I presume, in plain clothes; and Maggie, in her dressing gown, which of course is in much better nick than mine. Her hair appears to be doing what it's meant to do too. Has she just brushed it?

'You read her her rights?' says Lupton to one of the people crowded around Maggie.

'Do you want the honours?' comes the male reply.

Maggie's almost in touching distance, as I seem to be being ushered towards the stairs, feeling in a way as if I'm in a dream, or at least having an out-of-body experience. And though Maggie's so close, fleetingly anyway, I fail to catch her eye, or maybe she's avoiding looking at me; and up the stairs I seem to be going, Detective Sergeant Ellis right behind me, and suddenly Julie's in front of me on the landing at the top of the stairs. An expression of shock or perhaps disbelief on her face – what faces she can pull (of course).

There's an air about her too, quite tangible, of excitement, as I look at her, not knowing what she might say, not knowing what I want her to say. Then I notice she's wearing a shockingly short, rather clingy, cream-coloured nightie, which for someone of her age (not that I know what her age really is) seems faintly inappropriate. I swiftly avert my gaze, as I head for my bedroom.

'What the hell have you done, David?' Julie says, behind me and my escort.

Not answering her, I walk over to my wardrobe, with the detective sergeant still shadowing me. The weight of the situation, the shock finally starting to register and making me tremble and shake and gasp for enough air. What the hell have I done, Julie? Maggie?

Then, like a thick, heavy curtain suddenly being drawn, there's blackness, followed by a hard, heavy thump. Not a crash, no, but a thump – seemingly coming from the inside.

And spreading slowly, like something wet, but inside me too, there's this thing, this pain, somehow quickening in pace and intensity as it spreads, and now sort of shoots, down one side of my body. Yes, it's like pins and needles, but much hotter and much more unpleasant. I can't breathe.

My head's spinning, making it hard to focus, but I find I'm half on the bed, slumped on it (yes), feeling like I'm going to be sick.

Someone's saying, 'Should we call an ambulance?'

'Mr Slavitt?' It's a female voice. Not one I recognise – well. It's not Maggie, or Julie. It's not Poppy. 'He's breathing all right,' says the voice and the nightmare gathers shape.

'He just fainted,' someone else says.

'Mr Slavitt, are you able to stand?'

'I don't know,' I think I say, as figures and faces form around me: my new reality becoming clearer. I'm under arrest. I'm actually being pulled up, by the arms, made to stand – marched across the room.

'He's all right. Just grab some clothes for him,' the female voice says. Lupton's. That's it. Tired-looking Detective Superintendent Lupton. 'He can put them on at the station. You accompany him, I'm taking her.'

'Is she in a car already?' a man says. But I can't place this male voice – just one from the crowd, in my bedroom. However, it's not Lupton's sidekick, the Ellis fellow.

'Yes,' says Lupton. 'She's missed all the fun and games.'

'I wouldn't be so sure.'

There's laughter. Laughter!

'Don't worry, David,' comes Julie's voice, as I'm manhandled along the landing. 'The kids will be fine with me, for the rest of the night.' But I can't see her. Is she in one of the bedrooms, hiding from me? Hiding them from me, from this? Why can't I see her? Them?

'My children,' I say. 'I need to see the children.'

'You're coming with us, to the station, right away, Mr Slavitt, I'm afraid.' Lupton? That pressure on my upper arms. Something prodding me in the back, as I try to slow. 'I believe they're still asleep,' she adds.

'Maggie?' I call. Where's Maggie? 'Have you got them, Maggie? Are they OK?' We're down in the hall already, by the front door. The freezing wet night is grabbing at me.

'Your wife is already in a vehicle,' says Ellis, definitely Ellis this time – though I'm still having problems focusing, hearing, taking everything in. My new world is certainly a fast, harsh place. 'She'll be taken to a different station,' continues Ellis. 'We have social services standing by, but we understand your friend who's staying will be looking after the children, for tonight. Your wife has agreed.'

'Oh.' And I'm pushed into the blustery darkness, mugged by it, and on along the wet path. Fuck, it's cold. But it's not until we're on the pavement, under the glare of that trusty street lamp, moving towards a brightly marked police car and quickly past another, with Maggie – yes, my Maggie – already in the back of that one, her head in her hands, and what lovely, delicate hands, that I realise, the slow, thick idiot that I am, as I'm helped, actually shoved down hard, into the rear compartment of the second marked police vehicle (a Volvo estate, same model as mine, if I'm not mistaken), that she's also been arrested.

Then up it comes – finally and, yeah, unsurprisingly – my burnt pork loin in that lemon-infused, over-curdled milk sauce; instantly warming my lap and swamping the car with the stench of fresh vomit.

'You sad wanker,' says the policeman sitting in the front passenger seat.

PART THREE

Another Kind of End

Eleven

Keeping my eyes firmly shut, I can still see, still feel my hands, my wrists working overtime to keep all these balls in the air, and in some form of order. It's pretty frantic, and I'm beset with a growing feeling of panic as the pace, the arc, increases – the balls flying higher and wider. Just within grasp.

This is fingertip stuff all right. And I've never been exactly dextrous. Fat fingers, fat hands. Bad balance. A serious lack of coordination. Little competitive spirit. No puff. No wonder I've never taken up sport. No wonder I've failed to take advantage of all that's on offer locally, as Julie would have it: the tennis club, the squash club, the golf club (wherever that is, or they are – probably loads of them in my leafy corner of the world). Cricket, badminton, even fucking tango. Oh, they love their tango in my town.

But I can't let a ball slip through my fingers. I can't let a ball fly off, hit a wall and then drop to the floor – for it all to come to such a rushed, messy end. Besides, right now I need to hang on to something. And this is pretty much all that's there.

Someone's rooting around in Britt's house. Yes, this very moment.

But we need to step back for a moment, or at least sideways. Visit a different locale, a different perspective.

* * *

The rain had eased, though the night had got so much darker, and colder. Fonda looked up at the pitch-black sky, felt something shiver right through him.

He still wasn't on top of the situation. Far from it. He couldn't help wondering whether this was it, that it really was all collapsing around him, finally. And he'd worked so damn hard, for years – here in Kingsmouth, in Colchester before, and Bedford before that – to build his operations. To keep them tight. Of course he had to rely on trust and, when that failed, force.

Girts Kesteris had had it coming for years. No wonder he'd squeezed the trigger. Bam! It'd felt good to see the Latvian's brains splattered against the inside of the windscreen.

But Fonda wasn't feeling so good about the amount of force that had been required in the last few days and weeks. He knew it would be impossible to avoid all repercussions. Too much blood had now been spilt.

He began walking up the deserted Victoria Road, in the middle of the night, wondering how he'd manage without Girts Kesteris, or his brother. The local tart who'd vetted the punters at Victoria Road – what was her name? Sal? Sal currently lying on her filthy bed, with a plastic bag over her head and a pair of tights stuffed into her mouth; she was replaceable of course. There were plenty like her.

The Kesteris brothers, though? Harder to replace. Plus Fonda wasn't sure he could stomach the hassle. Not at the moment. Maybe it was time to move on anyway. Develop a new line, elsewhere. Before it was too late.

Looking over his shoulder, he crossed into Havelock Road, then almost immediately turned right into Well Road – half the street lamps out of action, half the houses boarded up.

Sure, he'd paid Shreve handsomely over the last couple of years, done the lad a load of other favours too. But could he trust him to pull this one off? No one else had proved that reliable, in the end.

Fonda should have taken care of it himself. The only way he could be certain of anything.

He beeped his car unlocked. Slid behind the wheel. Found no solace in the smell of new leather.

And then too, I mustn't forget (as if I could) – but they don't give you a pen and any paper, not even a book, nothing in this solitary, dank holding pen – where we're at with Britt.

For a second her mind flashed to the carving knife, still with Forensics. That was the sort of thing she wished she were armed with, as she stood on the landing, back against the wall.

Whoever it was down there had put a foot on the bottom step, another on the next one. The intruder was coming up the stairs – slowly, but surely.

Plus, of course (and as if I could really forget him), Alex Smith. The other, the other . . . Where's he right now? What's his next move? Presuming we don't already know. Presuming we, or rather I, haven't missed anything.

Trying to get comfortable, I bang my head against the thick bar on the metal frame that I suppose is meant to serve as a headboard. Ouch, that really hurt.

I turn onto my side, but it's not much better. My arm, now cushioning my head, quickly becomes numb. All right, all right, Julie. I'm still trying. OK? Anything to distract from the reality of my situation – anything to aid my future. It's truly awful in here, already. Incarceration's no joke. Nor this procedure.

It'll come, Julie, in graphic detail, that most sordid, disturbing moment of posthumous mutilation. And other stuff, whatever you want. See, I can do it; I can, for real, Julie. I'm not a fake.

But right now I still feel monstrously sick – that appalling pork loin.

And know that I have to hang on to those balls, those threads, flying wildly around in the fetid air. I could scream, not that anyone would hear.

Jesus, the smell in here is awful. Though it's on me, isn't it? I'm the one who stinks, from the inside out. I'm in no position to stand up for myself – my rights. Let alone for my family. My family? My children anyway – as if they need me to protect them, when they've got Julie of course. Not content with my soul, I guess, she's now got my kids.

I retch and writhe on my slab, banging my head on purpose this time. Arrgh!

But Julie has never had children. She's never expressed much interest in them, either. How does she know what to do? Oh God! And I'm suddenly overwhelmed by the idea that I have to keep those balls flying . . . otherwise – I don't even want to articulate the thought. All sense seems to have gone out of the barred window, leaving me in some sort of Kafkaesque hell, as Ashish might declare.

But isn't hell the sort of thing that everyone wants, Julie? Brought gloriously, entertainingly alive?

There'll be more, and more and more, I promise, Julie – if you keep Poppy and Jack safe, if you keep them calm. Keep them happy. Keep them ignorant.

What the hell have you been doing, David? You might well ask. My job, Julie. My job.

'Mr Slavitt?'

Opening my eyes, I see, slowly, a shape forming in front of me: a man. In uniform. Dark trousers, short-sleeved white shirt, black tie, black-and-silver epaulettes on the shirt. A massive gut straining the shirt buttons.

'You're needed in the interview room,' he says. 'You want to put these clothes on?'

He throws a bundle of clothes onto the bench beside me. I think I recognise them. Delicately, nervously, pushing myself off the bench and climbing to my feet, it seems I'm still in my nightgear, and bare feet. My pyjama bottoms feel damp around the crotch and slightly hard and crusty too, and God, do they – do I – smell. The front of my T-shirt, the T-shirt I always sleep in, is also damp and yet crusty and stinks, and there are flecks of food, or rather drying smears of vomit, down the front of it and on my pyjama bottoms – sort of everywhere obvious.

There's no sink in the cell, but a stainless-steel toilet without a seat. For a moment I think about dipping my hands into the toilet. Water, I'm so thirsty. But I dread to think who else has inhabited this place, who else has used that bog, and turn to the clothes on the bench and remove my T-shirt, pull on one of my old shirts. Then, while the huge man in the strained uniform blocks the doorway, but keeps his eyes on me – I can feel them, boring into my back – I remove my disgusting pyjama bottoms (they were bad enough before I puked on them) and pull on a pair of old jeans.

Seems like whoever grabbed these clothes for me forgot my boxers, and socks. Though on the floor, by the bench, I see my old, knackered slippers. Bit of puke on them too, by the look of it. Nevertheless I slide my large, cold feet into them, though there's little sense of comfort (or warmth), despite the familiarity.

Standing, my stomach suddenly feels very empty. My mouth, my throat absolutely parched.

'This way,' says the officer, leading me out of the cell and along the corridor, though letting me go first. In fact making sure I can go no other way; nor, I reckon, too fast the way we're going. Obviously I'm not cuffed, nor does he have hold of me, of my arm, but he seems more than adept in the art of transporting prisoners to and from the cells. The way he's walking, plus his bulk, his uniform, the epaulettes and tattoos, all clearly suggesting who's in charge right now.

Weirdly, the corridor is exactly how I've always imagined such a corridor to look and smell and sound. Shiny, bland-coloured surfaces, ear-piercing squeaks, a strong whiff of industrial cleaning fluid (much more cloying than whatever they use at Poppy and Jack's school). Thick double doors. Another set. Then stairs up and round and up and round again. Don't they have a lift? I can't help wheezing and gasping for breath.

'Take your time,' my jailer says. 'Don't want you collapsing.'

'I think I've already done that,' I say. 'Last night.'

'That so?' he says. 'No one told me. No one tells me anything. Better that way.'

It's light out, I realise as we pass an unbarred window. There's a brief view of a grey sky and the side of a large building, though I don't immediately recognise it, not being sure which way we are orientated. I've never been inside this building before. Can't quite remember the last time I was inside a police station. How slack of me!

'What time is it?' I ask. I don't know where my watch is (another lost timepiece).

'Nine-thirty.'

'In the morning?'

'In the morning,' he says, almost laughing.

Perhaps he feels sorry for me. Perhaps not.

We go through yet more double doors and then on to another corridor, though this one doesn't quite smell or look the same. It doesn't squeak, either. There is carpet, or rather the floor's covered with dark-grey carpet tiles, while the walls are a more pleasant creamy off-white. A couple of framed pictures, prints of the city in a bygone age (a proud cathedral in one, the castle in the other), hang at slight angles – having probably been knocked by guards restraining unwilling, unruly prisoners. Though this corridor doesn't quite seem the way such folk, such criminals, would be marched or led, or perhaps dragged. Seems too corporate, too businessy. It's a bit like my accountant's, I realise.

More windows, more natural light, even if it's a grey old day. Ahead, yet another double door, and as I'm thinking double doors probably make sense if everyone round here is even half the size of my new friend, though I'm probably bigger than half his size (but considerably younger, I think, even if seemingly much less fit), we suddenly stop, and I'm not sure how this happens, because he's still not put a hand on me (just his commanding presence, I suppose), at a door on our right. A dark mounting to one side, at chest height, says, in small, embossed white letters: *Interview Room Two*. We appear to have passed Interview Room One.

He knocks and pushes open the door before waiting for a reply, though, as he was probably expecting, the small, windowless room is empty. There's a desk and four chairs, two either side. A box covered with dials and switches is on the table, secured to the wall.

'Make yourself comfortable, they'll be with you shortly,' he says, exiting the room and closing the door slowly but firmly.

And making me think: he's OK, this big officer, for someone who could clearly inflict quite a lot of damage, very easily. I sit at the nearest chair, trying to calm my breathing.

Leaning back, a great wave of tiredness suddenly floods through me, so I lean forward, prop my head up with my strangely cold hands. But soon finding this position not exactly restful – as if I could relax, even nod off here – I start paying more attention to the box. Aside from a now-obvious set of recording controls, there's a whole bank of other switches and dials. I've not seen anything like it before.

Looking up, I spot a small lens mounted in a corner of the ceiling, another in another corner – ah, the full purpose of this box of tricks suddenly making more sense. But even I know video interview evidence is not admissible in court. Not yet anyway. The tape, and formally the transcription, is what still counts. Everything I say, or don't say. The inference of silence now legally, prejudicially considered.

However, a feeling that everything here, in this police station, everything I've seen and heard, and what's happened, how I've been treated and processed over the last few hours, even the cold, slimy hardness of the bench in the cell, is not just not quite what I think I expected, or anyway how I've been portraying much of it in my work, but that it's all startlingly different. Plus the stuff that's hard to pin down too, the sense of it, I suppose – a sense not of real menace, even of heavy threat if you like, but more of lame futility. This is almost more worrying (for my career) than the fact that I'm actually here, in this situation. Accused of . . . well, we'll see.

My arms are now crossed on the table in front of me, white and flabby. Gently, resignedly, I rest my head in their chunky cradle again and shut my eyes.

Hayes edged into the spare bedroom, hiding behind the door, just as the intruder reached the landing.

Through the crack in the door she could see a tall, slim man. There was something athletic about his build. He was dressed in an anorak, the hood up.

He had his back to her as he slowly approached her bedroom, and he was hunching a little, as if to make himself smaller.

She had left the door to her bedroom open, inadvertently, but she was thankful now, and light from her bedside lamp was trickling into the landing. It was the only light source upstairs.

Hayes sighed, almost audibly, with relief, as the man seemed intent on heading for her bedroom. He was like a moth being drawn to a bulb.

Then, putting her hand in front of her mouth, she gasped. As more light fell on him she could see he was wearing gloves, latex forensic gloves, and in his right hand, by his side, was a large kitchen knife, the blade glinting.

It was a carving knife, one of her cheap, blue-handled knives, by the look of it. From the rack above her barely used cooker.

How I'm going to remember these exact words I have no idea. I can see them in my head, as if I'm looking at my computer screen. And oddly, given where I am, given that I'm not at my desk, they seem to be coming out fine (but then going straight into the ether?).

Perhaps it's easier to write in your head, without the temptation, the equipment, to constantly rejig and rephrase and replot. But I was always utterly useless at remembering lines from poems or plays at school (pretty useless at school, full stop). Have never been able to recall verbatim significant (or not significant) quotes or anything remotely learned (or crass or banal, for that matter – I can't even remember jokes), unlike Maggie of course (though, thinking about her plagiarism problems, perhaps it's no bad thing to have a crap literary memory).

Though on it goes, on it must go (for you, Julie), in any fashion I can proceed with it. As if, too, it's my one link to something controllable, to something rational; to a bit of the past and the future, a bit of me, and the outside world. Besides, I have nothing else to do right now.

Hayes still couldn't believe the man hadn't heard her move across the landing, hadn't thought it odd that her bedroom door was open. But his lack of awareness, his lack of professionalism, gave her a chance. And perhaps a clue.

There's no way I'm going to remember all this, exactly. Though does it matter? From where I'm sitting, it will be a wonder if it ever sees the light of day.

The window in the spare room opened onto the flat roof of the kitchen. From there it only had to be a short drop to the back garden. The ceilings in her small, modern house were not high.

Silently, breathlessly stepping over to the window, she was suddenly aware of another noise, but coming from downstairs. A door opening. The back door? Footsteps. Were there two of them? More?

Stay calm, she told herself, undoing the catch on the window as quickly as she could. Now she was opening the window, hauling herself onto the ledge, getting one leg over, with the freezing wind blasting into the house.

The draught must have caught, because the spare bedroom door slammed shut with a deafening wallop.

Hayes scrambled the rest of the way out and onto the kitchen roof. Rushed to the edge, hearing voices, shouting, behind her.

The door opens and in walks a woman I've seen before, but can't immediately place. She's not too tall, with a trim body, tucked into a neat black suit. The collar of a white blouse is sitting over the collar of her jacket in a rather stylish way, and her hair, short lightish brown, has a definite gamine look to it. She has pretty, penetrating blue-green eyes (though, I can't help thinking, they are not a match for Katya's – oh, Katya, now look where I am).

'Mr Slavitt,' she says. It's not a question. And the tone makes me focus on her mouth, her face, which seems overly, in fact prematurely, lined. From smoking too much? From hard living? From all the stress of having to solve unsolvable cases? From dealing with people like me?

Yet there's something very sensual about her. Or rather sexy, actually. I find I've stood up and am holding out my hand. 'Hello,' I say.

She doesn't shake my hand and promptly pulls up one of the chairs on the other side of the table and, placing a folder and a clutch of papers in front of her, swiftly sits, folding her skirt under her. A waft of coffee and a perfume I can't place, and also a smell of cigarettes, hits me all at once, making me realise how deprived I've been of such sweet, intoxicating smells – and it's only been for a few hours. I have a sudden, desperate, overwhelming urge to be out of here, out of this situation and wandering freely among such happy scents.

'Please sit down.' She makes it sound very much like an order.

So I do.

'You feeling all right this morning?' she says, lightening up a bit, with dimples appearing in those tightly lined cheeks – which really are familiar.

Of course, she's the detective who came to my home last night, the person who read me my rights (wrongly, at least ungrammatically), the person who arrested me, and then never bothered to go into any specific details as to why – unless I wasn't able to pay attention by then, wasn't able to take it all in. Detective Superintendent Dora Lupton, that's it; at least I've now remembered.

'Couldn't be better,' I smile. 'Actually, I feel awful. What do you expect, having been dragged here in the middle of the night and then locked up in that stinking cell, no one telling me anything much? I feel absolutely bloody awful.'

'Not as awful as Alex Smith's parents are feeling, I bet,' she says, in a tone that makes me really not want to get on the wrong side of her. (Are these where the lines, the wrinkles, come from, a barely concealed toughness, an inner rage?) 'How do you think they feel about losing a son?'

'I have no idea. I don't know them. I don't know him.'

'Didn't know him,' she corrects. 'He's dead. Except I don't believe you for one minute.'

We look at each other for a few moments (though I doubt for a full minute), and though I'm increasingly aware of my position and what I'm up against, I still can't stop finding her quite alluring, more than quite actually, and wondering (when I seriously should be thinking of something else, anything else, which is perhaps why I'm doing it) whether she's married, or in a stable relationship, whether she has kids, whether she's happy.

Whether, like Britt Hayes, and that other detective with a complicated, if not compromising personal life (which Julie so decisively brought to my attention) – Nicky Blunt – she has an appetite for casual, no-strings-attached sex, possibly even with known criminals (or former criminals, or those still on some form of remand, those currently under investigation).

'Can't be nice losing your own child, in such a way too. Can it? Those poor people, Mandy and Graham Smith.'

'No,' I look at her, smiling grimly, forcefully, feeling my own fleshy cheeks wrinkle and line, 'must be dreadful. Beyond imagination.' Though I know that not to be true. Nothing's beyond imagination. 'There can't be anything worse,' I find myself adding, lamely, as if I somehow need to reaffirm a certain sense of intellectual, artistic, literary even, propriety. Or perhaps the nerves are getting to me. It's not easy trying to sound innocent. Especially when part of me is somewhat relieved, quite possibly delighted, that Alex Smith (the real Alex Smith) – as she's just said – is dead.

'Do you have children?' I ask her, surprising myself. I'm really not interested. Simply don't care, right now.

'You know what: that's none of your business,' she says.

'Fair enough,' I say. 'But you're the one who seems to want me to try to imagine what these people – Mandy and Graham, did you say? – whom I've never heard of, are going through, because, as you say, their son is dead. I simply wondered whether you might have some idea, if you have children.'

'As I said, at this moment in time that's very much none of your business.'

'Sorry.'

'What is your business is the death of Alex Smith.'

'To a degree,' I find myself saying. 'To a degree.'

She immediately leans forward and presses a couple of switches on the recording device, turns a knob, says into thin air, or rather into heavily (heavenly!) scented air, while glancing over my head, 'Detective Superintendent Dora Lupton, March the twenty-sixth, nine-twenty-two a.m. Interviewing David Slavitt, arrested under suspicion of murder.'

She alters her focus: those penetrating pools of blue-green now firmly fixing on me. Hard.

'Of course, Mr Slavitt, you are entitled to have a lawyer present,' she says. 'Though, if you don't mind, I thought we might be able to progress with this investigation much more quickly and efficiently if we can just clear up a few things straight away.'

'A lawyer? Right. I don't know.' I rub my chin, feeling the stubble, and try to recall exactly what I'm legally entitled to. I should know this stuff.

'When you were booked in last night the duty officer noted that you were quite adamant in not wanting to contact a lawyer,' she says.

'Was I?' The only lawyer I can think of is Ben Hargreaves, our solicitor. In London. The person who did all the stuff when we sold and bought our last houses. I wouldn't want him involved in anything like this. Besides, he's our solicitor, the family's. I have no idea whether he's ever done any serious criminal work – presuming that's what I'd need him for. 'I really don't remember that much about last night. I certainly don't remember being booked in. Though I do now remember being ill. Sorry, if I made a mess. Perhaps that's why I didn't want to contact a lawyer. Wasn't feeling up to it.'

'I'll repeat, you are entitled to have a lawyer present,' she says, 'but this will obviously delay things.'

Maybe it's because I was ill (probably still am, one way or another), and barely slept a wink, but I'm having a lot of trouble thinking what to do next. How I'd even go about getting the right sort of lawyer

I did once have a long chat over a great lunch with a criminal barrister, a friend of a friend, about a point of procedure, regarding the novel I was then writing. I can't now remember the issue, the plot, which novel it was (*The Watcher* sort of rings a bell), let alone the name of the lawyer. But I do remember the restaurant: Cigala, on Lamb's Conduit Street. I had a duck paella, which sounded odd, but wasn't. Best paella I've ever had in fact. This barrister – big, red-faced chap, complete with pinstripe suit, blue shirt with white collar and red braces (you couldn't make him up) – and I shared it, as they only did the dish for two or more. We shared a lovely bottle of white Rioja too, and then a couple of bottles of red – top-notch Spanish stuff also.

'It's fine. I'm happy to proceed, for the moment,' I say. I'm hungry, I realise. Could do with a drink as well, so I can't still be that ill, or that sort of ill. Why wasn't I brought any breakfast? Maybe my rights have already been infringed. Not that I would know. (The legal thriller obviously not being my area of expertise – not that I'm sure, sitting here, what my area of expertise actually is.)

Maybe Julie could enlighten me. Perhaps she'd even know the name of a top criminal lawyer; surely, in her line of work she must have come across a few. But presumably, hopefully, right now Julie has her hands full. No?

Oh God, she doesn't even know where Poppy's and Jack's school is. Or where their book bags are, their PE kits (do either of them have PE today? one of them must), where their lunchboxes are kept. Something tells me Julie has no idea how to even make a sandwich. Sandwiches are not her thing – just like legal thrillers or, possibly, frankly, police procedurals are not my thing. Wrong time, wrong business, wrong life I seem to have stumbled into.

'Mr Slavitt,' says Superintendent Dora Lupton, loudly. That stare. 'Did you hear me?'

'Sorry,' I shake my head. 'I was miles away – as ever.'

'Where were you last Wednesday? That was the eighteenth,' she says, still loudly, firmly.

'Last Wednesday? Shit, where was I? Seems like an age ago. At home, probably.'

'Mr Slavitt, I'm sure I don't need to remind you of the seriousness of the situation you are in,' Lupton says. 'But I think it would be greatly to your advantage if you could try and remember a little harder. Where were you on Wednesday last week?'

Try to remember, I'm thinking. It's try *to* remember. But we've been there before. 'I was at home, almost certainly. I haven't been anywhere for ages. Though I was meant to be in the States. Right now in fact.'

'Yes, we're aware of that,' she says.

'You are? How come?'

'We don't just arrest people for the fun of it, Mr Slavitt,' says Lupton. 'Obviously we've spoken to people. Done what we can so far to have tracked your movements. Electronic surveillance is pretty simple nowadays. Most information you don't even need a warrant for – it's all there, on the Internet. And then there's CCTV.'

'I guess,' I say, again seeing more mistakes that I might have made.

'The fact you suddenly cancelled your US trip has caused a bit of a stir, hasn't it? Have you seen the comments? Readers are a passionate, opinionated lot, aren't they?'

'Some are, yes, I guess.'

'Seems like you've let rather a lot of people down, Mr Slavitt.'

'I don't know about that,' I say.

'In Pittsburgh, Cincinnati, Cleveland, some other places too,' she continues. 'Why would you do that, so suddenly?'

'It's complicated,' I say. Do the police need to know just how dismal the American tour was really looking? And how personally expensive? 'For one reason or another, I couldn't face it. I work in a pretty tough, ruthless environment.'

'Yeah?'

'Let's just say in the end it would not have been worth my while.' Though I'm thinking maybe it would. Perhaps I should have got on a plane. Wouldn't be here now, being interrogated, if I had. And Julie would be happy, wouldn't she? The American publisher also. Peter too. However, the look on Julie's face last night, as I was being manhandled out of my house, flashes into my mind. I don't want to contemplate the meaning of it.

'We'll come back to this, I'm sure,' says Lupton. 'For the moment, then, I want to concentrate on Wednesday of last week. You're telling me you were at home all day? Please think very carefully before answering.'

I'm not sure I'm capable of thinking very carefully, right now. There's too much to grapple with. Again, this is so not what I might have expected. 'Yes – I'm pretty sure I was. Well, I usually am, apart from when I'm doing the school run. And when I'm shopping. Food shopping, I tend to do that. Not Maggie.'

'Do you always do the school run?'

'I usually take them. And we have this girl, Emily, who picks them up sometimes – perhaps a couple of days a week. Maggie claims she does as well, but she's been very busy at work recently; been to a couple of conferences too. So, yes, it's mostly me. Though not, I suppose, technically always.'

'Last Wednesday?'

'Let me think.' Please. 'I guess I took them and, yes, thinking about it, I did pick them up. Definitely.' I pause; take a long breath, sucking the air in through my mouth, which makes me realise I haven't cleaned my teeth today. They feel sort of furry, quite horrible. 'Though it's not the sort of thing I put in my diary.' I huff a laugh.

'And you say you were at home then all day, the Wednesday of last week? That's between dropping them off and, as you say, *definitely* picking them up – at the normal times.'

'Yes, I'm pretty sure.' Though I'm not, of course; not about the normal times, either, which makes me breathe faster. I don't know whether to confess or not, right now. Where it would lead.

'Is there anyone you know who can verify your whereabouts last Wednesday? The fact that you did the school run and were then at home. Because the thing is, we don't think you were at home all day.'

Why not? This electronic surveillance? CCTV? Oh God! 'Maggie?' I say. 'I'm sure she can. She usually knows where I am.'

'Other than Maggie?'

'Poppy and Jack? I don't know. Someone at the school? One of the parents?' I think of Clare. I think of attempting to avoid Clare – that could have been a mistake, yet another. 'A teacher? I don't know. I'm still trying to remember whether I absolutely definitely picked them up, at the normal time.'

Dora Lupton sighs, loudly.

'Can I ask why you need to know, exactly?' I say. Hesitantly.

'How about yesterday evening?' she says, avoiding my question. 'Where were you yesterday, from late afternoon?'

'That's easy,' I say, brightly, sitting forward. 'At home, absolutely definitely – cooking dinner for Julie, my agent. Though I burnt it.' However, the thought of that wretched pork makes me think of bacon. And not in a bad way. I'd kill for a bacon sandwich. And a proper coffee.

'Were you in all evening?'

'Oh yes – until you lot turned up and took me away.' When I try to laugh this time, nothing but a wheeze comes out. Have I suddenly developed asthma? Can you get it from shock? Can you catch it – from dirty cells? More likely it would be early-stage TB. That you *can* catch, from people who inhabit such places. Would probably serve me right.

'From what time?' she says.

'I don't know. I was there all afternoon, waiting for Julie. Her train was late. Emily was picking the kids up.'

'We're talking about Julie Everett, your literary agent?'

'Yes. Though, frankly, I'm not sure for how much longer. As I think I implied earlier, my career's not going brilliantly at the moment. I narrowly missed winning a big award. And Julie's not very keen on what I'm currently working on – my new book.'

Lupton nods, knowingly.

'And, well, I suppose she doesn't think I've been promoting myself properly. You see, the market's changed a lot recently. Is changing all the time. It's hard to keep up, especially while you've got your head down. And I suppose, to be honest, I've made a few mistakes.'

Lupton definitely raises her eyebrows at this – eyebrows that have been carefully, brutally maintained (not sure I really like over-plucked eyebrows). So I decide to stop talking, thinking that perhaps I've revealed too much already about my recent problems, knowing how important confidence is in my game. Putting on a front. Having belief – and having people believe in you.

But wouldn't it be nice to have a truly sympathetic ear. Even an empathetic one. I should have gone to a shrink, as Maggie suggested only the other day. Except I wasn't very positive about the idea. 'Why? Why the hell should I?' I said to Maggie – shouted more like. 'You're the one with all the issues. You're the one who's behaving so erratically. Slamming doors, bursting into tears. Upsetting the children, when you're here.'

'You expect Julie Everett to corroborate this?' says Lupton.

'What? That my career's down the pan, or that I cooked her a horrible dinner yesterday evening?'

'That you were with her, in your home, all yesterday evening?'

'Yes – yes, of course.'

'We'll be talking to Ms Everett further,' says Lupton.

'She's still looking after my children?' I say. 'She's still there, isn't she?'

'I believe so, for the time being,' says Lupton. 'Certainly I haven't heard anything to the contrary. And in fact a team should be searching your premises as we speak. Though I do believe your wife has been kept fully informed of your children's care and whereabouts, and some further plans have been instigated to cover all eventualities.'

'Well, she's the primary carer, isn't she? Fucking hell! Why am I never considered responsible for them? And what do you mean: all eventualities? What else can happen?'

Lupton looks at me. Says nothing.

'Oh, God, what time is it? What bloody time is it?' I look at my watch, which is not there.

Lupton looks at her watch, then up at a large clock on the wall behind her, which I'd somehow failed to notice. It's nearly 9.45.

'Nine forty-three,' she says.

'Did Julie take them to school, on time? Do you know even that?'

'I'm sorry, I don't have all the details. But rest assured, your children will be fine.'

'How can they be? Julie doesn't know where the school is, or what they need for the day. She doesn't know what to put in their packed lunches – that Jack hates apples, but loves oranges, and Poppy won't eat any fruit, though she loves these School Bars. And they'll be too shy to tell her, I can just see it. They're shy, my children. They don't really know Julie, and Julie certainly doesn't know how it all works. Can't do.'

I pause, gulp some air, but can't seem to breathe properly (is it the TB?). It's certainly hot in here now. My hands have finally gone clammy. I can feel perspiration on the back of my neck.

'They can't have taken themselves to school,' I continue. 'They're too young to go on their own. I hope Julie realises that. But why should she? She doesn't have children. What would have stopped her from letting them wander off all on their own? My children like school, and Poppy's always anxious about being late. She wouldn't want to miss school, I'm sure. Even if it meant going on her own. Oh no! Help me. Please.'

Lupton looks at me. I look at her – in a sort of blind panic. But she gives nothing much away, certainly no sense of sympathy. Then, like a sledgehammer knocking me into a different plane of consciousness, I realise there's something else I need help with, and which surely my interrogator can provide. 'Where exactly is Maggie? Where's my wife? Where's she been taken?'

'Mr Slavitt, try and remain calm. And seated,' Lupton says. 'I'm sure you'd rather we went through all this now and got it over with as quickly as possible. Just think of your children, and of getting back to them as soon as possible. Though I can stop this interview at any time and have you returned to the cells.'

'No, don't do that. Please.' I don't fancy that stark, lonely space, that slab of a germ-ridden bench for a second, obviously. The barred smudge of a window looking onto nowhere. Or the toilet without a seat. No toilet paper, either. Plus of course no phone, no Internet. No contact with the outside world. The fact there's no escape. I don't want to be locked up in there again. Whatever I've done wrong.

'OK,' says Lupton, leaning forward herself a little. 'Just so I'm absolutely clear. You didn't leave your house all afternoon or evening yesterday?'

'Yes, that's right,' I say quickly. This I can be confident about. 'I know I went out in the morning – late morning – briefly, to the butcher's and so on, to get the food for dinner. And that was it.'

'What about your wife, Maggie?'

'Well, she was out all day, as usual, at work.'

'What time did she come home?'

'I don't know. Six-ish? I can't remember exactly. Emily picked up the kids from school yesterday, as I said, and brought them back. Maggie came in some time later – I was chatting to Julie, while trying to cook the food. There've been a lot of distractions lately. Look, please help me. Where's Maggie now? What's happening to her?'

I do and don't want to know. I do and don't want to help her. Whatever's gone wrong recently, we've been married for a long time. Have two children together. What should I be saying, revealing?

Lupton just sits there, as if she has all the time in the world.

'How much longer is this going to last?' I say. 'What exactly are you accusing me of?'

Still that hard, lined look.

'There's something I'm missing.'

'That seems to be the case, certainly,' she says, speaking finally. 'But we'll get there. However long it takes. The thing is, you appear to be able to remember what you did yesterday. Where you were, where your wife supposedly was, to the hour. But what about last week, last Wednesday, the eighteenth? During the day?'

'Much the same.' But it wasn't much the same, by any stretch. 'A week is a long time ago,' I add, lamely.

'Not when you have the benefit of the technology we have,' she says. 'And we'll be utilising all of our resources, believe me. We have some pretty impressive stuff.'

'I'm behind the times.'

'Yes, it appears so, Mr Slavitt.' She brushes her mouth with her hand. 'Would you say you and your wife are happily married?' She leans back in her chair, crossing her arms in front of her. 'Do you have a close relationship? Have there been any tensions, any difficulties recently?'

'Where to begin?' I say, though fortunately I don't have to continue.

Someone's knocking at the door, and Lupton turns her head as the door is opened and a man edges in. He's tall, youngish, has an athletic build, and immediately there's something of an over-confident air about him, also something very familiar.

'Can I have a word?' he says, nodding towards Lupton. He doesn't come any further.

It's the man from last night, the one who was going to cuff me: Detective (Sergeant, I think) Grant Ellis. I don't know many Grants.

'Right,' she says, getting up. 'Excuse me,' she adds over her shoulder.

They disappear and the door is shut firmly behind them and I'm left on my own once more, in this airless, windowless, now very hot and stuffy interview room, with a growing sense of how time seems to have dramatically slowed since my arrest – just when you really want it to speed up and zip along. It's part of the process, the procedure, I suppose; the point of it.

Life's too short, except when you are banged up.

But before I have time to contemplate what a real stretch might mean – years and years of incarceration – the door is pushed back open and in strides Lupton, accompanied by Ellis. Lupton returns to her chair, while Ellis remains standing, to her left.

'I'd like to ask you again about your whereabouts last Wednesday, during the day,' she says.

'Right,' I say. Here we go. 'Sure.'

'You say you were at home all day, apart from dropping off and picking the children up from school?' she says. It's a definite question.

'That's what I said, I think. Well, I said I was pretty sure I was. But I have been under a lot of stress recently.'

'So much so that you've forgotten that you were in fact at the university that day?'

'Possibly, actually, I guess.' I rub my sticky forehead.

'New information has been passed to us which strongly suggests you were at the university that day.'

'Oh, OK.' But what information? From whom? The Porter's Lodge? Ashish? Fucking hell, would he do this to me? Then why not? Why wouldn't he admit to such a simple thing as seeing me on campus that day – whether I was behaving oddly or not? Or perhaps it was Julie. I suddenly remember speaking to her on my mobile, when I was sheltering from the wind and the rain. We were talking about America, why I wasn't there.

'Yeah, now you mention it,' I say, 'I sort of do remember being there. I had to go to the library, you see. So it must have been that Wednesday, then. They have a great local-history section.' She's staring at me; so is Ellis. 'Sorry, my mind's not what it used to be. But I couldn't have been there very long.'

'Why not? Is there anything else you have forgotten to tell us?' she says. 'I would think very carefully about how you reply. If what you say contradicts our information in any way, this process will only continue, of course – until we get to the truth. The thing is, you see, Mr Slavitt, I've been doing you a favour, trying to get all this done with as quickly as possible so that you can go home, to your children, your family. But you're not doing yourself any favours.'

'OK, I understand. I'm trying to help – I am.' I don't have an option. I should have come clean before – obviously you can't hide anything nowadays, CCTV or not. 'Look, this is a little hard to explain.' I try to clear my throat. 'But this is the truth, I promise you. I went to the university, not just to do some research, but because I wanted to see Maggie. And she wasn't in her office, which sort of worried me. And I guess I began to panic.'

'Why?' says Ellis.

'I didn't know what she was up to – with whom. We have been having some troubles, marital troubles.'

'Let him continue,' says Lupton.

'Anyway, when I was driving out of the car park, I did see this chap, in a big trench coat, walking along the road. I'm pretty sure it was him, Alex Smith, and he was on his own; at least he wasn't with Maggie, which was a great relief.' I pause, cough. 'Nevertheless I followed him for a bit. I know this probably doesn't sound great, but it's the truth. He was walking along the pavement, just on the other side of these bushes, and I was driving, slowly, at his pace, I suppose; and I did want to stop and get out and have a word with him. Just to see what he had to say about things. You know these rumours, et cetera, had all got a little much. Maybe I was being paranoid – I don't know. But I wanted to clear the air, I suppose. Be certain, one way or the other.'

'Is that so?' says Ellis.

Lupton looks at her colleague, as if to shut him up.

'But he turns into Bluebell Road,' I continue, 'and there's this bus waiting at the stop, with quite a few people milling about, and he suddenly starts jogging towards it, and eventually he gets on and the bus drives off – and that's it. Almost.'

Twelve

Hayes got onto her knees, turned and slid over the edge of the flat kitchen roof, cursing the sharp plastic guttering, then finally letting go. It wasn't far to drop.

Picking herself up, she ran down the side passage and out onto the small drive, passing her car. Yellow light from the street lamps bathed her end of the crescent, but all the houses were in darkness, curtains drawn tight. There wasn't anybody about that she could see.

Despite the wet, squally wind she heard a thud, then another coming from behind her – from inside her property.

She knew she had to get further away from here fast. She looked at her car. But she didn't have her keys, or her phone. For a moment she thought about waking a neighbour. However, she knew she would only be putting them in danger.

Whoever was after her seemed intent on one end.

Keeping away from the pavement and cutting across drives and front gardens, she began moving around the crescent, her bare feet already numb with the cold – but perhaps that was masking any pain.

She hadn't got more than four houses along when she was aware of footsteps on the road. Of someone trying to cut her off. She looked over her shoulder, gasped.

* * *

My large friend has just opened my cell door with some determination and walked straight in.

I suppose I should already have got to my feet, to greet him. But no one usually seems in much of a hurry around here – the hours (the days, already?) stretching on and on. Except that my guard seems full of purpose right now. The way he's rocking on his enormous rubber-soled shoes and clenching his tattooed forearms.

'You're wanted upstairs again,' he says. 'Popular man.'

Hardly, is my immediate thought. 'OK,' I say eventually, hauling myself up into a sitting position. I do believe I'm growing accustomed to the hardness of my slab (not to mention the bright, tight cosiness of my cell).

Our bed at home is probably far too soft. Maggie is always complaining that it dips badly in the middle (not that it doesn't dip at the edges too). That she's forever finding herself rolling my way. Has said why don't we get two single mattresses and push them together? How lots of older couples accommodate each other's sleeping requirements; how some couples of strikingly different weights do. Standing, slowly, I'm not sure how accommodating either of us will be in the future.

The door's being held open for me, so I shuffle out and wander along the corridor (the way we've been before), as if I have all the time in the world, which I suppose I do – but my guard is hot on my heels. Yet why should I be rushed anywhere? Certainly not towards another round of obviously leading questions.

Despite banging on about electronic and witness evidence, and new sources of information, they haven't come up with anything that specific, that damning actually, making me wonder whether they are trying to trip me up – to get me to incriminate myself. For something they still haven't exactly spelled out, either. Not of course that I was as specific, as clear, as I could have been at the beginning.

We now all know what I was doing on the Wednesday of last week. And I know it's hard to explain, to justify; even harder under duress. I'm still not sure I can quite explain it to myself. Besides, I don't know how this will impact on Maggie. Whether it will make things worse or better for her – for us. Where we stand, where I want us to stand. But being banged up quickly makes you very forgiving. And remorseful. (If not forgetful.)

We've at least, I think, categorically established my whereabouts yesterday evening (and how long ago that feels). And I've since been advised by a duty lawyer – Cathy Daniels, what an incredibly bright, patient woman she is – of what to put my name to and what not.

However, the police still appear not to be satisfied with their intelligence surrounding that Wednesday – and of course part of me doesn't blame them. I haven't helped myself, and revealing also that later that day I set off for Kingsmouth, only to return quickly to pick up my children from school, unexpectedly, appears to have added to the mistrust, the disbelief. The fact that they can't take me seriously.

But life isn't always clear, obvious, logical, without confusion. And I have to say the relentlessness of this process, this procedure, seems to be inducing in me, in all of us (except perhaps Cathy Daniels), not just exhaustion and frustration, but quite a considerable amount of indignation towards the police, the system.

Especially it appears that not only have I not been able to help them to a satisfactory degree with what Maggie was doing on that Wednesday, but yesterday evening too. How the hell should I know: where she was, with whom, doing what, when? She is her own person – Dr Maggie Robertson. Nor have I been able to help them enough, so it seems, with their understanding of the state of our relationship.

Some things just seem too private, too personal, too complicated, if not inexplicable, to discuss in depth, and rationally, with strangers in such an impersonal environment as Interview Room Two.

Even if certain freedoms, certain rights, are at stake.

'We've both been under a lot of pressure,' I told them during the last interview session. Adding, 'A lot of work pressure.'

'When were you first aware of your wife's closeness to her student, Alex Smith?' Lupton then immediately asked.

I'm beginning to think that the police believe Maggie and I might have acted – indeed, enacted this supposed crime – somehow together. The irony.

'Keep walking, can you?' says a now-familiar voice behind me. 'We haven't got all day.'

'Long shift?' I say, looking over my shoulder.

'What do you think?'

Hayes stopped dead in her tracks. Her head still turned his way. She couldn't move.

'It's all right, Britt,' Jones said, as he reached her. He held up his hands, in supplication. 'I'm not going to harm you.'

'I don't understand,' she said. 'What the hell are you doing here?'

'Let's go back inside, and I'll explain.' He gestured towards her house, where the front door was wide open. 'You must be freezing.'

'You're a crime writer, Mr Slavitt?' says Ellis.

It's the double act again. Ellis and Lupton. Good cop, bad cop, except I can't work out who's playing which role. They seem to keep changing. I look to my side, to Cathy Daniels, all frizzy hair and smiles next to me. Maybe I got her wrong. Maybe she's not quite so bright or patient.

'Yes,' I say, knowing they already know quite a lot about that – is he still questioning my credentials? We've even gone into my working routine, why I work from home and don't rent some office space elsewhere (as if, on my earnings), and why, just because I'm working from home, I might not necessarily be logged onto the Internet at all times. 'I do need some peace and quiet,' I said at one point. 'I can't be endlessly distracted. I do have to switch myself off from all that.'

'I can see why,' Lupton quickly added.

'And it's hell of a lot better if the house is empty too.'

'So,' Ellis says now, 'I'm just going to run through a scenario, and I'd like your expert advice. What someone with your imagination might make of it, because we're a little stuck here.'

He looks at his colleague, his superior, but her expression doesn't change. Those furrows on her face remaining deep-set, rigid. For a second I wonder whether she is uncomfortable with the line Ellis is taking.

'Mr Slavitt does not have to enter into any such supposition,' says Cathy Daniels, still smiling, at them, at me. 'Indeed, I'd strongly advise him not to. David, I recommend you don't say anything and exercise your right to remain silent.'

And I don't say anything (even though I know that my right to remain silent could become prejudicial). But part of me is intrigued, both professionally and personally. I'd like to hear his hypothesis, or I suppose his suspicions really. I too am still in the dark about a number of things. Funny what they tell you and what they don't – while trying to catch you out.

'I'm going to present this anyway,' says Ellis, looking straight at me – for a reaction? 'Your client can ignore me, Ms Daniels,' he continues, 'but I'd also like him to know that he hasn't yet been charged with anything, and we'd really like him to help us with our enquiries.'

That old euphemism; I smile to myself.

'No, he hasn't been charged,' says Daniels, 'and I'd like to remind you that you've only got another couple of hours or so to hold him here.'

'Unless we apply for an extension,' sneers Ellis.

'I'd like to remind everyone,' says Lupton, 'that a young man, who was closely connected to Mrs Slavitt—'

'Robertson,' I interrupt. 'Dr Robertson.'

'Who was closely connected to Mr Slavitt's wife,' says Lupton, 'is dead, and the manner of his death remains highly suspicious. What's more, it appears that Mr Slavitt had a clear motive for murdering Alex Smith. Call it a crime of passion, if you like, and as you know we could very well be looking at mitigating circumstances and a heavily reduced sentence. But the fact remains that Mr Slavitt's wife was having an affair with one of her students, this Alex Smith.'

'I'm sorry,' says Daniels, 'but this has most definitely not been categorically established. In fact, Detective, you are stepping way out of line here – aside from the personal trauma you are inflicting upon my client. For which there will be legal redress, believe me.'

I hadn't got Cathy Daniels wrong – she's the real deal. But what the hell am I meant to say, to think? Clear motive? Yes? I look at Ellis, sort of willing him to get on with his supposition, his hypothesis – these legal wrangles are driving me nuts. I would like him at least to reveal what he thinks he knows. Perhaps he knows the truth. Let's see. I smile grimly and nod, willing Ellis on.

'OK,' he says, blinking.

He does that – blink – a lot, I've just realised. Maybe it's a nervous condition. It makes me feel for him. Quite possibly he's the good cop after all and Lupton is the tough, prejudiced one, trying to nail me because . . . well, I don't know, I'm a man. And she's been on the wrong end of more than her fair share of shitty relationships. Why in fact she looks so worn out, and it's not because of her police work, which must surely be a breeze in this fine, calm, provincial city, this leafy backwater. Where murders are very rare indeed – if not entirely imagined.

'A man disappears just over a week ago. On a Wednesday, as it happens,' says Ellis.

'You don't have to listen to this,' says Daniels.

'It's all right,' I say. 'He can continue. I'm interested.' I lean forward a bit, but there really isn't much elbow-room. Though Cathy and the others all visibly sit back. Wow, I must stink!

'Tells his flatmate he's having lunch with his girlfriend, on campus,' says Ellis. 'His flatmate, of course, believes she knows exactly who he's referring to. In fact this flatmate has been very helpful with a lot of the background to this case. Plus we've studied the messages, the phone, text and email trail, so there's enough corroborating evidence as to the identity of the woman.'

I glance at Daniels and she's pulling a face and shaking her head, implying that she has no idea of this. Hasn't seen or heard of any such evidence.

'As far as we can establish, hypothetically speaking,' Ellis stresses, 'this woman, and more specifically this woman's husband, aren't where they should normally be on that day, that Wednesday – not all afternoon. In fact we even have a location for the man, the husband (who admits to following this young man earlier), picked up from a mobile-phone signal. This puts him within a thousand metres of where we later find a body, the body of a young man.'

A kilometre is quite a long way, I'm thinking.

'I don't know where this is going,' says Daniels (reading my mind?), 'but you're severely testing my patience, Detective.'

She looks at her watch, for effect. I catch Lupton looking at hers too. So I look up at the clock on the wall.

'The young man in question is reported missing, on the Friday morning, by his flatmate,' says Ellis. 'Now, a man of his age – he was twenty-eight – going missing, there's nothing unusual in that. Adults go missing all the time. Mostly because they choose to. But this flatmate, she's very persistent that it's entirely out of character. What's more, she alerts us to – how shall I put it? – the young man's complicated love life.'

'Compromising, I'd say,' says Lupton.

'I'm sticking with out-of-order – all of this,' says Daniels, firmly crossing her arms in front of her.

'We log it,' says Ellis, ignoring her, 'and put out the necessary alerts. We do a little investigating ourselves, it being one of those quiet weeks. Find out one of the people involved, the guy being cuckolded – to use an old-fashioned term – is a crime writer. This gets us thinking; me, anyway.'

Daniels sighs very loudly, though I suppose I'm a little flattered – someone taking me and my profession seriously, or at least thinking it's interesting (or is that 'of interest'?) that I'm a crime writer. That I have certain skills and attributes.

'Then nothing,' Ellis says, putting more effort, more theatricality into his delivery. Does he fancy himself as something of a storyteller? A novelist? Perhaps he's a fledgling crime writer himself. Maybe not even fledgling. Maybe he's well on the road to some considerable success (aided – just don't tell me – by Julie, or Peter, or both, and I've somehow missed his stuff, which wouldn't be remotely surprising, given the amount that's out there).

'Until,' says Lupton – so she is in on his *hypothetical* line, happy with it after all – 'a body is found in a car, beyond the water, at the far end of Fratlingham Lane. The car had been driven off the track and into a clearing in the trees, and wasn't spotted for some time.'

'How long exactly?' says Ellis. 'Well, that's the key. Because the decomposition of the body, which was found in an unusual position in the car anyway, was unnaturally advanced. There are other factors too, surrounding the scene, that lead us to believe that we're dealing with a murder.'

'How did you say the person died?' I ask.

'How do you think they died? How would you have them die?' says Lupton.

'Presuming I'd want them dead in the first place,' I say. 'But the thing is, I'm not sure I'd want anyone to die, if I could help it. Come on, death is a pretty serious business. You might think that because I'm a crime writer, who writes about murder for other people's entertainment, it comes easily. But I hope I'm never that rash about it. At least I try not to be, which I suppose might be one of my failings.'

I don't look at my lawyer, but can feel her staring at me, probably in exasperation. 'I don't like people dying, all right – even fictionally.' I'm tempted to laugh, but don't, and find myself saying, 'Ask Julie, ask my publishers, here and in the States. And in those few other territories that once took a punt on me.'

'We're looking into everything, very closely,' says Lupton.

'A body in the car, which had been deliberately hidden from view,' says Ellis.

'Sounds like suicide to me – not that you're telling me how they died,' I say. 'Some sort of overdose, slashed wrists, I don't know; could even be the old hosepipe from the exhaust. And what about this: the unusual position you found the body in could be the result of someone going through death throes? No?'

Lupton suddenly straightens her back. No mistaking the pricking up of her ears, the further furrowing of her furrowed face.

Ellis blinks, almost manically. 'Ah, that's just it,' he says. 'We're meant to think it's suicide. That's what it's meant to look like. And there are quite simple ways of covering tracks, notably through enhanced decomposition. Awful things happen to a body in a car full of carbon monoxide. Though I expect you know all about that, don't you, Mr Slavitt?'

Daniels sighs yet again, but this time so loudly I wonder whether she might deflate – at least enough for the frizz in her hair to collapse.

'I think whoever committed this crime was unusually careful, and clever, yes, I'll give them that,' says Ellis. 'But the fact remains: you are the one with the motivation and have acted more than suspiciously. And, given your occupation, you are someone who could obviously envisage and plan such a thing. You mentioned the word suicide, after all. We believe you wanted us to think that Alex Smith killed himself, when in fact it was you who lured him to that isolated spot and murdered him, before hooking a hosepipe into the exhaust and running it into the car, then turning on the engine.'

What can I say?

'The thing is,' says Lupton, 'we've evidence that you were in the vicinity at the time that we now estimate he died. There's no evidence, that you've given us, or that we've discovered, that categorically places you elsewhere. What's more, you've since admitted to following Alex Smith as he walked out of the campus on that very day.'

This perhaps was my biggest mistake, though I'm sure they would have located the CCTV footage sooner rather than later, if they don't have it already (and are waiting to trip me up even further). 'But as I've also told you,' I say, 'once he got on the bus, on Bluebell Road, I drove off. I just wanted to have a close look at him. I probably would have had a word with him, had there not been so many people around. That's not surprising, given the circumstances, is it? And it's not illegal, as far as I'm aware.'

'How do we know you didn't follow the bus?' says Lupton. 'Until he got off.'

'Because – how many times do I have to tell you! – I went home, typed up some notes and then I set off for Kingsmouth. To do more research, on the ground.'

I think about reiterating what then happened. How, not even halfway there, I was called by the school and told that Jack and Poppy were waiting to be picked up, so I turned round and made for their school as quickly as possible. But an uneasy feeling is creeping up on me once again. It's to do with Maggie. Her whereabouts, her intentions and actions. And my allegiance to her, the mother of my children – to our family. Despite everything.

So all I say is, 'And following a mix-up about who was picking the kids up, I never got to Kingsmouth. Check with the school, if you haven't already. Check with Maggie.'

'You remain our prime suspect,' says Lupton.

'I've never heard such flimsy, circumstantial evidence,' says Daniels. 'You're holding my client on a completely preposterous supposition. Is the Chief Constable aware of this? Has your major crime unit stooped to an all-time low?' She gathers her things. Stands.

'As I said, there are other factors, which we are not at liberty to reveal just yet,' says Ellis, 'either pointing to Mr Slavitt's involvement or his motivation.'

'Plus a significant development occurred yesterday evening, leaving us no option but to act,' says Lupton.

'Really, you couldn't make it up,' says Ellis, staring at me.

'Don't look at me,' I say, 'I'm not much of a crime writer – any more. Perhaps I never have been.'

'Mr Slavitt, I wouldn't say that. Your work is much more revealing than you might imagine.'

So he's been reading my stuff. For clues? No, you couldn't make it up – I couldn't make it up. But plenty of others have, haven't they?

'I've heard enough,' says Daniels. 'I suggest my client is released immediately.'

Hayes finally let Jones put his arm around her shoulders. Let him guide her back inside.

'You're not going to like what you see,' he said, shutting the front door firmly behind him. 'But I didn't have any option – he came at me.'

'It's OK,' she said, but knew it wasn't. Of course she couldn't be sure what, if anything, the neighbours had seen or heard.

'No, it's not,' said Jones. 'But you are alive, aren't you? Isn't that what counts?'

Hayes had to think about this for a couple of seconds. 'I was out the window, well away,' she said, as they climbed the stairs, Jones leading. 'He wouldn't have got me.'

'You want to bet? Besides, I didn't know you were safe. I didn't know you'd already got out. When I entered the house all I could hear was someone upstairs. Then I heard a door slamming – I knew what he was going to do.'

'You could have shouted, have warned me anyway.'

'And warned him of my presence? He wouldn't have held back then, would he? I couldn't risk that.'

Hayes still couldn't place Jones' accent. There was something northern in there. Also something North American. He sounded like he'd spent a lot of time abroad. Maybe one day she'd find out – join the dots.

However, there was definitely something very calming about his voice. About him. Which was one of the reasons she'd put her trust in him. And there was no going back now, that was for sure.

'Shit!' she said, stepping into her bedroom. 'Oh God, help us – I had a feeling about him.'

Jones was a little further in and to her right, in front of the chest of drawers. His hands were by his sides, and he seemed remarkably composed.

On the floor, at the end of the bed, lying on his side, his limbs at strange angles, his anorak hood still up, his head at a strange angle too, was DS Tom Shreve. Hayes could see his eyes. They were wide open, unblinking.

'How did you do it?' she said, looking at Jones. 'How did you kill him?'

'You don't want to know,' he said. 'It's not important.'

'Were you in the army or something?' There was no blood. Little sign of a struggle. He must have broken Shreve's neck, almost instantly.

Jones laughed, quietly. 'No. They wouldn't have me.'

'So what the hell do we do now?' said Hayes. She was almost beyond feeling – beyond being able to panic.

'Isn't that your call?'

'Do you know who he is?'

'I've got an idea,' said Jones. 'One of yours?'

'But this wasn't all his idea, can't have been,' said Hayes. She still needed a sense of perspective, of rationality, to know exactly why Shreve had wanted her dead. 'He wouldn't have had it in him, not on his own,' she said, moving around the body. The knife, her cheap kitchen carving knife, was next to the body. Jones must have swiftly disarmed him too.

'No, you're right,' said Jones. 'Heard of a man called Adrian Fonda?'

'Yeah – a big shot at the council. In charge of development and regeneration, something like that.'

'Is that where he is now? Some front!'

'He's behind this?'

'Could be,' said Jones. 'You wouldn't believe what he's been involved in.'

'Tell me.'

'Another time.'

'Come on. Look at the mess I'm in. I need some answers.'

'Britt, please, you don't need to worry about it now – it was in another part of the country anyway.'

'Bedford? Cheltenham?' She was thinking of where the name Kesteris had also cropped up.

'Were you closing in on him?' Jones moved away from the chest of drawers.

'I don't know how close we were really getting,' said Hayes. 'What I was being fed, and what would have stacked up. So what's the link?' She looked at the body again.

'I've seen those two together, more than once,' said Jones. 'Your guy must have been on Fonda's payroll. That's how he operates – knows how to get information, how to plant it. How to keep his back covered. And make a mint.'

'That town,' said Hayes. And her colleagues, she thought. What a lethal combination. She looked at Jones again, shook her head, wondered yet again whether she could really trust him. But knew she didn't have any choice. Not now. 'Tell me,' she said, 'how come you followed that wanker here, in the middle of the night?'

'I don't sleep well,' Jones said, a smile cracking on his strong, undeniably handsome, but well lived-in face.

Hayes took a deep breath.

'I walk my dog at night,' he continued. 'Cover a lot of ground – Baz needs his exercise. Tonight I saw something I didn't like the look of.'

Sleep deprivation is of course a form of torture, I'm thinking.

Always a light sleeper, always up early, perhaps I've been torturing myself for years. But this is something different, on a different scale;

compounded by an atrocious headache and still being badly parched. My cell, my new existence obviously doing strange, disturbing things to my equilibrium, my metabolism, my state of mind.

And yet, small fortunes (or is it mercies?), I've been allowed a pad and a pen. 'To enable me to map out my confession,' I can just imagine Ellis saying. 'In my inimitable style.' Ho-ho. But at least I have something else to occupy me, to worry about. Plus I'll have no fear of forgetting, or rather losing, the thread. Though what if they then confiscate my notes? What if DS Ellis somehow tries to use them against me?

Yet I'm on my feet, not working, trying once more to look out of the tiny, smudged window. But it's dark outside. Darker than it was. Night-time – finally? The bars barring my exit still firmly, thickly, menacingly in place. Nothing but blackness beyond.

Perhaps I am worried that Ellis and co. will try to use whatever I now write down against me. Perhaps I do feel limited in what I'm able to say and do with the plot. (In a way, I suppose, I've always been limited.) But please don't tell me I'm going to be one of those crime writers (real, or more commonly fictional) who implicate themselves through their work – the master of my own downfall. Surely I'm not that stupid.

Though haven't I done just that, as far as Ellis is concerned? Being a crime writer, in his book, is almost enough, so it would seem. Because what exactly did he mean when he said my work was *much more revealing than you might imagine*?

Come on, David. Cathy Daniels, who gave me her legal pad and a pen in the first place, would see a way to avoid them using this material (as if it's remotely revealing of anything important to their investigation, or anything else for that matter). I'm sure.

Though am I? How the hell did I end up here? Who has the answer to that one?

All the legal issues my characters have been involved with over the years, and here I am, knowing so very little about the law, about my rights. Another lunch with that fat barrister must be long overdue. Oh, I'd love that right now. Or it would be dinner, a late dinner, I suppose – with plenty of wine.

My God, have the children eaten? My heart misses a beat. A wave of anger, at my incarceration, my helplessness, floods through me. Did Julie feed them, properly, before putting them to bed? She's still there, so I've been informed. While Emily, too, apparently has been helping out. Nevertheless my children must be suffering. Just how terrible a father am I? What the hell will Jack's and Poppy's future be like now? Will they be teased at school?

Maybe the barrister can help get me out of here. Why didn't I think of him before? He's a criminal expert, after all. Years of experience. And sumptuous dining. But the expense, I can just imagine. Plus Cathy Daniels has grown on me. She takes a firm stance, and is not remotely overawed by the investigating detectives. I wouldn't want to go above her head (even if I could afford it).

I move away from the small, barred rectangle of blackness and retire to my slab, my gurney. Weak with hunger. Yet none of my characters ever seem to eat anything, I'm suddenly thinking. They manage to keep going. Or did.

'Feeling better?' said Jones. They were in the sparsely furnished lounge, drinking over-sweetened tea.

'I don't know what came over me,' Hayes said.

'Shock?' said Jones.

'I thought I was immune,' she said. 'The things I've seen.'

'Dead bodies weigh more than live ones,' said Jones, smiling, trying to raise the mood.

Hayes had helped him get the body wrapped up, in an old Ikea rug, and down the stairs. Before she started to really wobble. He made her sit down. Made her a brew. Though he couldn't find any biscuits in her kitchen. Couldn't find much food of any kind. Wasn't the only thing that made him think she didn't spend a lot of time at home. He liked that.

'So how many have you dealt with, then?' she said, placing her mug on the floor, and sitting back.

'What?'

'Dead bodies.'

He wanted to concentrate on making this one disappear. On what he had to do next. Not on his past. A past he'd hoped he'd long left behind. But he hadn't, of course. Would he ever?

'That's another place I don't want to go, not now,' he said. 'Some things take more explaining. I need to deal with this first. To get it into the car before it's light. Must be plenty of curtain-twitchers out there. We've been lucky enough as it is.'

'Lucky?' said Hayes, rising to her feet.

I must have been deeply asleep, because I'm not sure I'm properly awake now. That what's happening is really happening.

'And here,' the officer behind the counter is saying.

I sign the form, feeling somehow that this is all a bit of an anticlimax, and hand back the pen. Which is when I remember the other pen, and the pad Cathy gave me. They're back in the cell. A storey and endless corridors below where we are now. My incriminating notes!

'OK,' says Cathy, next to me, 'let's get out of here.'

'Goodbye, Mr Slavitt,' says the man behind the counter. 'Pleasure doing business with you, as they say,' he says. 'Let's hope we don't see you again too soon.'

'OK?' says Cathy, now taking my arm, trying to lead me away and to freedom.

'Hang about a minute,' I say, easing myself from her gentle grasp. 'I've left something in the cell. Sorry, I was still half asleep when they brought me up here.'

'What?' she says, looking at me from head to toe, 'your socks?'

'That pad you gave me. I was making some notes.' It was inevitable.

Maggie has always said I need her to organise me, that on my own I'm completely shambolic.

Cathy exhales, loudly (she does this a lot – must drive her partner nuts; if she has a partner). Says to the officer behind the counter, 'My client has left something in the cell. A legal pad, actually. It's pretty important. Any chance you could get someone to fetch it?'

And I'm immediately thinking: hang on a minute. I don't want just anyone fetching it, and taking copies so that they can pore over my words and the latest developments. No doubt someone will be able to see something – I never realised quite how dangerous this game was, that inspiration is inevitably, or perhaps obviously, more personal than anyone might hope otherwise. I want to get that pad, my new words. I say, 'If it's OK, could I pop down and retrieve it?'

'No, it's not OK, my friend,' he says. 'You think just anyone can walk down there?'

'No, I suppose not,' I say. 'Look, I'm sorry. It's been a very tiring twenty-four hours.'

'I'll see what I can do,' he says and disappears through the door behind him, leaving Cathy and me alone in the brightly lit reception area.

Posters decorate the walls – mostly advertising (if that's quite the right word) knife and gun amnesties, though there's one warning of rabies, and another extolling the perks of being a community officer. There's a large clock high up on the wall behind the counter: cream face, Roman indexes, and looking, because of those indexes, strangely out of place. From a different time, certainly a different context. It's a fraction to midnight. 'I can't wait to have a shower,' I say.

'I bet,' says Cathy.

'Then once this has all died down a bit, perhaps it would be good to have a holiday – take the kids somewhere fun. I can't remember the last time we all went away.' It's not just the last twenty-four hours, but it's clear I've been letting my children down for months, for years.

'David, you do understand the bail conditions?' says Cathy.

'Yes, yes.'

'You can't leave the country. You can barely leave this city. You have to be in your home between six in the evening and six in the morning. You are on police bail – still technically a suspect.'

'I know.' Though did I exactly? 'I suppose I was just thinking about when all this is really over. Imagining that day.'

'Well, yes. But while these conditions are in place, I must advise you to adhere to them strictly, otherwise you could very easily be locked up again. Not just in a cell here, at the station, but you could find yourself in prison, on remand. And any such move could be highly prejudicial to your case. Once you get in front of a judge, in front of a jury, should it ever go that far, impressions count almost as much as facts. Shouldn't be the way, but believe me, it is.'

I look down at the piece of paper I've just signed, as if for further clarification. I was awake enough, alert enough, wasn't I, when the duty officer and Cathy were quickly explaining my release?

Where were the investigating detectives, Lupton and Ellis, however? I presume they'd already gone home, allowing the system to proceed automatically. Plus maybe they were too embarrassed – that it could be seen as some sort of failure on their part not to be able to persuade a magistrate to keep me here, not to be able to actually charge me, yet.

He's suddenly back, brandishing the pad (though not the pen) and something else. A fat smile on his reddening face. 'There you go,' he says, handing over the pad, my barely legible scrawl page-up.

'Thank you so much,' I say, grasping it.

'Now I've got a favour to ask you. I nearly forgot. Would you mind signing this book for me, Mr Slavitt?' He hands me a thick, dog-eared hardback, one of mine, *The Liberator*. Says, looking away, 'It's the wife's. She's a big fan.'

Not a big enough fan to have bought my most recent title. 'This has seen some mileage,' I say. 'Who to? Her name?'

'Suzi,' he says. 'Spelt with a z and an i.' He hands me a pen. 'She'll be chuffed – especially given what's happened.'

'Right.' *To Suzi*, I scribble, adding, *A real fan. David x.* I close the cover and hand him back the copy. 'There have been a couple since,' I say. 'Books, that is, not fans. Well them too, I hope.' I laugh, lamely. No one else does. I do a sort of wave-and-smile combination (though it's probably more of a grimace), reversing away from the counter.

'Yeah? She likes this one best, I think.' He pats the book. Nods a goodbye.

'Must be a lot of pressure,' says Cathy, as we turn and head across the lobby towards the main exit, 'to keep making them better.'

'You try to up your game, I guess,' I say. 'But in the end you can only do what you can.' I pull on the door and am immediately slapped in the face by a wall of freezing air. But despite the temperature drop it feels good. It smells good. Freedom, of a kind and for a bit anyway. 'Like you, I imagine. You can only do what you can to get people like me out of places like this.'

'Oh, it was pretty easy, in your case,' she says, arranging her coat, her collar, to defend herself better from the cold and drizzle. 'That wretched DS Ellis, what an agenda he's got. You shouldn't have been arrested, in my book. They never had much to go on, that I was aware of. And then they ran out of time and evidence to keep you. Plus the fact that you picked up your kids from school – I don't think they could dispute that.'

'So they did check?'

'If they haven't, they will. They check everything – in time. Certainly this could be a big help, should the investigation go any further, should they bring charges. There'll be CCTV, I expect.'

'Yes,' I say, suddenly picturing the entry security system. How did I forget that? 'Of course.'

'Though you might have mentioned the school earlier too, and the mix-up about collecting the children,' says Cathy. 'Could have saved you a few hours in there. The police really don't like it when they think suspects are withholding information.'

'It's hard to think of everything, at once,' I say. And while of course I remember mostly what I was doing that day, that afternoon, and while some of this now seems to be accepted by the police, no one's assured me of Maggie's movements. Her actions all day, all afternoon – before she also arrived late at the school. Not everything fits, for either of us, hence the bail, I guess.

'If I should never have been arrested,' I ask, 'what about Maggie?'

'You're my client. I can't answer for her. But the police were looking for discrepancies. Trying to catch one of you out, playing you off each other: standard practice. Though clearly that hasn't happened.'

Yet (as ever), I'm thinking, as something flashes in my face and Cathy jumps to one side, pulling me with her. Regaining focus, I see a small man backing off the edge of the pavement, onto the road, pointing a large camera at me. There's another flash. And another. He turns, begins walking quickly away, the hood of his cheap, dark anorak flapping on his back.

'Who the hell told the press?' Cathy says, recovering her poise.

Thirteen

'Get some stuff together,' said Adrian Fonda, flicking on the light.

'Hey, what the fuck!' said Tanya, her head lifting from the nest of pillows.

'Get the kid – we're going on a trip.'

'Have you gone mad?' she said, sitting up now. 'It's like – what time is it?'

Fonda had moved over to his wardrobe. Was opening drawers, pulling out clothes, and from the back of the sock drawer a fat envelope containing €5,000 and a passport.

He knew the picture looked just like him – it was him. Though the name with it was someone else's. It was a good fake. Cost him enough. He threw the envelope into a holdall. Chucked in more clothes on top. Looked over at his young wife, who was still half under the covers. Was tempted to put a bullet in her head and leave her there.

As it was, there was no false passport for her, or River. But then they weren't going as far as he was. He just needed to get them out of this stinking town for a while. Couldn't trust what she would say, and to whom. He needed some time, some distance.

Knew he should never have relied on Tom Shreve; the man had always been weak. Bent coppers usually were.

Fonda walked over to the bed, pulled the duvet off his wife. 'You've got three minutes.'

'I'm not going anywhere,' she said.

He put his right hand into the deep pocket of his overcoat. Pulled out the small pistol. Pointed it at her head. 'I'm not going to say it again.'

'What are you doing?'

I look up to see that Maggie has pushed open my study door. Though she hasn't come in. She's standing by the entrance, wrapped in her dressing gown, her head a mess of brunette bed-hair. Gone the sharp styling. Gone the need to look good, to look the part. Her face is pale and lined (comparatively). There are deep bags under her eyes too. Stress and distrust (distrust?) written all over her face. She leans against one side of the frame, heavily, as if she'll never be able to pull herself free and stand unaided. Be truly independent. Herself.

'What are you doing?' she repeats. 'It's the middle of the night.'

'I couldn't sleep,' I say, finding that my voice is rather hoarse. 'That spare bed's bloody uncomfortable. Cold too.' I feel myself smiling.

'How did this happen?' she says.

'What do you mean?' I glance at my screen, unused to its dimensions (though at least I should be happy that they didn't take all my computers; just my newest, which wasn't that new). Would Fonda really put a bullet in Tanya's head? Yes, I think he would. I think he'd sacrifice his son too. I look back to Maggie.

'This, David. Us. Our relationship. How did it go so wrong?' Despite her rising voice, despite a certain, growing animation to her delivery, she's still attached to the door frame.

'I don't know,' I say. 'I'm not sure I know anything any more. Do I know who you really are? I thought I did. At least everything seemed to make sense. Us, the kids. Our home, away from the hassle of London. Things were all right. My work could have been going better, for sure, but look at what we had. Then this extraordinary thing happens. Way out of my control.'

'So what are we going to do about it?' she says, pushing herself away from the frame finally – standing unaided, on her own two feet.

With her free hands, her free arms, she wraps her dressing gown tighter around herself. She suddenly looks rather small. Shrunken perhaps. She edges into the room.

'I don't know,' I say, standing. Though not moving out from behind my desk, not walking over to her. I slam the thick lid of my very old laptop shut (not that it does shut properly any more). 'I don't know whether I can even trust you.'

'And I'm meant to trust you?' She pauses. Runs her right hand through her hair (which is so unusually messy, though perhaps not for the middle of the night – but she's not normally up in the middle of the night, that I know about), then wraps her arms tightly around herself again, pulling taut the thin, satiny material of her dressing gown. 'I'm sorry, but it's you they really suspect, you know.'

'Well, it would be, wouldn't it? I'm the man.'

A flicker of a smile appears on her tired face. 'You should have heard what they asked me about you. I was shocked, as was Ben.'

'Ben?'

'Ben Hargreaves, our solicitor. He blames your job for making things worse.'

'My job?'

'I'm just saying what Ben said.'

'What on earth was Ben Hargreaves doing there anyway?'

'I was told I needed a lawyer and he was the only person I could think of.'

'But he's just a solicitor. Our mutual solicitor. The family's solicitor.' I've walked out from behind my desk now. Too tired, too full (how I've stuffed myself since I've been home) to sit on my tiny office chair any longer. Maggie is almost within touching distance.

'He seemed to know what he was doing,' she says. 'I was rather impressed. Those detectives can be very threatening. Sort of puts what

I've been dealing with at work into perspective. I tell you, that university could learn a thing or two about questioning techniques. My colleagues have a long way to go if they really want to crack research misdemeanours, let alone issues of harassment, et cetera. The police are so much more imaginative. Suggestive anyway. They get things out of you that even you didn't know were there.'

She smiles at me, properly and much like she used to. Maggie of old. Then her face drops. And it's a pretty galling thing to witness; this face that's so familiar, that's been so loved, suddenly looking so pained. And she turns away and steps into the hallway. Stops. Waits.

Giving me time.

But what exactly does she mean by saying that the police got things out of her that even she didn't know were there? Just what has she been telling them?

Walking across my study, and out into the hallway towards her, towards her back, I feel it would be so easy to throw my arms around her and clasp her tightly to me. Yet everything is so obviously, so remarkably different that I don't. Even when she turns to look at me, in the thick, heavy dimness of the hallway – in the hushed middle of the night.

Maggie and I haven't so much as touched each other since we've been back from our incarcerations (me in the city's central police station, Maggie in the city's second-biggest police station, out by the university). And it doesn't look as if we're going to now.

Suddenly she's shooting into the kitchen, turning on the lights. I follow, to see her walking over to where the kettle is, which is next to the knife block: a place that used to be out of reach for the kids, but isn't any more (how fast they grow).

She lifts the kettle, feeling how much water is in it. Enough, it seems, because she flicks it on without refilling it. She hovers by it as it almost immediately begins to hiss and rattle, glancing at me and back at the kettle and the knife block, I'm sure, which is when I wonder whether she might be scared of me. Who knows what the police told her, what

221

they tried to get out of her, what they insinuated, what she thought of their suggestive line of questioning, how she contributed to it all – what she thinks of me now?

'This is so weird,' I say, moving towards her again, this woman I once knew so intimately. 'You don't actually think I did it, do you?' The bare windows behind her, behind me, all around the kitchen, showing nothing but the cloudy night beyond – a fudgy dark. There's little light pollution. No stars.

No witnesses?

'I don't know what to think,' Maggie says. 'I'm very confused. For the moment I suggest we concentrate on the children.'

'But, Maggie, honestly, how can we do that if you suspect me? I am not a murderer. Believe me. Who knows exactly how this Alex Smith died – the police don't seem totally sure. For all I know, you could have done it.'

'You think I did it? Me, David? How on earth could I do it? Overpower a man?'

'Women have killed men before, you know.'

She laughs, scornfully. 'It's pretty rare.'

'Though you do know how he died then?' I say.

'No. What makes you think that?'

'Because you just mentioned overpowering a man: that you wouldn't be able to. But how do you know he was overpowered, that that was how he died?'

'Perhaps the police suggested as much. I can't remember everything they said; it was very intense. One interview after another, with various detectives, and all these scenarios they kept presenting – could have been one of your books.'

'If only,' I say. 'Though I'm not sure my plots are that inventive.'

'Maybe you're right,' she says. 'But perhaps that's why they work, for me.'

'Thanks.' And I mean it.

She looks over her shoulder at the sighing kettle, and at the still, silent knives neatly sheaved in their heavy wooden block. Turns back to face me.

'I'm sorry, for suggesting that you might have done it. That was mean,' I say.

'I'm sorry for not knowing what to think about it all,' says Maggie. 'It's not just you. Though I guess it's going to take some getting used to, being here with you now, especially as there's no option, as we have to be in this house, every evening, every night, every morning together – until the police drop these ridiculous bail conditions.'

'If they drop them,' I say.

'They haven't even charged us with anything, David. I don't understand how they can do this. How can they put us through this, if there's no evidence, nothing concrete? Seems utterly ludicrous.'

'A minute ago you seemed to be praising them for their thoroughness, if not inventiveness.'

'Was I? Well, I said I'm confused. Very.'

'That's the police, the legal system for you. Makes you distrust everything.'

'I don't like it.'

'Neither do I,' I say, smiling. 'Did you want a cup of tea? Maybe we should have a drink. Is there any wine anywhere?' I start for the cupboard under the stairs. 'Or has Julie drunk it all?'

He watched as the front door opened.

As Fonda stepped into the end of the night, clutching a holdall. As Fonda beeped open his Audi, chucked his bag on the back seat, then climbed into the front.

He watched as Fonda quickly turned the car round in the drive. And he tucked himself further behind the large tree across the road as the Audi, headlights on, aimed his way. The car then went left, and accelerated towards the A12, the rear lights disappearing in the foggy dawn.

So he left his wife and child, Smith thought. That was thoughtless of him – he'd just been given the perfect opportunity to make Fonda do anything he demanded.

He crossed the road, walked towards the house. Glancing over his shoulder, seeing nothing moving, Smith slipped down the side of the house, making for the rear, and the cloakroom window. It was how he'd got in before.

Smith's breathing had increased. The idea of taking Fonda's wife captive seemed more attractive by the second. He didn't think the boy would prove too much trouble to keep out of the way.

When things got exciting.

'Hello, Dad,' says Jack, sitting up in bed. 'Is it school today?'

'Yes, and I'm taking you,' I say, walking across his bedroom to open his curtains.

'Good,' he says. 'I don't want Julie to do it again.'

'She won't, don't worry.'

'I mean she was all right,' he says, behind me. 'She's nicer than Emily. I like Emily the worst. But she kept laughing, really loudly. It was embarrassing.'

'I know what you mean. She does that. She used to be an actress.' It's dim out, but what daylight there is is almost too much for my eyes. I have a terrible headache.

Turning back to Jack, who still hasn't got himself out of bed, who's sitting there gazing happily at me (he does have this lovely smile – a sort of cheeky shrug), I realise that at least I can gaze freely at my son, and at a new day. These things I always took for granted. I look outside again, thinking that perhaps it's getting brighter, that the clouds are thinning.

'David, what are you doing?' says Maggie.

Quickly looking over my shoulder, I find Maggie's standing at the entrance to Jack's bedroom. How long's she been there?

'It's late. Jack'll be late,' she says. 'I thought you were getting him up and dressed. Poppy's getting her coat on.'

'It's OK, Mum,' says Jack. 'School's not the most important thing in the world. That's what Julie said. She said she didn't pass one exam.'

'Did she now?' says Maggie, flinging Jack's duvet off and hauling him out of bed. 'Well, I'm not surprised. Right, where are your clothes?'

'She said she didn't think Dad had passed any exams, either,' says Jack.

'I did,' I say. 'A few.'

Maggie looks at me – despairingly? But slowly a smile creeps across her face.

She shakes her head, turns to Jack. 'If your father had paid more attention at school, he could have got himself a proper job and saved us an awful lot of trouble.' Though her voice carries a hint of jollity.

'Me? A proper job?' I move into the centre of the room, not sure I can keep up any whisper of good humour or goodwill. 'Hang about. It's your so-called proper job that's actually got us into this trouble. Didn't anyone warn you about mixing work with pleasure?'

'David, later, please.'

'Yes, of course.'

'Can we go now?' says Poppy, with perfect timing. She's appeared in the doorway, her coat buttoned up, her book bag in one hand, her packed-lunch case in the other. She's even brushed her hair. 'I don't want to be late again.'

'No, I understand,' I say, looking at my watch (happily back on my wrist). 'But we've got time, sweetheart. Don't worry.' I follow Poppy out of the room, leaving Maggie to get Jack ready, thinking that actually we probably don't have much time, to pull through this. Perhaps some things are just too big, too difficult to surmount. Being under such suspicion – as devastating, as outrageous as it is – is not as bad as not knowing exactly where you stand with your partner, actually your wife and the mother of your children.

If Maggie and I had committed such an act together, if acting in tandem or at least within the knowledge that we (or one of us) had overpowered and murdered (somehow) this Alex Smith character, then I'm certain it would be much easier sticking together, believing in each other and in the family as a whole. We'd be able to weather the storm.

Could even be fun, in a way: keeping such a terrible, dark secret. Imagine the sort of trust, the sort of committed love that would have to be maintained. Much like Britt Hayes and Howie Jones will need to discover. If they are to have a future. But this seems even less likely now. I'm really not sure why I'm still wasting time on it – out of sheer stubbornness? Because no decent alternative has arisen. Because, one way or another, I've simply invested too much in it?

'Dad,' says Poppy, way ahead of me.

I trot down the stairs after her, thinking, and for the first time in a while: pace, pace, pace. As ever I must be aware not to give my characters too much interiority, too much say and desire, too much time.

Reaching the hall and Poppy (buttoned up and desperate to depart), I find I'm wondering not just about pace and timing, about time running out, but also about truth – again. Where is it really? Does it actually exist? 'What do you reckon, DS Grant Ellis?'

'What did you say, Dad?' asks Poppy.

You don't have to know everything about someone to trust him or her, I suppose, though when that trust has been severely tested, it's harder to ignore the gaps. Even if there's a common purpose.

But he wasn't mad. He wasn't some sexually depraved psychopath, despite surprising himself with the ease with which he did that thing to the prostitute's body. Fonda was to blame for it all, Smith thought, advancing on his next victim. Of course he was.

And it could easily have been so different. They could have worked together. Had Fonda bothered to notice him, to take him seriously – to realise his potential.

Smith knew a good opportunity when he saw one. He could be loyal, strong, ruthless. Cunning. Though he knew that that part of his plan, the most intricate and ambitious part, appeared not to be working. What were the police doing? Why were they taking so long to identify some DNA? It couldn't be that complicated, could it?

Meanwhile it seemed that Fonda was about to slip the net, leaving his family behind. Leaving Smith with no choice.

Having climbed through the downstairs toilet window and removed his shoes, Smith crept along the wide hall.

The police would thank him one day, he thought, reaching the stairs. Unless of course they were being paid to look elsewhere – by Fonda. That could explain plenty. Though surely not every cop, not every detective, was on his payroll. Some had to be clean.

Some crimes were too big to be covered up for ever.

The house was completely quiet and totally still, which was making Smith, as he headed upstairs, a little less excited and a little more nervous.

'David. Hello, David.'

The voice, right behind me, is loud and familiar, and slightly out of breath. But I don't want to turn round and face her. Not yet. Not now. Suddenly I don't think I'm quite ready – despite having thought it would be best just to carry on as normal. As if none of it had happened. Why did I say I'd take the kids to school and venture out in public?

I feel a tug at my arm. Am being physically pulled back and turned around, whether I like it or not. And there she is – those friendly round features, topped off by a helmet of thick mauve hair – as close as you can decently get on a pavement, at eight forty-eight in the morning.

'Hello, Clare,' I feel I'm forced to say. Billy whips past me and on towards Jack, and Poppy, who have pulled ahead. How I'd love to run on – run off – too.

'My God!' Clare says, loudly, bringing me abruptly to attention. 'You poor thing. I won't pretend I don't know.'

'What?' I say, hopelessly. 'What do you think you know, Clare?'

'David, it's everywhere. Everyone's talking about it. It's a big story.'

'Oh,' I say. 'Though what exactly have you heard?'

She pauses, frowns, says, 'That a young man's been murdered and that you and Maggie were arrested in connection with it, but have now been released on bail. It's been on the TV, on the radio. I guess it's in the paper – not that I read them – and no doubt it's all over the Internet.'

'Oh,' I say again, the memory of the photographer last night suddenly coming back to me. How could I have forgotten? Because, frankly, obviously, I had more important things to worry about, like the future of my marriage, my family. Because I've been forgetting a lot of things recently.

'Besides, everyone always knows everything around here,' says Clare.

Except perhaps me, I'm thinking. We start walking towards our children.

'Actually, I'm rather surprised to see you,' she says. 'Pleased, of course, David, don't get me wrong. Though you were arrested, weren't you? Both of you? And, like, accused of murder? It must have been a pretty frightening experience.'

'Clare, can you talk a little more quietly, please. We obviously haven't told the children anything about all this. I hope they still think we were in London – for an event, a last-minute thing.'

We're having to slow, and are being bunched up by other kids and parents and carers as we advance on the school gates, and I'm suddenly aware, as I look around me, as people and children close in, that I'm being observed, stared at. Picked out.

'Yes, of course. Sorry, David,' Clare says, only fractionally quieter. 'Though you know what children are like. You might want to alter your story a little. It's going to be hard to keep all this from them.'

Of course we should already have thought about gossip and public knowledge and what our children might hear. But I suppose, with our wish to try to carry on as normal, and our attempts to come quickly to some sort of grown-up agreement between ourselves, this has been overlooked. We should have been thinking of our children first. As ever.

The guilt, yet more guilt, burns through me, instantly bringing me out in a sweat. Maybe it's hotter out than I thought. And muggier.

'Children, wait up,' I shout, urgently wanting their attention, wanting them to hear me loudly and clearly, before we have to cross the road (and not be – accidentally? – hit by a fast-moving, dark-coloured Audi, driven by the corrupt head of a local council regeneration board).

Everyone now most definitely feels free to gawp at me, as I try to focus on my children, who are jostling each other and being jostled by others.

'David, if there's anything I can do to help,' says Clare, smiling, though perhaps more in a pitiful way than a friendly, even flirtatious way, the way she used to look at me. But suddenly she does smile, excitedly, wildly almost.

'Yes, of course,' I say, trying to ignore all the other grown-up faces around me and not make anything of Clare's expression.

'Just ask,' she says, maintaining eye contact and that wild, rather mad look, while backing away, in the general direction of her son. 'You know where I am.' Then she winks. She actually winks.

'Yes,' I say, grabbing the collar of Jack's coat, reaching with my other hand for Poppy's. I think I would have asked her for a coffee, over one of those big, organic flapjacks in The Green Grocer, seeing as I haven't had breakfast – as if I had time, getting the kids ready this morning while trying out life as a suspect, life on police bail – and seeing as I reckon I'll be in need of friends, and (as ever) fans. But the wink put paid to that.

There was something almost complicit about it. As if she thinks I am responsible for Alex Smith's death, and that she's not unhappy with the notion. As if, suddenly, I've raised my game, am even hotter property (ha!) – in her eyes.

Which makes me wonder what Liz, for instance, will think of me now;

and Katya, with the extraordinary eyes. Would she wink? That would be a different proposition.

And something else comes to me: the wife of the desk sergeant. My incarceration and the accusations don't seem to have reduced her enthusiasm. Though of course it wasn't a recent book she wanted signing – seems like she'd already been put off at least my latest work (the one that didn't win the award). But what about what's coming next?

Finally I seem to get the email working, because there's this sudden, ferocious stream of pings alerting me to new mail – the number in the box rapidly multiplying. I quickly quit the application, take a sip of coffee and plough on, my stomach rumbling away. Thoughts of a flapjack not far away. And women of a certain inclination winking at me.

Hayes parked her car in the usual spot. Got out, beeped it locked and hurried across the forecourt.

Just before entering the building she glanced back at her staff Vauxhall saloon, checking that the boot hadn't somehow opened. Of course it hadn't.

She swiped herself in and, rather than wait for the lift, pushed through the double doors, turned left, carried on down the corridor for a short while, then hit the stairwell. Jogged up the three flights, determined to keep moving. As if this would somehow stop her thinking about last night and help her plan what to do next.

Though starved of sleep, adrenalin was still coursing through her.

I purposely left my mobile in the kitchen and thought I'd turned it to silent, but I can hear it ringing, again.

It's no good. I get up and cross my study, open the door, power along the hallway – slippers scuffing on the carpet – enter the kitchen, pick up my phone, which is on the worktop, switch it to silent, while being careful not to look at the screen. I don't want to know who's calling. I don't want to know how many calls I've missed. I don't want to be contacted right now. I'm busy. I'm trying to concentrate. I want to be left alone – shunned (as before), if you like. Otherwise I'm never going to finish this thing, and there's no turning back now: you stubborn old fool.

Returning to my study and firmly shutting the door, which actually rattles the door frame, if not the surrounding walls, I realise that being banged up had its advantages. And might still have its advantages. I can't rule anything in or out, it would seem.

Given how the police have handled it so far. But who's really to blame? It can only be my fault, can't it, if people interpret my work incorrectly? Was I not being clear enough? Another one of my flaws – along with, this morning anyway, an inability to concentrate for long.

Somehow my email has opened again (this ancient contraption), and the new-message figure in the mail icon is multiplying as I look. I can hear them coming in too. Ping, ping, ping.

There's another application, of course, that I should open, if the operating system can handle it, if indeed it can still access the Web – one that I've somehow managed to resist so far today. Perhaps it's dread. Though I'm sort of used to that. Maybe it's excitement, and wanting to hang on to the unknown, the unconfirmed; that sense of uncharted territory to come, for just a little longer. 'Wait and see,' my mother always used to say when I asked her what was for dessert.

'Where's DS Shreve?' said Hayes, finally emerging from her office. She stood in the doorway, facing the operations room. 'Anyone seen him?' She could feel perspiration on her back. It was making her blouse cling to her skin.

'Still not in yet, I think,' said DC Jo Niven, looking up brightly. 'Pete Leonard's been trying to get hold of him too.'

Hayes noticed that Niven had a large cup of vending-machine coffee on her desk. Crap coffee or not, what she'd give for a sip of it right now! Her mouth was suddenly parched. And she felt faint with tiredness.

'OK, we'll just have to begin without him. Everyone,' Hayes raised her voice, 'let's get on with it.'

There was the sound of chairs being pushed back, people standing, gathering papers, drinks, jackets, whatever they needed, and advancing on the incident board. Phones were left gently ringing behind them.

Hayes, avoiding eye contact with the officers, skirted the compact room until she was standing in front of the large screen. She waited for everyone to get settled before she took in the assembled crew – larger than normal

Shreve was the only person missing.

'Guess what?' she said, trying to calm her nerves. And to sound normal, casual.

'There's nothing new?'

For an instant Hayes thought Shreve had spoken. It was exactly the sort of thing he might have said. But it wasn't him, of course. It was DS Peter Leonard, on secondment from Vice, and making a rare appearance.

'No, actually,' she said, thinking she just had to focus on the moment, get the right information out. 'For once Forensics have come up with something.'

'A DNA match?' said DC Niven.

'You bet,' said Hayes. 'They've found a near hundred-per-cent match with DNA on the knife and DNA on the passenger door of Kesteris' car.'

'And it's not this guy Kesteris' DNA?' said Leonard.

'No,' said Hayes. 'Obviously Kesteris' DNA has been isolated, and the cold-case unit are running checks. Not something that's been done before apparently, despite his previous form.'

'So are you saying the person who killed Kristine and the person who then shot Kesteris could be same?' said Leonard.

'I love this unit,' said Hayes, 'I really do, with the amount of attention you lot pay. Or perhaps you weren't here for the last briefing, Leonard?'

She'd always disliked Leonard. The lazy slob, currently slumped at the back of the room. There was no one in the bland, airless room, except perhaps Niven, whom she had any time for. But Niven's enthusiasm, her energy, was offset by her naïvety.

And aside from the ineptitude, the cynicism, the corruption, none of them ever made much difference anyway. The world still turned on its flawed axis.

Suddenly she wasn't sure she wanted to do this any more. Wasn't sure she could do this any more.

'The nature of Kristine's death still hasn't been ascertained,' Hayes said. 'It's possible it never will be. So no, I'm not saying the person who killed Kristine then shot Kesteris. But what I am saying is that we can positively link someone out there with the deaths of Kristine and Girts Kesteris. They're still analysing Bernard Kesteris' clothes. The water damage is not helping.'

'But we don't know who they are, right?' said Leonard. 'This DNA's not on the system?'

'Yeah – sadly that's correct,' said Hayes. 'And I can't tell you the grief I'm getting from the people upstairs to find the source.' She paused. Wiped her forehead with the back of her hand. 'The great British public aren't helping, either, as I'm sure you are all aware. They don't care about the forensics. They want arrests, like yesterday. If not the day before.'

But Hayes couldn't even feel angry. She was too tired – of it all. And was simply going through the motions, putting on an act. Not that she should have been shouting at them. There had been a development. The net was tightening.

Perhaps that was the problem. She had too much of an idea where it was heading.

'The bullet,' said Niven, breaking the unsettled quiet, 'anything from that yet?'

'It was a .38-calibre,' said Hayes. 'Probably from a Smith & Wesson – some kind of snub.'

'Discreet piece,' said Leonard. 'Tricky to use too. Not something an amateur would necessarily want to handle. Don't see many of them around, either. That might help.'

'It's hardly going to be registered,' said Niven.

'No,' said Leonard. 'But you never know who might have belonged to a club, who might have trained to use such a weapon.'

'Don't hold you breath, anyone,' said Hayes. 'We need to concentrate on the Kesteris brothers, Girts especially. Who knew him, who worked for him, how his operation was run. Come on, Peter, this is your world, isn't it?'

'DS Shreve's been working this angle, as you know,' Leonard said. 'We've been liaising all right – but I don't want to step on his toes.'

'Well, now you're here in person, for once perhaps you can pull your weight.'

'Sure, Boss.'

'And Kristine,' she said quickly, hating the way Leonard called her Boss, 'let's not forget her. We urgently need some more background. Who knew her? Why did she die? Why her, and not another sad, drug-addicted hooker? This wasn't just an overdose, a body being dumped. We know that. Is there anything in her background, her family, we haven't connected yet? She and the Kesterises were from the same country. They were Latvian. How far back do we need to go? And how far from here?'

Though Hayes knew it wasn't far.

I can't wait any longer, so I double-click on the Firefox icon, watching the screen slowly whirr into action. After a couple of minutes and a few more clicks the front page of the *Daily Mirror* eventually stabilises. I still always go to the *Mirror* first – don't ask me why. And, perhaps unsurprisingly, there's nothing there, except the obvious, the usual. Same with *The Sun*, except even more obvious stuff.

But I get a hit with the *Daily Mail*, having scrolled a long way down. There's not much, a couple of paragraphs. Though there's a picture of me – looking startled, at night, on the pavement, outside the police station; Cathy Daniels' arm is in the edge of the frame.

The Guardian goes bigger. I'm near the top. In the middle column. That photograph again, and the subtitle: *'Crime writer on murder rap sees sales soar overnight'.*

Can I complain? To the PCC? I mean, I would have expected a bit more accuracy and restraint from *The Guardian*. As far as I'm aware, I'm not on a *murder rap*, yet. I'm just a suspect, helping the police with their enquiries.

'After losing out on the Crime Thriller of the Year, David Slavitt hits the jackpot following the suspicious death of his wife's lover.'

There's even a quote from, of all people, James P, though I'm not entirely sure it's a new quote. Not sure it should be attributed to him, either. *'Crime writers like to think they are cleverer than the criminals they write about, but they are also human. We all make mistakes.'*

But fucking hell! Beyond my wildest dreams. I navigate over to Amazon, as fast as the Apple will go. Come on, come on! And yes, blimey, bingo: *The Tortured* is up in the top hundreds: 568. Its highest ranking ever – the last time I looked it was 268,192. *The Showman* is doing even better, at 327. And what about this? *The Watcher* is now at 119. It's nearly in the top hundred. *The Watcher* has consistently been my best-selling book. Still is.

There it goes again, the faint trilling vibration of my mobile on silent (all the way in the kitchen). But I must resist – and savour this moment. Gather strength. Capitalise further. Believe in myself, my work, for once; as others now appear to be doing.

'Sorry if I'm being stupid,' said Niven, 'but what if Kesteris – that's Girts Kesteris – murdered Kristine, and someone was not very happy about it?

Then this person decides to kill him and his brother for it. Like they were acting out of revenge. Or, I suppose, what if Bernard killed Kristine, then Girts killed Bernard?'

'And who then shot Girts? And why?' said Leonard. 'Come on, guys, this is not some love triangle, some personal vendetta. People don't go to those sorts of lengths for a junkie on the game. This is organised crime, a power struggle of some sort – Girts Kesteris was executed. We need to look closer to home. That poor prostitute happened to be in the wrong place at the wrong time.'

'As they always are,' said Hayes, wondering why no one, apart from Leonard and Niven, had anything to say. But then there was no Shreve – normally the most obstreperous person there. 'Besides, Kesteris' DNA wasn't on that knife.'

It wasn't on the watch, which she'd quietly passed through the lab, either. Though more perplexing perhaps was the fact that the DNA on both the knife and in the car also wasn't on the watch.

The DNA since found on the watch had another code entirely. Which was beginning to make Hayes question its significance. Perhaps Howie Jones had been trying to deflect attention.

But from what?

'Jo,' said Leonard, 'didn't DS Shreve suggest the possibility that someone might have inserted the knife into Kristine after she had already died? That they came across her body and then planted the knife, knowing what DNA was on it. That they were trying to frame someone? The person whose DNA it is?'

'That seemed a little too sophisticated, for round here,' said Niven. 'But maybe he's right.'

'It's an interesting angle,' said Leonard. 'I would like to know whether he's got any further with that line,' he continued. 'Shame we can't ask him right now.'

Hayes quickly turned towards the incident board, which was crowded with images, names, arrows. Things underlined and circled, but the order to the colour-coding was now lost on her. The whole board seemed more confused and duplicitous than ever.

The right things still weren't linking. And too much was out of view. Much having been deliberately withheld, and not just by her.

She didn't want to contemplate the idea that Howie had misled her from the start with the watch, with what he said he'd seen. She couldn't go down that road. She had to trust him. He had saved her life.

Besides, there was no alternative. Forget tampering with evidence and withholding information, she was an accessory to murder. Shreve's. And now Peter Leonard, Shreve's closest colleague, seemed to be on her case.

What the hell did he know?

Fourteen

'Yes?' I say, into the phone, perhaps rather sharply. The mobile in the other room is one thing, but the desk phone right next to me is another. I could only ignore it for so long – not being able to turn it to silent. Plus there's this edge of nervous excitement bubbling through me: this need to know what's being said, what's being bought.

'David?'

'Who the hell do you think it is? James Patterson?'

'OK, I've seen the figures, but calm down. You're not quite up there yet.'

'Sorry,' I say, a bit embarrassed, and surprised too to hear Peter's voice. Actually perhaps I'm not surprised. He's a clever, careful (some might say calculating) guy, who can be very enthusiastic when he wants to be. When he feels it's justified. Why he's such a good publisher, I suppose. 'It's been a rather fraught twenty-four hours or so.'

'I can imagine,' he says.

I wonder whether I should change Peter Leonard's name, his first name at least. I don't want any libel problems, no hint of that, or any further careless or frankly unnecessary real-life associations – seeing as there might now be something of a market for my next book (however it turns out), and people do seem to have a habit of coming out of the woodwork when they sniff money. 'I doubt it,' I say. 'When were you last accused of murder and locked up?'

'You're sounding rather hysterical again, David. No surprise, though – no surprise. Look, hang on, someone wants me. Just wait there a sec.'

There's a clunk as the phone is put down (on a desk?). The sound of Peter talking to someone else. A woman. In his office? I presume that's where he is. Neither is talking particularly quietly. In fact the conversation sounds rather animated, though good-humoured. Peter laughing for a moment. A squeal (of delight?) suddenly coming from the woman. Peter shushing her.

Looking up, at my empty study, papers and crap everywhere (far worse than usual), I realise, like a jab in the ribs, that perhaps I should be having a good laugh with someone. It's not every day you surge up the charts. Maybe I should ring Clare. Then maybe not. Perhaps I should try to get hold of Katya. Ask her round for lunch, or dinner, with her hairy bloke, I suppose, and Michael and Liz also; and, why not, Ashish too – that could be very interesting. The bail conditions don't stipulate that we can't have guests. But would anyone still want to eat my food?

Surely, if they still want to buy my books, in suddenly ever-increasing numbers. Maybe there's a whole world of new guests that we could ask.

'What's going on?' I say into the phone. 'Who are you with, Peter?' But he must still be holding the handset away from him. There's another squeal of laughter. And a guffaw. I hate that word, but that's what it sounded like: a guffaw. Sometimes, of course, often indeed, you're stuck with the words that first come to you, stuck with what you know and how you express it. Your limits, I guess.

And look where they seem to have got me. But it's these limits that you need to turn into strengths, of course. At last, perhaps, I'm recognising this.

Fortunate for some, for many now possibly (including Kristine, definitely), that I'm not a quitter – Maggie, take note. I couldn't have got where I am, if I were. This business takes a certain sort of commitment.

'David, you still there?' Peter's suddenly saying at last. 'Sorry, look, things are going mental here too.' He laughs. So does someone else close by him. 'You do realise you're all over the news, the Internet. You're even trending on Twitter.'

'Yes, I'm aware of that,' I say, though I haven't checked Twitter or any of the key blogs. That joy is to come.

'Not everything being said about you is – how should I put this? – complimentary, so don't take it all to heart,' says Peter. 'But the attention is there: that's the key thing.'

For a second I wonder if my closest rival, the guy I lost the Crime Thriller of the Year to, is jealous of all this attention. In fact I need to see on Amazon whether I'm now outperforming him.

'People are even checking out your backlist, which is great news for us,' Peter continues. 'In fact they seem to be trawling through everything you've written. Seeing if they can establish fact from fiction – what other crimes you might have committed.' He laughs again.

'What?' I say, reaching for the trackpad with my free hand, and thinking: like that idiot DS Ellis?

'So,' says Peter, quickly, 'every cloud, it seems, has a silver lining.'

Maggie's never really taken to Peter (I'm desperately trying to link into the *CrimeTime* blog, see the comments there), not comprehending how he's done so well. 'There's not an original thought in his brain,' she once said. I've tried telling her that's the point, where I'm coming from, with what we do. Though she doesn't even buy that. Judgemental lot, those academics. And, as far as I can tell, they're forever copying ideas and plagiarising each other's work anyway (isn't that so, my darling Maggie?).

My attempts to open up the *Shots* e-zine as well freeze the Apple solid.

'All these people think I did it?' I say.

'I can't control what the public think,' says Peter, 'how they interpret what's recently happened to you or what they read into your work, for that matter. But no, I'm sure they don't think you actually did it. You've been let out anyway.'

'On bail,' I say. 'Police bail.'

'Yes, well, presumably if they were convinced you had something to do with it, they wouldn't have done that.'

Doesn't he know how the process works – this great crime editor? 'They ran out of time,' I say. 'They either had to charge me or release me, and they didn't have enough evidence for the first.'

And now I'm thinking of not just Detective Sergeant Grant Ellis and Detective Superintendent Dora Lupton, but of all these people, these members of the reading public, scouring my work for signs and clues – of my culpability, my guilt? And I'm thinking, too, of what Peter just said about it not being up to him what people read into my work. That was up to me, originally, I suppose. And now the stuff is out there, it's too late. All these years I've craved readers – finally, when I appear to have some, they might prove to be something of a mixed blessing. Could this make matters with the police, the investigation, worse? But surely whatever these new readers think about my stuff is better than them not thinking about it at all.

'Talking about running out of time,' says Peter (ignoring the issue of evidence, I can't help noticing), 'Julie and I have had an idea.'

'You and Julie?'

'Yes, Julie and I. Well, to be fair, it was Julie's idea – but makes perfect sense in the current climate. She's here in fact, in my office, now. She came straight over this morning.'

'Right. So that's who I heard laughing.' Theatrically. Though I can't be openly critical of Julie. I can never be critical of her again. She stepped in (not that she had much choice) and looked after my children that fateful night. Although Maggie actually wondered, shortly after we both returned from our separate interrogations, our separate incarcerations, and having found the kids tucked up in bed (with Emily calmly in charge – Julie having left for London), whether we were entirely necessary to their upbringing. 'Well, it's possible we won't have that option,' I said to Maggie, not being able to look my wife in the eye then. 'If we're both given life.'

'David,' Peter's saying, 'if we're right and move now, we'll all be laughing, all the way to the bank.'

Notoriously there was once an earthquake in this city, or rather a tremor. So it can happen, here. Yet surely I'm imagining that the walls of my study are rippling and swaying, are closing in on me. No, it's not happening. Even though the floor beneath my chair, my desk, my feet, feels also like it's become liquid. An ocean, a sea at least – the cold, grey North Sea, frothing and fuming away, and sweeping me out of my depth with it. 'How do you mean, move now?' I manage to say.

'We want to slot you into the schedule this spring, and go to town with it.'

'But it is already spring, or meant to be.'

'Yes, David, well observed. So how about it?'

'My new novel? You want to bring that out now?'

'That was our thinking, to capitalise on all this interest – yes.'

'But it wasn't meant to come out for another year. It's not finished. Not edited. Besides, I was under the impression that Julie, and you for that matter, weren't very keen on the premise. Which was why I'd been relegated to next spring (and that seemed to be in some doubt) and not this autumn.'

'Things have changed, David, haven't they?' says Peter.

'Not the book, not that much,' I say. 'OK, I've tried to spice it up a bit. Took some advice from Julie – am doing what I can.'

'I hope you haven't gone off on too many wild tangents,' says Peter. 'I mean, we do still want the authentic David Slavitt – that's what people will be looking for.'

'They weren't before, much,' I say.

'They will be now, believe me,' he says. 'I mean, obviously if your recent experiences filter into the book, in any shape or form, then so much the better. I'm not going to say write about what you know, anything as basic as that, but I think you get the point.'

'Do I, Peter? What are you really saying?'

'Nothing more than the obvious: we need to get your new book out fast.'

'Who else backs this up?'

'The people in marketing and sales. The whole team. It's been a busy morning. But we've got to move quickly.'

'How fast are we talking?' I say. 'Printing alone takes time, doesn't it?'

'We can go straight into e-book,' he says. 'The print copies can come later. It's a brave new world out there.'

'But I'm still a while off finishing.' The room's stopped swaying. And I no longer feel I'm being sucked out to sea, but my old computer's still jammed. Maybe it will remain so, and I'll never be able to retrieve my most recent work. Besides, I suddenly realise, the police still have my main laptop, containing the bulk of the novel. Of course I should have backed it up, put it on a memory stick or emailed it to myself. But I didn't (perhaps thinking – not surprisingly, having been told so – that it was all rather worthless). 'And there might be one or two other logistical problems.'

'You think you could be rearrested? Put on remand?' He doesn't even bother to hide the excitement in his voice.

'No – well, I don't know,' I say. 'I hope not. But there's a chance, I guess.'

'Then we really have to hurry,' says Peter. 'You need to get it to me as soon as you can. When do you reckon? Next week?'

'Next week?' The room starts trembling again – about 8.6 on the Richter scale. I get to my feet, grasp the desk with one hand. 'Look, I don't even have everything I have written. The police have most of it. Or rather it's on my laptop, and they've taken that away.'

'You didn't back it up?' he says. 'This material could be crucial.'

'No, I didn't back it up.'

'You fucking idiot!'

He still felt sick. Perhaps he would always feel sick. It wasn't something you saw every day. Something he would ever want to see again. But he knew the image was not going to go away.

The thing that was getting to him was that it was so much worse than the first time he saw a dead body. When he'd done those things to the corpse as well.

This time he'd not even got that close.

Then he'd panicked.

It was only a matter of time before they came for him. And when they did, they were never going to believe the truth.

Hayes slowly replaced the receiver. Looked up. Looked around her. There were no personal touches in her office. No photos, no cheery postcards, no personal icons. She didn't think it right. Not here.

She wasn't the sort of person who collected stuff like that anyway. She didn't have close friends. Not much family left, either.

She'd survived just fine on her own, keeping relationships brief, keeping her distance – until now.

Slowly she gathered her things: her mobile, her keys, a new packet of disposable latex gloves. Dropped them all into her bag and walked out of her office.

'Jo, you need to come with me,' she said out in the operations room. 'Peter, you stay here, wait for Tom. And can you check out Kingsmouth Council for me – the development and regeneration committee? This thing's just exploded in our faces.'

'What the hell's happened now?' said Niven, standing.

'Double murder, over the river in a house in Gorleston,' Hayes said. 'A young woman and a child. Both shot at point-blank range.'

'Oh shit!' said Niven. 'Not a child too.'

'A neighbour noticed the front door was open. Nice big house. Went in to have a look – got the shock of her life,' said Hayes, who until last night thought she was immune to shock. 'The whole area's been cordoned off,' she continued. 'And Forensics are on their way.'

She paused for a moment. Scratched the back of her head. Her scalp dry from the hour-long shower she'd had earlier today.

'The good news is we've already got a lead on a suspect,' she continued. 'A man was seen running down the street, about five in the morning, by a guy working in the Texaco garage. There's one at the end of the road. He thought it was a bit strange at the time, especially when the man got into a Toyota Prius and sped off. Texaco's CCTV should have picked it all up.'

'Why didn't the guy at the garage ring it in at the time?' said Leonard.

'It's Kingsmouth,' Hayes said. 'Strange behaviour is par for the course. Let's just be grateful someone noticed something.'

'So whose house is it?' said Leonard. 'Why do you want me to check out the development committee?'

'Heard of Adrian Fonda?' said Hayes. She looked straight at Leonard. Straight into his small, dark eyes.

'Yeah,' he said. 'Who hasn't?'

'It's his house,' said Hayes, turning for the exit.

Kristine, I'm thinking: it's a fight for justice (for her friends, her family – if she had any and wherever they may be – for her soul), always has been.

People like Kristine – trafficked, enslaved, drug-ravaged women, girls really – mustn't be forgotten. Even if subsequent events grab more attention, more headlines, are conceivably even more tragic. A young mother and child, shot dead in their home, in a quiet English town, by a wide, tidal river? It could eclipse everything. The poor boy especially. Just imagine – he was Jack's age too. Though Britt Hayes won't let Kristine be forgotten. I won't let Kristine be forgotten. But it's hard, though.

The road was clear as she accelerated, but Hayes' mind wasn't.

Could Howie have gone to Fonda's house, after he dumped Shreve's body? And before he then calmly returned her car?

'No one will ever find your colleague,' he'd said, as if he'd done this before, more than once – which she guessed she'd always suspected.

Why had he insisted on taking her car in the first place?

Simply because his was hot? On what CCTV was hers now going to show up? She just hoped the guy acting suspiciously by the Texaco garage, who'd then driven off in a Prius, was going to provide some answers. He'd better.

She couldn't see why Howie would go after Fonda anyway. Because he was enraged that Fonda might have ordered Shreve to take her out? He was that bothered about her? Though, of course, he had tailed Shreve to her house.

But what might have happened at Fonda's? Why the wife and the son? Was Howie Jones that dangerous, that lethal?

Hayes hadn't been in a fit state to question such moves, such motivations, at the time. She was still getting her head around the fact that Shreve had been murdered in her house and she was now helping to protect the perpetrator.

She was so fucked.

She glanced over at Niven in the passenger seat, thinking: you've got so much ahead of you, girl. But how easy it was to make a mistake, and how quickly more mistakes then followed. One after the other, until you couldn't see anything properly any more. The view ahead blurred and foggy.

Be careful who you fall in love with.

Be careful who you let fall in love with you.

Crucial stuff, hey?

'Oh, hello.' I seem to have shuffled into the kitchen, and there, sitting at the table, slumped really (yes – we know you can slump over a table), is Maggie. She turns her head, looks at me, smiles. She's been crying. Her eyes are red and puffy and her mascara has smudged, and though she's smiling, or trying to smile, she looks completely wretched. I want to go over to her, put my arms around her, rest my face against her cheek, run a hand through her lovely hair and mutter something about how everything will be all right. But will it?

I keep my distance. Partly because I feel that if I do rush over to her she won't just recoil, I might indeed frighten her. We're still getting used to our new status of course, the new dynamic.

She's still looking at me, not really smiling any more. Turns back to her mug. Takes a sip.

'I didn't hear you come in,' I say.

'You were on the phone. Who on earth were you talking to – seemed a rather animated conversation?'

'Oh, Peter, mainly. They want to . . . actually I don't really want to talk about it.' Something tells me that now's not the moment to reveal the good news, if indeed that's what it is. Doesn't quite feel like it.

Sunlight is streaming into the kitchen. It's warm in here. It's the middle of the day. I walk over to the back door, undo the lock, step outside, where it's even warmer. And suddenly so very quiet. Just the sound of birdsong and a gentle breeze rustling through the trees beyond our garden – the new leaves lush and green and flickering. Though I begin to pick up, faintly, the distant rumble of provincial traffic (no screeching, no sirens, nothing menacing). I take my eyes off all this pleasantness, look at my watch, look back at Maggie. 'What are you doing here, Maggie? Shouldn't you be at work?'

'Work – at a time like this?' she says.

'Isn't it best to try to carry on as normal? I thought that's what we were attempting to do. For the sake of the children, if nothing else.'

'David, are you so out of touch with reality? We're all over the fucking newspapers, the Internet. Everyone is talking about us.'

'I am aware.'

'There was another photographer, one of those paparazzi people, chasing after me on campus this morning. You should see the faces of my colleagues when I walk down the corridor.'

'I'm sorry.'

'Well, it's not your fault, is it?'

'I thought you said it was.' I think about laughing, to lighten the mood, but don't. I've stepped back into the kitchen. 'That because of what I do, the nature of my work, all this outrageous suspicion has been generated.' I try to look into her eyes. She won't meet mine, and something more than avoidance is there. 'If it wasn't for my bloody books,' I say, 'we wouldn't be in this mess.'

'OK, sorry. I take some of the blame – of course. He was my student.'

'Yeah, well, in your world these things happen, I guess.'

'My world? At least you've still got a job.' Her eyes are watering up again. 'People still take you seriously.'

'Yeah, but it looks like all for the wrong reason now. You should have heard what Peter's been saying. Have you any idea what's happening out there? What people are saying about me, and my books? Jesus, Maggie, I've become something of an overnight sensation. But it doesn't feel right, and I don't know what to do about it.'

'Carry on as normal?' she says.

I move towards her, but something (the truth?) pulls me back once more.

'Enjoy the moment?' She sort of laughs. Not quite a full Maggie giggle.

'That's just it – it is a moment. And not exactly of glory. And who knows where it will lead. More trouble, I reckon. As Peter said, there's no accounting for what people see and read into things. Fuck knows what I'll be accused of next.'

'Maybe you're taking yourself, your work, too seriously again.'

'Me? I'm not sure that's the case. It's suddenly everyone else. I tell you, it's never straightforward, my bloody job. I should have been a poet – would have got myself into a lot less trouble.'

Maggie laughs now, properly. 'Not from what you've ever shown me. You were crap.'

'An academic then.'

'You don't have the qualifications.'

'I could have got them. I'm not that stupid.'

'You'd have hated it. You couldn't have coped with your colleagues, let alone the students.'

I decide not to mention anything more about how Maggie copes with her students. And say instead, 'I'd have loved the security, the pension plan, the very generous holidays. A nice designer campus.' The insecurity, the precariousness, the fickleness of what I do takes its toll, that's for sure. In a way it makes you into someone you're not. Certainly makes you behave in a way that's not normal, that's not you. Whether you are dealing with the failure, or the sudden success. 'A job for life, too,' I add.

'Well, they've suspended me,' Maggie says. Her shoulders suddenly give and she begins to sob.

And I'm not sure whether I should rush over, fling my arms around her in comfort, in support – that's what I'd like to do. But yet again I can't help feeling that it would be inappropriate somehow; that Maggie would reject the gesture anyway.

'Oh,' I say, staying where I am, 'Oh, Maggie, I'm sorry. I'm really sorry.' Her shoulders continue to heave and shake. 'But you haven't been sacked!'

'Not yet,' she gulps. 'Not that there's much difference. It's just a matter of time.'

'Once this business is cleared up, they'll have to reinstate you,' I say. 'Simple as that. I know enough to know that that's how those organisations work. They can't just suspend you, if you've done nothing wrong – not for ever. Otherwise you could sue them. Get Ben Hargreaves on the case – not that I'm sure he's quite the right person. You could try Cathy Daniels, the lawyer who was appointed to me. She's pretty smart.'

'What if I have done something wrong, David?'

The sobbing has all but ceased and Maggie's voice is strangely clear and calm. Chillingly so?

'What do you mean?' I'm on the other side of her now, standing between her and the door into the hall, and staring down at the faded denim shirt stretched across my stomach – a button missing just above my navel; at my legs in faded, scruffy denim too, and at my feet in the knackered slippers. The sun pouring into the kitchen and straight onto me, striking the denim, seems to be highlighting the fade and weave. 'What have you done?' I say, still looking down. 'Are you saying you did kill him – your student, Alex Smith?'

Yet it's my slippered feet that have really hooked my focus, where I'm rooted to the floor, the ground. It's in the shade down there.

'No, of course I didn't kill him,' she says. 'My God! I barely knew him. He was simply some student who had a bit of an obsession with me. A crush, I suppose. He was always knocking on my office door, and there were times when I'd catch him following me around campus, and in town too actually. I probably should have reported him. But I didn't, because these things happen – goes with the territory. Plus there was always so much else on my mind.'

She's wiping her eyes on some kitchen roll. The paper greying with mascara.

'Though obviously it hasn't exactly helped, having this hanging over me – over us,' she continues. 'But they would have suspended me anyway, so they said: for "misconduct in research" is technically how they phrase it. Misconduct in research, not apparently bringing the institute into disrepute or anything like that, which would have made a lot more sense to me. Though I guess, and as you implied, they have to be pretty careful of their position, legally. They're terrified of being sued.'

'Sorry, Maggie, I'm not quite with you.' I stop looking at my feet and pull out a chair. Not the one next to her. The one at the end of the table, a little further away, and sit down, heavily.

'You never are, darling.' She blows her nose on the already soggy and greyed bit of kitchen roll. She balls what's left of it. Drops it on the table.

'Misconduct in research?' I say. 'What exactly does that mean?'

'What it says. That I didn't do everything I implied I'd done.' She sighs. Leans back.

Didn't do everything I implied I'd done? 'But that's OK, isn't it?' I say.

'It's others, Lupton and co., those bloody detectives, who've implied you've done something you shouldn't have.'

'Wrong track, David – please. Do you ever listen to me, properly?'

'Sorry, you're going to have to spell it out.'

'I took a few shortcuts with the research of this paper I was doing on John Barth. Remember me telling you – days, weeks ago now? I've lost all sense of time.'

'It's coming back.'

'Well, anyway, it was about Barth. Remember who he is?' she says.

I look at her as if to say: yeah, of course.

'He wrote this essay, *The Literature of Exhaustion*, back in the Sixties. It was all to do with the death of the novel. That was how it was interpreted anyway.'

'He should have a word with Julie,' I say. 'No chance of that, she'd tell him – if you put enough deaths in the novel.'

'Honestly, David – I'm being serious.'

'Go on.'

'Actually Barth did have a rethink and change his tune a number of years later, in another essay. Anyway, I was looking at these two key works, trying to be clever, I suppose, and suggest that far from recanting his original thesis by implying, as he appeared to, that literature could be replenished by fiddling around with the role and objectivity of the author – it's postmodern stuff – Barth had in fact gone even further than had initially been supposed, and that what he was really saying all along was that the novel wasn't just dead, but had never truly been alive. Only the reader had.'

'OK, sort of makes sense, I guess.' Maggie's right, I would have hated being an academic. 'So what's the problem?'

'Someone else had already suggested as much. Someone who worked with Barth in the States. He's saying it's not just his research and thesis, but that I'd even lifted whole chunks of his material.'

'Did you?' I can hear the desk phone in my study ringing. Can hear it ring out.

'I don't know. Not on purpose. Certainly not word-for-word. Michael's had a look. He's pretty certain there are enough differences with the text, the prose itself. Though the premise is similar. No denying that.'

'So, are you always meant to come up with a new idea, a new interpretation?'

'Yes, obviously if you are publishing original research, especially if it's already attracted funding.'

'That must be hard.'

'Yeah – it is my job. Or was,' she says.

'I'm so sorry.' I get up, feeling the need to return to my study – my bolthole. Even though the phone in there is going, yet again. It's not just the intricacies of Maggie's work that are difficult to comprehend, but now the sudden collapse of her career, her reputation too. The poor thing, and I don't know where to look, what to say, how to support her.

Maggie stands too, though she walks over to the sink. Grabs a glass from the drainer and pours herself some water. She drinks it quickly. 'You don't know how lucky you are, David, working for yourself. Doing exactly want you want every day. Not having people constantly looking over your shoulder. The freedom must be wonderful.'

'I can't be suspended, I suppose,' I say, moving towards the doorway. 'But that doesn't mean people don't tell me what to do. You know what I have to cope with, Maggie. How it's always been. There's not a lot of freedom. Not for someone like me. But perhaps you should try it sometime. See what you can make of it. You're cleverer than me.' I leave the kitchen.

'As if I don't have enough to do,' I hear her say behind my back.

'Not now you're suspended,' I reply, trying to make it sound humorous, but quickly slipping into my study – catching my old, dirty white laptop open and ready for me on my desk (will I ever see my tough, powerful, resilient MacBook Pro again – the machine I extravagantly bought, thinking it would be perfect for my travels, for my book tours and especially trips to the States, and which only ever went to London on the train and, I guess, is still being sullied by DS Ellis' dirty paws?).

'OK,' Maggie says, making me jump, before I've even sat down. She's striding into my study, my space, my hallowed turf. 'Where do I begin?' she says.

'Good question.'

New Year didn't mean anything to Jones. He'd made his resolutions a while back.

He pulled aside the curtain, stared down at the dismal street. Daylight was having another problem exerting itself. More freezing mist was rolling in. He'd had enough of this place. And this place had had enough of him.

Where the hell was Britt?

He let the thin curtain fall back and stepped away from the window. On his bed lay his rucksack. Everything he owned was stuffed inside.

Baz lay on the rug by the foot of the bed, snoring away. The bloody dog had given him away, Jones couldn't help thinking – exposed him to a routine, and a person, Adrian Fonda, who had never made any resolutions, because he didn't have the conscience, the heart. Wouldn't know where to begin. Wouldn't bother.

Jones knew he was different. That he'd always been different.

He gently kicked Baz. But Baz barely stirred.

He should leave him behind. Put him to sleep for good. Though he had a feeling it would be a lot harder to break such a dog's neck than a man's.

Besides, if Britt wasn't going to show, he'd need the company. A man and his dog.

'OK,' says Maggie. 'Will that do for the moment? I need to stretch my legs.' She gets up. 'Glad I saved the dog's life at least.'

Hayes walked out of the bedroom, clutching her stomach. But she was determined not to be sick. It was one thing seeing the body of a young woman, blasted in the chest at close range. Another, a young boy – curled in a foetal position, on his bed – missing half his head.

Blood, bone and brain had splattered the headboard and the blue *Toy Story* wallpaper behind. Hayes estimated the boy to have been six years old.

Niven was downstairs, talking to the scene-of-crime officers.

The Prius driver, Alex Smith, had already been arrested and was at the local police station.

Hayes was going to head straight there: hear what the man had to say, while his car and home were checked and a DNA sample was taken and rushed through the lab.

She wasn't a ballistics expert, but she had a feeling that the gun used to kill Tanya and River Fonda was the same gun that killed Girts Kesteris. She also had a feeling that Alex Smith, who appeared to be a council employee, wasn't the one who'd been pulling the trigger.

Adrian Fonda, who hadn't been seen since yesterday evening – currently no trace of his car, no trace on his phone – was on her mind. As was Howie Jones.

She knew she should call him.

'David?' It's Maggie, my companion, my collaborator, my soulmate – yes? She's by the door to my study, that lovely head of hers peering round the frame. A smile on her face – a determined smile. 'Don't you ever let it go?'

'You can't,' I say. 'That's part of the problem.'

'I'm going to pick up the kids,' she says.

'Gosh, is that the time?'

'Yes.'

'Is Emily not doing it today?' I say.

'She was, but I sent her a text. Said I'd like to.'

'OK.' I glance back at my screen. Bollocks! It's so much harder on your own. 'Maggie, wait,' I shout, standing and leaving my desk.

Coat already on, she's reaching for the handle and then pulling the front door open. She looks over her shoulder, looks puzzled. Hesitates.

'I'd like to come,' I say, shuffling her way. 'We can pick up the kids together. They'd like it. I'd like it, very much. Is that OK?' I've almost reached her.

'Yeah, that would be nice,' she says, a less determined, but more natural smile forming on her so very pretty face. Then it's gone, replaced by a frown – oh, those lines on her forehead, at the corners of her mouth. All my fault? Or is it more this guy John Barth's? His former colleague's, anyway? What was his line? Something about exhaustion, but really meaning the opposite? The academy, hey!

'Don't you need to put some shoes on?' she says. 'We are walking, aren't we?'

'Oh yeah, of course,' I say, looking down at my slippers. 'I could do with the exercise, as well.'

Fifteen

Another fine day and sun is slapping the Volvo's windscreen, picking up the dust and the grime, making it hard to see ahead. I slow, get the squirters going again. 'Swish-swash.' I say it.

Fortunately the roads are pretty clear, almost empty – the joy of driving around this city in the middle of the day. Who'd want to be stuck in London, in a traffic jam snarling up the Old Kent Road? Even if great material was so close by: the economic and social polarity, the menace. It's all in here anyway, isn't it, David? I tap my head.

Volvo for Life. I catch sight of the back of the tax disc and then tap the steering wheel, as if I somehow haven't just tapped my nut. *Life*. Would hum, if I could think of anything to hum – maybe I should start listening to music again. Maybe Maggie and I could catch some concerts, some gigs. But I don't want to fill my head with music. I don't think there's enough space, with everything else that's going on – that constant juggle. As it is, I desperately need to clear some room. Soon, soon.

Round a bend (oh, this calm, curvy city) there's more blinding sun. Crap squirters in this Volvo for Life. Or maybe the manufacturers just don't want you to see everything too clearly, all that life, for what it really is. Better that way – maybe.

There's no mistaking the weather we're having, however. What a patch! What a sudden, late spring. I could get used to this. Maybe I already am.

Odd how quickly you get used to things, both pleasant and unpleasant. How, anyway, your attitude can change about what's pleasant and what's unpleasant – this stuff constantly switching around. Swish-swash.

I glance at my watch: the watch! Bags of time until curfew. Though not bags of time for Britt Hayes. Or Howie Jones. I can see, hear, taste their mounting anxiety: Britt's eagerness to make the necessary breakthroughs; Howie working out the mistakes he'd now just made, what he could have done differently, whether he'd been as professional as possible.

Hayes was struck by how harmless, how gormless really, Smith appeared. He looked like a geek – or was that an emo? – with his limp, straggly hair, his sad attempt at a beard. Sitting in the interview room, in his light-blue, police-issue jumpsuit, his clothes having been removed for analysis.

He'd admitted to being in the house. To discovering the bodies, of Tanya and River.

The guy was a shaking wreck. Quickly confessed to wanting to exact some sort of revenge on his boss, Adrian Fonda. Though wasn't that forthcoming on exactly what form that would have taken. Why he even hated his boss so much.

'Were you thinking of kidnap?' Hayes had asked. 'Doing something to Tanya, or River? That was why you were there, wasn't it? Were you going to torture them?'

'I wouldn't have harmed them,' he'd kept saying. 'I know what I was doing was wrong, but I'd never have harmed them. Not a young boy.'

'What about the woman? What about Tanya: what had you planned for her?'

'I would never have touched her, I promise – she was beautiful.'

Hayes knew they didn't have any forensic evidence to go on yet. Though the search at Smith's flat had only just begun – his computer equipment was being taken away, before they started the stripping and lifting.

However, he appeared to have little money. There were no immediate signs of being involved in organised crime.

His connection with Fonda seemed to stem from the workplace. Enquiries there would quickly have to be made. And obviously they urgently needed to speak to Fonda himself.

But Fonda – whom Britt knew was soon to be declared Britain's most wanted man, presumed armed, very dangerous and not to be approached by the public – had disappeared.

Hayes might have been struggling for something concrete – that link, that crucial piece of evidence – though despite everything she realised she couldn't just quit, not yet, for a new life. Jones meanwhile knew at least that Shreve's body, dumped in a disused grain silo eight miles from Kingsmouth, would never be found in this story. The silo was too deep, and anyway he'd covered his tracks (in Britt's car, nevertheless) too carefully.

Odd! I now seem to be on the ring road. Moving fast in the sparse traffic. Even during rush hour these wide arterial roads (40 mph mostly) are hardly clogged. I'm way past the butcher's. The award-wining bakery. The greengrocer. Sainsbury's, Waitrose and Majestic. It seems that the shopping will have to wait. I've passed football pitches, games fields and the tennis club too. That idea I once had of getting fit (or was it Julie's?) and smartened up (to please Maggie, and Julie, my audience) will have to wait. I'm enjoying this road, this space, this sense of movement. Being out and about (I've never got out enough – existing in my little bubble, my world, as Maggie once used to describe it). Not knowing where the hell I'm going in my big, blurry Volvo for Life. Though I do know where I'm going. Don't I?

Fonda should have kept driving. He had planned to go south. To Kent – Ashford. And grab the train to France, before any alerts were issued. He could have been on the continent by now, heading east, to some old friends.

How he'd always believed it might end.

Instead, he still had business here, in Kingsmouth. Where they wouldn't be looking for him. Besides, he thought, glancing up at the massive chimney of the redundant power station – clouds bunching, gulls swirling – he'd grown to like this town.

Liked the way it was sandwiched between a wide, fast-flowing river and the sea. How it was out on a limb – vulnerable, helpless. Hopeless.

Fonda didn't know how Shreve had failed, how he could have failed, but he had an idea who might have played a part: the cunt with a dog. That was where he was heading. To prove that, yes, no one messed with Adrian Fonda.

He wasn't going to hold back, especially as he'd nothing to lose. Except his life, and he didn't care about that much any more.

Fratlingham. Midday (actually it's later than that now, more like mid-afternoon), midweek, seems pretty deserted. Despite the exceptional weather. A *Country Park*, recently so-named, with a glistening broad, which was once a gravel pit. People should be enjoying the space, the careful landscaping. And the wild woodland surrounding it all. A woodland coming into full leaf.

A woodland – as I progress further along what has always been known as Fratlingham Lane, which looks just perfect for playing hide-and-seek in, perfect to get lost in. Perfect for hiding a vehicle in, too – perhaps over there, to my right. There seem to be tracks in the dirt, the undergrowth. But after this amount of time?

We used to come here with the kids, a lot, when we were new to the area. It's where Jack learned to ride his bike. Poppy, having already learned on the mean streets of London, would race ahead, far out of sight. Can't imagine being able to run after her now. Can't remember the last time we all came here, as a family.

My Volvo for Life seems to have a mind of its own today, because it's stopped. Half on, half off the lane, just a little further along from where I thought I saw those tracks. Though I'm certainly not nosing the vehicle into the undergrowth. The weight of this Swedish thing, it's bound to get stuck. The weather might be brilliant at the moment, but it has been awfully wet. I reach for the door handle. Though I pause, thinking about the DNA found on the passenger door in Girts Kesteris' car. And the DNA on that Sabatier carving knife. And the DNA on the watch. Incriminating DNA all over the place. And how, surely, facts are pretty easy to come by nowadays.

There's little need for doubt, for suspicion, for supposition. And all the fucking drama that goes with it. The truth must always be there, staring everyone in the face.

How then do people still get away with things? With murder?

Hayes tapped in the number, put the mobile to her ear.

She was on the pavement, in front of the station, walking towards her car.

A container lorry lumbered past.

She tried to shield the handset so that she could listen more carefully. Wishing he'd hurry up and answer.

Climbing out and standing on the soggy earth, I realise that there's no way anyone could have pushed the car Alex Smith (the real Alex Smith) was found dead in off the lane and far enough into the woods so that no one could immediately see it from the road. It would have to have been driven in. So either he drove it in, or whoever he was with drove it in. And either they were both happy about the situation, about wanting to get out of plain view, so that they could embark upon . . . Actually I really don't want to continue with that train of thought. Or one of them didn't want to go such a way (off the beaten path) and was making something of a fuss about it. *What the hell are you doing, Alex? Where the hell are we going? Stop! Stop the fucking car now.* I can sort of imagine – something like that (hey, Detective Sergeant Ellis? Hey, Superintendent Lupton?).

Or perhaps it was Alex demanding the car to be stopped. Perhaps it was Alex struggling to be let out, knowing what was coming next. But the childproof central locking was activated and he couldn't get out. Then the car came to a stop and he was attacked.

But how, exactly? I don't even know whose car it was. His, or someone else's. Don't think the police ever said as much – probably for tactical reasons. Ever that: what they do and don't tell you.

A flock of birds (blackbirds? crows? not sure I know the difference) settles in the nearby trees. There's much flapping and squawking, startling me further. Unnerving me, actually.

Looking round, I see that to my left, through the woods, are glimpses of sun on rippling water. I walk back along the lane a little, to where there are clear tyre marks. I then head into the woods through the undergrowth and overgrowth (what's the difference?), going their way, aware still of not just the birds, but of no one else being around in this suddenly quite isolated patch of the park (which is such a popular local draw, though not, so it seems, midweek, mid-afternoon, and not this bit).

Certainly this particular spot appears to have been well chosen. But by whom?

There's an echoey crack behind me. I turn, catching my breath, though I can't see anyone. Perhaps it was a falling branch. Or an animal – a muntjac maybe. Or simply twigs and foliage, settling after I'd walked over?

I continue pushing through to the water's edge, the ground becoming soggier and soggier, until I enter a sort of clearing. Here the ground is much more trampled and traversed. People have definitely been about, and recently too. Are those tyre marks again? Not sure, though I suppose a car – a small, light car – could just about have squeezed through and got this far. But then been towed back out?

Maybe this particular spot was, or is, used for something else, something other than death and murder. Something much more life-affirming.

But I guess if you weren't feeling in that sort of mood, and indeed were feeling the very opposite and were on your own (for whatever reason), there's still the isolation, the privacy. And if you didn't want to create an immediate fuss, if you wanted to leave a few people worrying, sweating even, about your whereabouts, your well-being (which I guess is mostly the point), here's as good a spot as any, to end it all.

How long had Maggie's student been missing before they found his body?

Was Maggie one of the people who were so worried that she did some driving around and looking herself? Where did Maggie really go earlier that evening we were arrested: when I was home, being harangued by Julie and overcooking that loin of pork?

Did Maggie venture this way, sparking the police's attention? But it was pouring with rain. It was a truly rotten night. No night for sneaking off to the woods, that's for sure. She went to her office, like she said she did – why can't I just accept that?

Accept too that people, even those closest to you, need a certain amount of freedom, of space to live and breathe on their own, to be able to think freely, imaginatively (or darkly, or erotically, or actually similarly, as a couple of academics might). Space to have dreams and desires, secrets and lies.

All is not lost, all is never lost. How can it be on such a wonderful spring day?

Turning away from the water, that sparkling openness, and heading back through the woods for my car (*for Life*) and a pretty, provincial civilisation, I'm suddenly overwhelmed by the idea, the conviction no less, that something very simple (and to me now startlingly obvious) happened here.

And that while it is tragic for some, it doesn't have to be tragic for everyone – certainly not for Maggie and me, and Poppy and Jack. Belief, and some proper police work, it doesn't take much more than that. Does it?

Howie was right about the watch. It was important. It was incriminating. It was Smith's – not that they'd ever be able to use the evidence.

Fortunately Smith had finally confessed to a highly elaborate and deeply disturbing plot, not just to frame Fonda, but to destroy his reputation for ever. However, there was no disguising Smith's depravity: drugging a prostitute, then stripping and mutilating her corpse, with a knife stolen from Fonda's house.

Smith thought he was being so clever. Though it didn't take them long to find items of women's clothing and a quantity of acetomorphine in his flat.

But Girts and Bernard Kesteris played their parts too, by trying to rid their sordid premises of a tragic young woman OD'ing. Girts leaving her already dead, if Smith was to believed, out on the dunes on Christmas Eve.

The season of goodwill had long been forgotten.

It was almost too easy to see how an increasingly distrustful and paranoid Fonda embarked upon his killing spree.

Hayes peered through the windscreen. Took in the empty side road, Marine Parade ahead, a wedge of dark-grey sea merging with the threatening sky.

The corner of Howie's crumbling hotel was to her left. Where was he? She couldn't get him on the phone.

She was about to try yet again when her phone began ringing, caller ID blocked. 'Hayes,' she said.

'Where the bloody hell are you?' said DS Peter Leonard. 'Even the chief constable's been asking. Small matter of a press conference this afternoon.'

'Still in Kingsmouth.'

'Well, you better get your arse back here, pronto,' he said.

'Get Shreve to handle it, can you?'

'Shreve's still not in. We've sent a car round to check his home.' Leonard paused, coughed, came back on. 'Where is he, Hayes?'

'I've no idea – why don't we ask Fonda, when we find him. You know what Shreve was up to.'

She ended the call. Climbed out of her car. Almost walked straight into someone, a man, who then grabbed her round the waist, putting a hand over her mouth.

No, not lamb this time. Or pork. Definitely not pork. I'm not sure I'm going to cook pork ever again. And not beef, for that matter – even if I can suddenly afford it.

Howard Jones (not the pop star, or the former – former? – hit-man) once got me a piece of beef that he claimed had been hung for fifty-six days. And he did this (for me) at a time when I didn't even know his name. What service! What an inspiration, I guess, that man has been. Though it's the effect he has not on me, but on others, of course, that counts. Maggie thinks my version of Howie Jones is rather cuddly. Cuddly! And she can quite see why Britt immediately fell for him.

Julie, and Peter, for that matter, have yet to air their thoughts. Actually they have yet to see any material – despite the constant barrage of calls and emails requesting anything, anything at all.

'Do I have to go to the police,' Julie left on one message, 'to ask them for a copy?'

I've been avoiding them, and will continue to avoid them until it's finished. I know they want it now, and I also know that by the time they do get it they might not want it quite so much. But Maggie and I have a little plan, a pact.

Anyway Howard Jones (the butcher) wasn't in again today, which is perhaps why I opted not for the beef (how could I trust an assistant?), but chicken. Simply chicken. Actually not simply chicken – I still splashed out. A couple of slow-reared, yellow-tinged, Label Rouge organic birds. However, no one needs to know that exactly, or possibly could know that except me, especially as they've been jointed.

Oh, come clean. Howard Jones' absence was not in fact why I opted for the chicken. I went for chicken (to be accompanied by an unfussy tarragon and white-wine sauce) because this supper, which Maggie has quickly planned (and probably against her better judgement, though I wasn't going to dampen her enthusiasm – we're a team, have to be, for now, for ever), is not meant to be seen as anything so crass as celebratory (given our current circumstances, given that there's been a death), but a casual (hence the chicken), last-minute-kind-of-thing thank-you.

A thank-you for a particular sort of friendship and support, over all the years (the last two or three anyway).

Beats me how she's decided that this particular sort of friendship deserves such recognition; indeed, I'm not sure how she's even identified it, what exactly constitutes friendship in her eyes. However, she's her own person, has her own (particular) ways, and I must respect that. Am more than happy to (God, I'll do anything, anything, not to actually feel the need to drive down that lonely lane and slip off into the bushes). Which is why I'm preparing this simple-ish supper – for the usual crew.

'David,' said Maggie a short while ago, 'I know Michael is a complete tosser, and Liz is a boring old shit-stirrer, but they never deserted me.'

Neither did I, I felt like saying. There is definitely something about that lane, that country park, that's spooked me (and not in the way I was expecting). 'It's fine,' I said. 'Anyway, you know how much I like cooking and entertaining.' I don't bother to laugh. There's no need to fake anything any more.

'I did seriously think about quitting anyway, you know,' she said. 'I came that close. It wouldn't have been so bad. I could've spent more time with the children at least – they more than deserve it.'

We were in the sitting room for once, jointly tidying up. The television was playing for the kids, who were sitting on the floor, far too close to the screen, completely oblivious to Maggie and me.

'But the thing is, David,' she said, standing up straight and looking at me, a clump of toys in her arms (all this plastic crap), 'I'm going to fight this – the work thing. I believe I have a lot more to give.' A little Buzz Lightyear fell from her grasp. 'They just didn't understand what I was trying to do. The whole point was about imitation.' She picked Buzz up.

'So you said,' I said.

'I know I took it a bit far, but it wasn't done dishonestly. It really wasn't.'

'Can I help?' I continued. 'Can I read it? You're now helping me, hugely.' Though even as I said it, I wasn't sure how exactly. I find her research papers, her monographs, very hard to read (the ones that I have read). I'm not sure I fully understand any of it. My brain doesn't quite work like that.

There's Maggie's world and there's my world. Shit, in mine we copy everyone's styles and ideas all the time. That's part of the point: giving people what they want, what they expect. Until, I suppose, they desire new things, done better – and by different people.

'It's OK,' she said, knowing the truth, knowing everything, I reckon. She's so smart, her mind quite able to deal with plenty of difficult and diverse stuff. 'Michael's been helping, as I said,' she continues. 'He seems to get it. Says he does. One of the reasons why I wanted him and Liz to come over. I'm going to fight this, David.'

'Good,' I said. 'Good. Good.' I probably scratched my chin, the stubble that seems to be turning into a beard. Maggie's not a quitter, either. Why our plan could work. You need plenty of determination in my world, and something of a thick skin.

'And the other thing,' she said, dumping the toys in the toy box.

We've been thinking about getting rid of the toy box for some time. The children don't play with the mostly broken things kept in there, so much as chuck them around the room, Buzz Lightyear included. Though the box has its uses.

Maggie and I were jointly tidying up – because people were coming and, for some unspoken reason, I believe, we wanted the house to look nice. To show how we're coping.

'And the other thing too,' Maggie reiterated, a wry smile breaking out on her lovely face (she can be so cool, but also so animated, without making anything like the effort Julie seems to put into her expressions), 'we're going to fight that, of course.'

'Oh, we already are, aren't we?' I said, winking. Adding, and not for the first time, 'Fucking police!', before hurrying through to the kitchen and my chicken. I wasn't going to burn this one.

'Hey,' Maggie says, right behind me now, making me drop the wooden spoon.

'Hey,' I say, turning. I'd been stirring in the tarragon. 'You creeping up on me, again?'

She leans forward, kisses me on the cheek. 'Smells good. On schedule?'

'It'll be OK.'

'I'm sure. You always manage it somehow. A glass of wine?' She's moving towards the fridge.

'Yeah, that would be good. Necessary, I reckon. It's going to be an interesting evening.'

She smiles – warily now.

'I'm joking.' Though I guess however good a relationship might be, there'll always be an edge over certain issues, always some baggage. Some things you've just got to live with, accept, and gladly.

'Is that your phone again?' she says, retrieving a bottle of Sancerre (we're living it up, while we can) from the fridge.

'Probably.' A faint ringing is coming from my study, once more.

'Are you going to answer it this time?'

'No.'

'But soon, yeah?'

'When I'm ready – when we're ready.'

Maggie looks at me, a knowing look. A conspiratorial look. 'Let's not kill Britt, either,' she says. 'I'm just beginning to enjoy this. I'd like to do more – help you from the start, one day. I'm not as naïve, as innocent about all this stuff, as you think I might be.'

'That hasn't occurred to me.' Has it? 'But let's see where it takes us,' I say. 'You can't always plan these things.'

'David, don't rush off into your study and do something stupid behind my back.'

'As if – after all this.'

'Why am I beginning to think you might not be the easiest person to work with?'

'Give me a chance, Maggie. Hey, I haven't kissed the children goodnight.' And I leave my place in the kitchen, and Maggie, and thoughts I'm not sure I can quite fathom, and rush out of the kitchen, past my study and along the hallway to the foot of the stairs, where I pause for a moment. The phone's stopped ringing, but I can hear Jack laughing.

Hayes desperately fought for breath. He had his hand firmly, crushingly, around her mouth and against her nose. She was going dizzy – her chest feeling like it was about to explode. She clawed at his hand, his arms. But her legs were buckling under her and she was being dragged further into an alleyway, thinking: so this is it.

Is this really it? Can it be? What about Maggie, her wishes? Our collaboration? I'd be a fool to ignore her help, her advice, the chance to do it differently – despite my enhanced (albeit temporarily so) status.

Things always had to change. Am I really that difficult and stubborn to work with?

'Mr Slavitt?'

'Yes.' Not thinking, or rather with my mind elsewhere, I seem to have answered the damn phone.

'It's Detective Sergeant Ellis.'

'Oh yes.' I look over the top of my old screen, at my study, with the door just ajar, with light coming in from the hall. I can hear the others, still in the sitting room, still on the Sancerre and olives.

'There's just something I want to ask you.'

'Do you have to now? This isn't a good time. We have people round. I'm cooking. Besides, don't I need a lawyer present? I don't trust you lot.'

'The investigation's moving forward very quickly,' he says. 'We're following new leads.'

Hasn't he said as much before? 'I'm very pleased for you,' I say. 'Look, I really have to go.' You can overcook chicken of course, but it's not as fatal as overcooking pork. I stand. There's just enough stretch in the telephone cord. With my free hand I close the computer for the night. I need further guidance, further instruction from Maggie.

'One quick question,' says Ellis. 'I'll get straight to it. Why didn't Fonda torch Kesteris' Mercedes, after he'd shot him?'

'What?'

'I'm a slow reader,' he says. 'I've just got to this bit.'

'Look, I'm pleased you're interested in it, but I need to go.'

'Please, Mr Slavitt – just this one question. Why didn't he set fire to the car? He made a mistake, surely, leaving evidence all over the place.'

'Who said that's what he was intending?' I can't help myself. 'Fonda was never going to torch Kesteris' Merc. There was no accelerant. The police made a wrong assumption.'

'We can do,' says Ellis, 'I'll give you that. I still don't get it, though.'

'Obviously he didn't want to draw any attention to what he'd just done, and wanted to get away from there as quickly as possible.'

'But someone as calculating as Fonda must have had more of a plan,' said Ellis immediately. 'He must have thought this through beforehand. And I'm not the only person who wants to know. There are a number of us at the station, involved with this investigation, who are interested. In fact, it seems like there are a lot of people all over the place who are pretty interested in you and your work.'

Flattery is quite peculiar. Easy to see how it can get you into so much trouble. I suppose it's always been a major weakness of mine (and Maggie's) – anything for an audience, a bit of love. I sit. 'What do you think he would be planning?' Am I thinking on the hoof, letting it see where it takes us (or should have taken us) – another one of my weaknesses?

'I don't know. I'm a little baffled with this bit. That's why I asked.'

Is that really why? I laugh. 'He was going to incriminate Shreve somehow, by linking him to the car, to that shooting – not that actually he'd yet planned exactly how. Shreve, you see, was another person on his payroll whom he could no longer trust.'

'Oh,' says Ellis. 'Yeah, that would make sense, I guess. Incompetence and corruption at the local nick – you've got to have that, I suppose.' Ellis laughs too (nervously?). 'Does Fonda then incriminate him? Is he successful? What does happen to Shreve?'

'Where are you up to?'

'David,' says Maggie, suddenly pushing open my study door, giving me her slightly irritated or perhaps exhausted look, but there's a wryness to it also, as if she not only knows all too well why I've snuck away, but doesn't entirely blame me, doesn't exactly condemn it (old habits die hard, and all that), even now. 'Are you going to join us?'

'Hang on a minute,' I say to Ellis, before holding the phone away and leaning forward. 'Yes, yes, of course – just coming,' I say to Maggie, pointing at the phone and then mouthing the word 'important'. Maggie retreats, pulling the door to, and I clamp the phone back to my head. 'OK.'

'Britt Hayes thinks she hears someone moving around downstairs in her house,' says Ellis.

'You're only there? Yes, of course you are. That's where I'd got to when you took away that computer. Hey, when can I have it back? It's quite a new machine. I love that thing. Bought it for my travels.'

'Not sure you'll be going anywhere just yet, but I'll see what I can do,' he says, 'if you do something for me. Answer that question, come on: what does happen to Shreve?'

'What do you think should happen to him?'

'OK, no one's squeaky clean in this business,' says Ellis. 'But he was probably under a lot of pressure. We are, you know. And police pay's really bad, and it's only going to get worse.'

'Look, why don't you wait until the book's published and you can buy it? It's not going to be long. They're rushing it through, the e-book. In fact, if you can wait a bit longer, I'll send you a printed copy, for free. We'll even sign it.' I'm about to put down the phone when I hear him squawking.

'Wait, wait, Mr Slavitt.'

'What?'

'Don't take this the wrong way, but I wouldn't want you to misrepresent the police. Or prejudice the case – if it goes that far. It's a legal minefield out there.'

'Is this a threat? A legal threat?'

'It's an offer of help, Mr Slavitt. You know – if you need any inside information, stuff like that. I've seen a few things, some you wouldn't believe. Always fancied myself as a bit of a writer. I think I've got a pretty good imagination.'

'You said it.'

'So how about it?'

'Right now, I've got all the help I need, thanks.'

As soon as Jones had noticed the car, he gathered his things, Baz and made for the door. Blood beginning to race.

* * *

Michael and that beard are on the sofa with Maggie.

But if this is what Maggie wants, that's fine by me.

Liz is looking like she might pop – with excitement. She probably can't believe she's here, with us and our predicament, and my sudden success. Maybe we can't. Except we're not talking about it, about that. We can talk about the plagiarism (or they can) and Maggie's intention to fight on at the university, but not the other stuff; it would be too gauche, too callous even. That's what Maggie and I agreed. Let them continue to make their own assumptions, as they – as everyone – will anyway.

'Sorry,' I say, having entered the room but remained by the fireplace. I'm not sure whether I should sit, not sure whether I want to sit, or whether I should just head into the kitchen and finish cooking the food. It's always hard, barging in on a conversation, and when you are a bit shy and unsure of yourself too (one of the reasons why I like cooking on these occasions, why I probably drink too much as well). 'I had to take that call,' I say, reaching for my wine, which I'd left on the mantelpiece, some time ago.

'Katya,' Liz is saying brightly, 'Oliver's wife? We were talking about her.'

'Oh, right,' I say, not paying much attention, but taking in our sitting room, hurriedly tidied and now complete with guests, and with fine smells drifting in from the kitchen, and with the children safely, soundly, asleep upstairs – and thinking this is how it should always be, in a fine, quiet provincial city. The curtains haven't been drawn. It's still light outside, and I can just see, through the abundant foliage, the lamp post that I spotted Alex Smith loitering by, more than once, in the middle of the night.

'Well, I'm not surprised,' Maggie is saying. 'She's very attractive. Isn't she, David?'

'What?'

'Katya,' says Maggie, 'who we met at Liz and Michael's the other week. She was rather taken with you that night, from what I remember.'

'What about her?' I finish my glass, suddenly worried whether there's been quite enough suffering, and pain, enough grief and loss. The currency that my genre must trade in. Whether this has been supplemented by matters of a different nature, a different genre. Funny how quickly we move on (given the freedom to do so). I'll seek Maggie's counsel later. She'll know the answer.

'She's left Oliver,' says Liz, sitting forward and beaming at me. 'You better watch out, David.'

'Oh, he's used to it,' says Maggie. 'All those mums at the kids' school. I've seen the way they look at him. What's her name, Billy's mum? And then there's your agent,' Maggie turns towards me, 'and all your readers, those fans. They've always been women. And think how many of them there are now.' She flicks some hair behind her ear, continues, 'Women adore David.' She looks back at Liz, proudly.

The brilliant thing about Maggie is that she's never been the jealous type. I was the jealous one, of course, and look what trouble it got me into. But I'm learning – so much.

'Is that the door?' says Michael.

'Oh yes,' says Maggie.

'I'll get it,' I say.

'About time,' says Michael behind me.

Shit! It is a little smoky out in the hall. Don't tell me I've burnt the bloody chicken. It's something of a relief to haul open the front door and let some fresh air in, and the smoke out.

'Hi, David,' says Ashish. 'Sorry I'm late.'

'It's OK, no problem. We haven't started eating.'

'I must say you're looking fine,' he says. 'Particularly so.'

'Thanks. And you,' I say. I back into the sitting room, Ashish following closely.

'Hi, everyone,' he says, removing his shoulder bag and unwrapping his vast mustard-coloured scarf.

'Drink?' says Maggie, standing and moving over to greet him.

'Yes, yes, I think I will have one this evening,' he says, kissing her on both cheeks. 'Lots to celebrate.'

'What?' says Michael, standing also. 'You're going to have a drink, Ashish? Blimey – what's brought this on?'

Liz too seems to be struggling to her feet. 'Do you know something we don't?' she says.

Maggie, on her way to the kitchen to fetch a glass, stops by the door into the hall. Turns to face the room. Frowns. 'Am I missing something?' she says.

'It was just on the local radio, in the taxi on the way here,' says Ashish.

'What? What was?' says Michael, glancing at me, and not in a particularly friendly way.

'They've arrested Alex Smith's girlfriend,' says Ashish.

'I didn't know he had one,' says Maggie.

'For what?' says Liz. 'Murder? Bloody hell!'

'Perverting the course of justice, apparently,' says Ashish. 'Seems Smith committed suicide, but his girlfriend had other ideas.'

'Poor woman,' I say, taking in the news. 'It can't be easy losing someone you love, like that.'

'I think the fucking police could have bothered to inform us, if this is the case,' says Maggie.

I think Ellis could have informed me on the phone when he rang, only minutes ago. He obviously knew. Was he concerned I might try to exact some literary revenge on him, on the police? And was therefore suddenly attempting to gain favour by offering his services – to impart some inside information, some of the stuff he'd seen (and no doubt been culpable for)? Perhaps he was just trying to keep the connection with me (and my notoriety), and make some money. A bit of both? The total jerk.

'David, where the hell are the police?' says Maggie. 'They really need to tell us what's going on now.'

'Maybe they're sorting out the legals,' I say. 'I'm sure you need to go through plenty of hoops before you can drop bail conditions. Get things signed by the right people. And at this time – can't be easy. But I don't know.' I should know, of course. Where are our lawyers? 'But this is good, isn't it, sweetheart? If it's true, if it sticks. Though I thought this would happen . . . I have been saying.'

'How did he commit suicide?' says Liz. 'If they thought, for so long, that he'd been murdered?'

'The body was badly decomposed, according to the radio,' says Ashish. 'It's what happens when you have a car filled with carbon monoxide. Like being in an oven, apparently.'

'Do we have to?' says Michael.

'I'm intrigued by his girlfriend,' says Liz. 'Did she think that he was having an affair? Is that it? Is she then responsible for Maggie and David being caught up in this dreadful thing?'

'I'm sure we'll find out all the details soon enough,' says Ashish.

'I'm not even going to suggest the obvious, David,' says Liz.

'Which is?' says Michael.

'Don't,' I say, suddenly aware of the fumes now drifting in from the hall, and turning away and gathering momentum, as I pass Maggie; gently, lovingly, conspiratorially tapping her on the arm as I do so, and breaking into something like a trot (pace, pace, pace – finally, easily) along the hallway.

She wasn't in the car. And he hadn't bumped into her on the way down from his room.

He scanned the pavement. Up and down Victoria Road. The dull wedge of Marine Parade in sight. There were a few people about, sheltering from the weather in their inadequate anoraks. No sign of Britt, however. He looked down at Baz. Baz looked up at him.

He tried the car door – surprised to find it wasn't locked. Her mobile sitting on the passenger seat. Her handbag in the passenger footwell.

A noise, he realised, was coming from behind him. A noise he didn't like the sound of. He spun round. Saw a figure down the alleyway, by the bins. Two figures. Struggling. A man and a woman. The glint of a gun in the man's right hand? But the woman, Britt, was holding the man's arm away. Fighting for her life.

'Go,' Jones said to Baz, and the dog shot off, almost immediately leaping into the air, leaping for the man. Sinking his teeth into Fonda's right arm and knocking the killer to the ground.

Epilogue
Something Like a Future

'Bit fucking late, David,' says Julie, down the blower. 'Especially now you're off the hook. I'm not sure what Peter will say, what his plans still are.'

'Julie,' I say, 'we've worked our arses off to get this to you so quickly.'

'Yeah, well, not much I can do about the market,' she says, and I hold the phone away from me, stretching, trying to get some feeling into my fingers. 'But I like the idea of Maggie putting her name to it,' I hear Julie say. 'That could help keep some attention. David Slavitt and Maggie Robertson. Hey, why not call yourselves Mr and Mrs Slavitt? I can see that on a jacket.'

'She's Maggie Robertson, Dr Robertson, actually,' I say, clamping the receiver back to my head. 'And Maggie hasn't just put her name to it. She's been integral. I could never have done it without her, never have finished it.'

'Mr and Mrs Roberston then. That has more of a ring to it anyway.'

'I'm easy.'

'Well, we'll see – or Peter will – whether we still need the name Slavitt. Whether he thinks we can't do without it, now. Who knows, in this fast-moving market. Nevertheless, I'm sure he'll like the idea of both of you being on the cover somehow. Lots of branding potential. You could be the new . . . what were they called, that Swedish couple?'

'Maj Sjöwall and Per Wahlöö. I'm not sure we've quite got their talent, their originality,' I say. 'Though we are planning to do more together: a whole series, featuring Britt and Howie.'

'Featuring who?'

He'd pulled off the main road, onto little more than a dirt track. Flat, marshy fields stretching relentlessly away to either side of them – just a massive grain silo piercing what there was of a horizon straight ahead.

'I thought you'd changed your mind,' said Jones. 'And weren't coming.'

'No,' said Hayes. 'I was always coming. Just got held up. I tried to ring.' She reached down, patted Baz, by her feet.

'Something must have happened to my signal. Perhaps the fog was too thick.'

'Maybe,' she said, smiling.

'He needs a walk,' said Howie. 'When I've taken care of – well, you know what.' He couldn't believe he was back here so soon.

'Yeah,' she said, 'then can we get a long way away?'

She needed to pinch herself. Was this really happening? Were they going to keep driving?

We're in bed. Light from the street lamps is edging round the curtains. Or perhaps it's dawn – already. We're both fully awake, holding each other tightly. Another night of passion, and we're not yet spent. Boy, am I getting fitter!

'So where?' she says. 'Where did they go? Because it sort of impacts on the next one, doesn't it?'

'I don't know. You tell me.'

'Do they really have to go that far?' she says. 'Can't they resurface, in

Kingsmouth? I mean, are all Britt's bridges burned, now Fonda's out of the way?'

'There's Leonard,' I say.

'He could just make it more interesting,' Maggie says.

'True. I do like continuity,' I say. 'And we've got the setting, even if it's a bit cold and damp and Julie hates it.'

'She'll come round. She always does,' says Maggie. 'Doesn't she?'

'I love your optimism,' I say. 'I love the fact we're here, tucked up together, too.' With plenty of duvet each (funny where the extra cover comes from), I could add, but don't. This, of course, is how it should always be. How it will always be – fingers crossed.

Shutting my eyes, I try to picture the view out of my study window, the trees in leaf, the buds turning to flower; some flowers, of which I'll never know the names, already in bloom – a gentle, soporific sort of scene. But, as ever, other images and thoughts soon come to me.

'Maggie,' I ask, 'what's the most gruesome crime you can imagine?'

The End

As ever writing is a collaborative effort. Many people were hugely instrumental in the realisation of this novel. I'd especially like to thank David R. Slavitt, the original 'Henry Sutton', my determined agent David Miller, my great colleague Andrew Cowan, and from the best publisher in my world: the supreme Bethan Jones; the inspired Liz Foley; and the truly insightful Alison Hennessey, who saw what was really here.

Henry Sutton is the author of six previous novels, including *Get Me Out of Here* and *Kids' Stuff*, which became a long-running stage play in Latvia. He's also the author of a collection of short stories, *Thong Nation*. He has worked as a journalist and critic, and is now Senior Lecturer in Creative Writing at the University of East Anglia. He lives in Norwich.

www.henrysutton.co.uk